A FATAL
INTERVENTION

by

Bill Rogers

C A T O N

Published in 2010 by Caton Books

First Edition

The author asserts the moral right under the Copyright, Designs and Patents Act 1988 to be identified as the author of this work.

Whilst this book is based on factual research, and actual police operations are referred to as background context, all of the characters in this book are fictitious, and any resemblance to actual persons, living or dead, is purely coincidental.

Published by Caton Books

www.catonbooks.com

ISBN: 978-0-9564220-3-3

Cover Photo courtesy of Andrew Brooks
Cover Design by Dragonfruit
Design & Layout: Commercial Campaigns

Acknowledgements

Brian Wroe, former Chief Superintendent, and
Divisional Commander, Greater Manchester Police.
Anthony Phillips FFS.DIP, former Senior Scene of Crime
Officer at New Scotland Yard, and Visiting Lecturer at
Thames Valley University. Joan Rogers, Barbara Caterall,
Jenny and Paul Whur, Mike Atherton, Andrew Brooks,
Andy Brydon, & the Urbis City Guides

And, not least, the amazing City of Manchester

Cover Photo
Culvert Report
Photographer: Andrew Paul Brooks
©2008 Andrew Paul Brooks
Commissioned by Andy Brydon for the Urbis exhibition
Reality Hack: Hidden Manchester, 2008

Images from **Reality Hack: Hidden Manchester are**
available to purchase from:
www.andrewbrooksphotography.com

1

A hammer thumped away at the back of his head, and there was a buzzing in his ears. A sliver of light seeped beneath the window blind. As he reached up to switch on the lamp a succession of pains, sharp as bee stings, raked his back. The flashing bedside clock mocked him; five forty three am. He sank back into the pillows, desperate for sleep to drag him down; to shut out the noise. The buzzing became more insistent, the hammering staccato. And now there were voices.

'Open up Mr Thornton! This is the Police!'

He levered himself up, pushed back the duvet, and swung his legs over the side of the bed. This wasn't how it was supposed to work. He came to them. Not them to him.

'Mr Thornton. Open up Sir, or we'll be forced to break it down!'

He shook his head, unscrambling the banging inside it from that on the apartment door. As he passed the wet room he took his silk dressing gown from the hook, and padded down the entrance hall, shrugging it on as he went. As the hammering intensified he feared that the door would break.

'Hang on!' he shouted. A firework exploded in his skull. Through sleep encrusted eyes he peered at the image on the video entry screen. The one in front he recognised, despite the way the fish eye distorted his head into a grinning gargoyle. DI Gordon Holmes, of the Force Major Incident Team holding up his warrant card. Beside him loomed two uniformed officers. Behind them, in civilian clothes, a man and a woman. He slid the door chain from its runner, unlocked the dead bolts, and opened the door. Holmes stepped forward, one hand against the door, his foot across the sill.

'Robert Thornton, My name is Detective Inspector Gordon Holmes. In accordance with the Police and Criminal Evidence Act 1984, I am here to make a Summary Arrest. I must also advise you that this is a Serious Arrestable Offence.'

Rob's mind was racing; close to a snail's pace. Who the hell were they coming to arrest? There was no one else in the flat. And since when did they trouble to use this form of words? *Summary Arrest:* for an offence that carried a fixed penalty: serious assault; murder. *Serious Arrestable Offence;* he knew the list by heart. Without realising that he was doing it he began to mutter it out loud.

'Treason, murder, manslaughter, rape, kidnapping, incest or intercourse with a girl under 13, buggery with a boy under 16, indecent assault constituting gross indecency, causing an explosion likely to endanger life or property…'

He looked down into the detective's face, hoping to find an answer. Across the corridor the door to one of the other apartments opened as far as the security chain would allow.

'I think that it would better if we did this inside, Mr Thornton.' Holmes said. Without waiting for a reply he pushed the door open, and entered the apartment.

Rob flattened himself against the wall as they trooped past, heads down, avoiding his eyes. All but the last of them; a thick set constable whom he recognised, but whose name he did not know, his frame accentuated by the regulation stab vest, stood resolutely in the doorway waiting for Rob to turn and follow the others down the hall. As he did so he heard the door close behind him.

The apartment was not small, but they filled it; standing awkwardly, in a bunch, between the sofa and the entrance to the open plan kitchen.

'I'd offer you all a seat, but I doubt there are enough.' It was an attempt to lighten the atmosphere; to give himself time to order his thoughts. It was wasted on Holmes.

'Robert Thornton,' he said. 'I have reasonable grounds for suspecting that earlier this morning you committed a serious sexual assault on one Anjelita Rosa Covas. We also have reason to believe that you may be in possession of a controlled substance. You do not have to say anything. But it may harm your defence if you do not mention when questioned something which you later rely on in court. Anything you do say may be given in evidence. Do you understand?'

Of course he bloody well understood. Holmes knew that he did. What Rob didn't understand was what these 'reasonable grounds' could possibly be.

'Do you understand Sir?' The detective persisted.

'Yes I understand.' Rob replied. 'And you won't be surprised to hear that I am completely innocent of these offences, and I have nothing to further to say until I've spoken with my solicitor.' Even as he spoke them, his words felt hollow. It was a mantra that he knew most policemen regarded as an admission of guilt.

Holmes took an envelope from his inside breast pocket, and held it out like an offering. 'I have here a warrant to search these premises for evidence relating to these alleged offences.'

Rob waved it aside. Given the nature of the offences a warrant was unnecessary. Holmes's warrant card, and a Notice of Rights and Powers would have sufficed. They were just being extra careful; closing all the loopholes. The magistrate who signed that warrant, not best pleased at being woken in the middle of the night, would have known it too. Holmes's boss would be getting an irate phone call.

'In that case, Mr Thornton, I think we'll start in the bedroom.'

Rob led the way. His head had begun to clear, adrenalin acting as an anaesthetic, dulling the pain to a constant throb. He just wished it would send him back to sleep. To wake around lunchtime, and find this was all a dream. No, not a dream, a nightmare.

Holmes pointed to the trail of clothes from the foot of the built-in wardrobe to the side of his bed. 'Are these the clothes you wore last night?'

No *Mr Thornton*, no *Sir*, Rob noticed. Not now that he had been read his rights. He nodded.

'Is this all of them?' Holmes asked.

Rob slid open the wardrobe door. His linen jacket hung crookedly on a hanger. It occurred to him that he couldn't have been that smashed, or it would have been crumpled in a heap on the bedroom floor.

Holmes signalled to the man and woman in civvies, both of whom had donned search gloves and carried a selection of evidence bags. Rob watched as they gathered up his clothes, tagged them, and placed them in separate bags. The duvet was stripped back. The pillow cases and sheets were removed, and individually bagged. Rob knew what would come next. Every cupboard, drawer, shoe, piece of clothing, would be examined. Floorboards checked to see if they were loose. Walls tapped for hollow spaces; then on to the next room. He didn't need to watch. If they wanted to plant something in one of these rooms there would be nothing he could do to stop them. But at least his fingerprints would not be on it.

'If you don't mind, I'd like to go to the bathroom,' he said, pointing to the ensuite wet room. 'I need to relieve myself, and take some paracetemol.'

Holmes nodded to one of the policemen, who then led the way. Rob stood back while the toilet cistern and the bathroom cabinet were searched. He had to turn out the pockets of his dressing gown before he was finally allowed to use the toilet. The policeman waited until he had finished washing his hands, then handed him two paracetemol, and placed the packet back in the cabinet. Rob looked at the tiny tablets nestling in the palm of his hand. Two weren't going to be anywhere near enough. Not today.

The ride to the station was uneventful. This early on a Saturday morning in December the streets of Manchester were deserted. At least they had allowed him to slip on a pair of underpants, his track suit, and a pair of trainers.

The station sergeant was known to him. His embarrassment was palpable.

'I'm sorry about this Mr Thornton,' he began, before taking refuge behind the formalities; a kind of protection for them both. 'Are you currently undergoing any medical treatment? Are you currently taking any medication?'

'Just paracetemol; for a headache.' Rob told him. The sergeant made a note.

'Are you in need of any medical attention? Do you, prior to questioning, require the presence of an approved person to assist you in understanding the documentation?'

This was ridiculous. Rob was on the verge of telling him so when the next form of words brought him up short.

'You will now be asked to accompany this officer to the medical room where you will be required to remove your clothes, submit to an intimate body search by a medical officer, and give either a blood or urine sample. You may, if you wish, ask for another appropriate adult to be present.'

An intimate body search. It was inevitable in view of the accusations, but he had conveniently pushed it to the back of his mind. He didn't require anyone else to be present, nor was he at risk of self-harm. He didn't need to listen to anymore of this. He just wanted it over with.

The search was every bit as humiliating as he had imagined it would be; more so, because he knew the police surgeon well. He had cross examined him on a number of occasions, for the prosecution, and for the defence. Whatever the outcome he reflected, their relationship would never be quite the same again. Samples were scraped from the inside of his mouth. His head, hands, genitals, knees, elbows and feet were closely examined. It came as a complete surprise when the police surgeon traced his fingers across his back, causing him to wince. He had no idea that his back had been injured, or how. Digital photographs were taken. He was further surprised, when they discovered faint bruises on his upper arms, and shoulders. He stared, transfixed, at the purple blotches blueing at the edges. The examination completed, his track suit and underpants were bagged and tagged. He was handed a white Tyvek all in one, and told to put it on.

'Since you've completed your examination, why do I have to wear this?' he asked.

DI Holmes stepped forward. 'Because Mr Thornton, depending on the answers to the questions which we have yet to put to you, we may, or may not, need to make a further examination, and take additional evidential samples.'

Rob was nearing the end of his tether. He knew exactly what those questions would be, and why they might need further evidence. But that only happened to other people. People he prosecuted, not to him. Not to Rob Thornton, Leading Junior Counsel.

'If you should come to feel that that is necessary,' he said. 'Then you are going to have to charge me first.'

'Don't worry Sir,' Holmes replied, looking him squarely in the eyes. 'If we do come to feel that it's necessary, then we'll charge you anyway.'

They gave him a cup of coffee in a plastic cup, and put him into one of the cells. Only, they explained, because the interview rooms were still being cleaned from the night before, and his solicitor had rung to say that he was delayed. None of that changed the nausea, and feeling of desolation, that swept over him as the door closed, and the key turned in the lock.

2

In the twenty minutes it took for his solicitor to arrive,
things were beginning to fall into place. It was funny
how being locked in a cell concentrated the mind. Rob
had been confused, irritated, and angry. Now he was
worried.

Henry Mayhew had his serious face on. Even
though they'd known each other for over seven years,
and worked together on a regular basis, this was the
first time that Rob had cause to study his colleague
closely. Immaculate, in pinstriped suit, crisp white
shirt, and red silk tie, he was every inch the gentleman
professional. Self assured, knowledgeable, incapable
of being fazed; a mirror image of Rob himself. Except
for the toll the years had taken. His silver hair was
thinning, and male pattern baldness advancing at a
rate of knots. The buttons of his suit strained to
contain his paunch. The lines on his forehead, that
had always seemed to radiate experience, spoke now
of anxiety. His podgy hands, perfectly manicured,
were dotted with liver spots. Mayhew stood there,
awkwardly clutching his briefcase; looking around for
somewhere to put it.

'Robert, I'm sorry I'm late. But worry not, we'll
have you out of here in no time.'

Stuffy, but ever proper, he always called him
Robert. The only person, apart from his Head of
Chambers, who did. Until this morning, when DI

13

Holmes had joined the fold. Rob looked past him to the open door of the cell.

'We?' he said smiling weakly. 'Have you brought the cavalry?'

'Well at least you've kept your sense of humour,' the solicitor replied. 'Come on, they've made one of the interview rooms available for our consultation.'

'Bugger that,' Rob told him, patting the bed. 'We'll do it here.'

'What on earth for?'

'Because you and I know that there are video cameras, microphones, and two way mirrors in every interview room in this custody suite.'

'Come on Robert. You know that lawyer-client conversations are privileged. The police are not allowed to listen in, let alone record them.'

Rob made himself comfortable on the bed, pulling his knees up, encircling them with his arms. 'And pigs can fly.'

'I'm sorry Robert, but you're simply being paranoid.'

'And you've never heard of it happening before? In the Isle of Man in the nineties for example.'

'Well even if it has, it can't be used as evidence. Any recording would be inadmissible.'

'What about Regina versus Wilkinson, 2006?'

'That was by accident, in the Crown Court cells. They forgot to turn off the tape.'

'Ho! Ho! Ho! But it still influenced the outcome.'

'Only because it showed that his lawyer had been coaching him. Now you're just being paranoid.' Mayhew glanced anxiously over his shoulder at the duty sergeant, standing impatiently at the door to the cell. 'Besides, according to your reasoning, this cell must be equally unsafe.'

Rob had to accept the logic. In any case he was freezing cold, and sick of this room. He unclasped his legs, and swung them off the bed. 'Fair enough,' he said,' lead on Macduff.'

Mayhew selected a new notebook, clicked his biro, and stared at his client. 'Robert, I simply don't understand how you can be so flippant.'

Rob folded his arms across his chest. 'Because this is so bloody ridiculous, that's why.'

'That doesn't stop it having serious implications for you, does it?'

He didn't have an answer to that. Well actually, he did. But it wasn't one he liked. Mayhew saved him the trouble.

'They are alleging rape,' he said. 'I don't have to tell you that it carries a maximum life sentence. And since you've been called to the Bar, the prosecution would be certain to ask for the maximum sentence, and the judge would be bending over backwards to make an example of you. They don't like the Bar being brought into disrepute.'

'Thanks for reminding me.'

Mayhew ignored the sarcasm. 'So why don't you start at the beginning?' he said.

Rob resigned himself to the inevitable. He ran his fingers through his hair, searching his memory banks. 'I was at a party. A friend of Harry's.'

'Before that, had you been at work?'

Rob nodded. 'I had a short appearance at Minshull Street Crown Court, requesting an adjournment.

Then I did some paperwork in the office. Had a light lunch with Anna at El Rincon...'

'Anna?'

'My pupil. Started about a month ago. You must have met her?'

'I don't think so.'

'We were going over some research she's been doing for me on the Rushton case.'

'What did you have to drink?'

He had to think about it. 'Two glasses of the house red. Some mineral water.'

'What time did you leave?'

'A quarter to two. Something like that. We walked back to the chambers together. She carried on with her research, I read a couple of briefs Stanley had put on my desk, then made some phone calls. One of them was to you.'

The solicitor nodded. 'Shortly before four pm. Then what did you do?'

'Harry Richmond stuck his head round the door, and asked if I was coming for a drink to start the weekend off. I told him to hang on, then I shut down the computer, locked the briefs away, and we left together.'

'Was that something you would normally do on a Friday evening?'

Rob's sigh was pregnant with frustration. 'Come on Henry, you know it's practically a ritual.'

Mayhew stabbed his biro towards his friend and client. 'And you know that we have to do it this way. These are the questions the police are going to ask you. Now stop giving me a hard time, and listen to your own advice; just answer the bloody questions, and let me do my work.'

It was the bloody that did it. Mayhew never swore. He was either very worried, or really pissed off. Rob suspected it was both. He cleared his throat. 'OK Henry,' he said. 'Let's do it your way.'

Mayhew looked down at his notes. 'You went to a bar?'

'Several actually. We started at Sam's Chop House. A few of the gang were there. Then Harry got a phone call and suggested we got over to the Rain Bar to meet some of the others.'

'What did you have to drink in the Chop House?'

'A pint of bitter. I was just about to order another round when Harry dragged us off. When we got to the Rain Bar it was heaving. You know what it's like on Fridays, never mind it was Happy Hour. We had trouble pushing our way through to join the others.'

'How long were you there?'

'About an hour and a half. I only had one pint. I didn't want to get into a big round, and in any case there were too many in the group by then. Then Harry told me that his mate Vince was having a party, and we were invited. A penthouse apartment in the Northern Quarter. Everyone was going to be there. The food and the girls were sorted; we just had to pick up some drink on the way. I had no intention of going straight there from the bar. A recipe for disaster.' He caught Henry's eye, and grimaced. 'You're right. Pretty bloody ironic given where I'm sitting now.'

'So what did you do?'

'I got the address, and said I'd be along as soon as I'd freshened up and changed my clothes. Then I set off for my apartment.'

'Alone?'

'Yes.'

Mayhew consulted his notes again. 'You said the food and the girls were sorted. What did you think he meant by that?'

'Exactly that. He must have already had the party planned. Ordered food in. Invited some girls.' He spotted the raised eyebrows. 'I get it,' he said. 'You want to know if they were working girls, escorts?'

'Well, were they?'

'No they were bloody well not!'

'And you know that for a fact?'

'Yes I do. One of them was Vince's girl friend. She'd brought some of her mates with her, and then there were ones belonging to some of the other guys.'

'Belonging?'

'Come on Henry, you know what I mean; partners of.'

'That's better. Less open to interpretation. Less likely to wind up...' he let it tail off.

Rob sat bolt upright. Gripping the edge of the table with both hands. 'The jury! That's what you were going to say wasn't it? For God sake Henry, you don't really think this is going all the way?'

Mayhew remained calm. For him this was a daily occurrence. Well, not quite. Not with a friend and colleague. 'That depends very much on you Robert,' he said. 'You know that. Assuming whatever is alleged to have taken place did so away from prying eyes, then your only defence is likely to be the credibility of your account. So think about this very carefully. Was anything said that might have led you to believe that any of these girls...hold that, let's stick to the term women, unless there's any reason why we should not?'

'No there bloody well isn't. Under the age of consent? What the hell do you take me for?'

'Fine. In which case, was anything said to you, or in your presence, before or during the party, which might have led you to believe that any of these women were of easy virtue, and invited for the express purpose of engaging in sexual activity?'

'*Procured* is the term Henry; procured. And the answer, emphatically, is no!'

'Good, but probably best not to be so emphatic.'

Rob had never before regarded Mayhew as pompous; measured, solid, meticulous, reliable, but not pompous. Until now.

'So, you went home first?' Henry said.

'Yes. I had a shave, and a shower, cleaned my teeth, got changed, and set off.'

'Did you have a hair of the dog?'

'No, I didn't. I'd already had two pints, and it was still early in the evening.'

'What were you wearing?'

'A beige linen jacket, over a white linen open necked shirt, blue jeans, and trainers.'

'You were hoping to pull?'

'No. Not especially.'

'Did you take any condoms?'

'No.'

'Why not?'

'Because I do not currently have a partner, and I was not – as you quaintly put it – planning to pull. In any case, I tend to be cautious about having sex at first meeting. And these days women who are up for it tend to come prepared.'

'It's a shame that you chose that evening to buck

19

your trend.' Henry observed caustically. 'And I should leave out the last part about them coming prepared if I were you. It suggests a lack of responsibility, and a cavalier attitude towards women that is not going to help.'

'Anyway, who says I did buck the trend?'

Henry shook his head, and sighed. 'Well, one Anjelita Rosa Covas, for a start.'

Rob bristled. 'What do you mean, for a start?'

'Did you or didn't you?'

'Yes.'

'Right, now that we've got that out of the way, can we press on? And stop being so coy, it doesn't suit you. And considering the circumstances, it's pathetic. Tell me about the party.'

'As I said, it was at Vince's apartment, in the Northern Quarter. He's got a massive penthouse apartment on the top two floors of a converted warehouse. Four bedrooms, three ensuite, Jacuzzi, sauna and steam room. Views on all three sides, across the city, and out towards the Pennines above Oldham. You know the kind of thing.'

'What does he do, this Vince?'

'Property I think. He bought some of the first apartments when the boom was starting, back in the early nineties. Made a big profit, bought some more. He moved into Spain, added Croatia as soon as the war finished there; now he's got a load of villas in Bosnia as well.'

'The party was underway?'

'There were about forty people there. I knew about half of them. Of the ones I didn't know, quite a few I'd seen around the clubs and bars. Three of them I recognised as footballers; a couple from Man City, one from Man U. There was a married couple from Eastern Europe – lawyers I think he said - and a very flash looking Russian guy. The drink was flowing, the speakers were uncomfortably loud. I was really hungry, but only the nibbles were out...nuts, crisps, Doritos, dips. So I filled a plate with those, grabbed a bottle of Keo, started to circulate.'

'Keo?'

'Lager. From Cyprus. Vince had a shed load stacked up in one of the windows.'

'How strong is that?

'I don't know, about 4.5%.'

'How big was the bottle?'

'A big one, just a bit smaller than a bottle of wine I guess.'

'You'd started to circulate.'

'I got chatting with some of the usual bunch. Harry dragged me away at one point to introduce me to a friend of his fiancée. Should have been a Jewish Momma, Harry; always trying to fix me up. I think he's jealous of my freedom.'

'This was Ms Covas?'

'No way. She was a five foot seven blonde; size four, heading for size zero. Works at the Royal Bank of Scotland. I've never understood how someone apparently intelligent can choose to starve herself to death. I made small talk for five minutes or so, then pretended I needed to go to the loo. Actually, I did go. When I went back into the main room the food had arrived; buffet style. Vince had got caterers in. There must have been nearly fifty people by then. People kept coming and going throughout the evening. I was ravenous, so I joined the queue. That was when I met Anjelita. She was immediately in front of me. It was impossible not to notice her. She had gorgeous black hair, flowing in waves down her back, and over her shoulders. A perfect hourglass figure squeezed into a silk red mini dress. Three inch red stiletto heels. Legs to die for. When she dropped her serviette I practically caught it before it hit the ground. I held it out, and she turned and smiled. Her eyes were pools of rich brown chocolate that drew you in. She had lips perfect for pouting; but they didn't. Instead, they gave her smile a sort of vulnerability, a sadness that made you want to take her in your arms, and tell her everything would be alright. Her lips parted, in slow motion. The tip of her tongue – light coral pink – rested for a moment between gleaming white teeth. She whispered, *Thank you.* It should have been drowned out by the throbbing music, and the wild chatter. But I heard it crystal clear. Like a profession of enduring love, from the only other person in the room.' He paused. Recapturing the moment.

Henry Mayhew had stopped writing. As Rob had begun to describe this woman his tone had changed, becoming wistful. She had accused him of rape, and yet here he was describing her with an emotional attachment bordering on obsession. In court, that could work for or against him. 'You clearly found her attractive?' Mayhew said, for want of anything else to say.

Rob looked up. The spell broken. 'She was the nearest thing I'd ever seen to Penelope Cruz, whom I happen to find stunningly attractive. Anjelita was more than that… she was mesmerising.'

'What happened next?'

'I told her my name. She told me hers. Anjelita Covas. We loaded our plates, looked around for somewhere to sit, but all the sofas were taken. We ended up sitting on the stairs.'

'What time was this?'

'By then it must have been getting on for ten o'clock. To be honest, I'd no idea of the time.'

'Go on.'

'We just sat there chatting. Like we'd known each other for years. Except that she told me her life story, and I told her mine. It seemed so natural. People kept stepping over and round us, but we were oblivious. I was intoxicated.'

'How much had you had by then?'

Rob shook his head in disbelief. 'Come on Henry,' he said. 'You know what I mean. By her beauty, her spirit, the way she hung on my every word, even laughed at my jokes; something you never do.'

'Even so. How much had you had to drink?'

'Another couple of bottles.'

'And Anjelita? How much had she had to drink?'

He really had to think about that. 'I'm not sure. She was stone cold sober when I met her in the queue. Said she'd only just arrived. I got her a glass of champagne with the food, then she more or less kept pace with me. So, three glasses of champagne I guess.'

'You fetched those for her?'

'Yes, except for the last one. She went to the loo, and came back with two glasses. Champagne cocktails, she said. Insisted I have one.'

'Then what?'

'She said she'd like to dance. Took my hand and pulled me up. People were dancing to Café Smooch. Those who weren't, were either into drink fuelled conversation, or snogging on the sofas. I lost track of time. There was soft music, low lights, sophisticated perfume, this beautiful body fused with mine. You know how it is.'

The solicitor shook his head. 'As a matter of fact,' he said. 'I don't. So tell me. I can't wait to hear. And neither can the police.'

'Well, it's like you're lost in each other's warmth. Floating in a dream of your own making. Oblivious of anything and everyone around you.'

'That could equally be a definition of being drunk.'

'Well I wasn't. This was too important to mess up. And I don't make a habit of getting drunk. For God's sake Henry, you know that.'

Mayhew had to admit that he had a point. Rob might go close to the limit occasionally, but he had never seen him drunk. 'So how would you describe your condition at that point?' He asked.

'Happy, relaxed, slightly tipsy. No more than that. Compos mentis enough to know what she meant when she whispered in my ear… *let's go upstairs.*'

'So it was her suggestion?'

'Yes. She led me off the dance floor, past the couples sprawled on the stairs, onto the landing. She was the one who tried each door in turn, until she found a room unoccupied. She was the one who drew me in, and locked the door behind us.'

'You assumed this was an invitation to have sex?'

'Come on Henry. What do you think? Anyway, she certainly didn't waste any time removing any lingering doubts I might have had. She found the switch for the lights above the bed, kicked off her shoes, put her arms around my neck, and kissed me; long, and hard. I take it even you know what a French kiss is?'

Mayhew didn't grace that with a reply.

'This was a Spanish kiss. Definitely hotter, accompanied by a touch of flamenco from her hips. When I came up for air she pushed my jacket over my shoulders, and tugged until it fell to the floor. Then she began to undo the buttons on my shirt. I reached out and put my hands behind her back, searching for the zip. She laughed, pushed against my chest, and pulled away. 'Give me a moment' she said, gliding over to the doors set in the wall. She opened one, and found it was a walk-in wardrobe. We both started laughing. The next one was the bathroom. She slipped inside, and closed the door behind her, leaving me standing there, wondering if she expected me to get undressed, get in bed, or stay as I was.'

'How were you feeling at that moment?'

'Surprised, elated...very horny.'

'Did you have any second thoughts?'

'If I did, I don't recall them. It was like Christmas Eve come a week early. All my Christmas's rolled into one.'

'Then what happened?'

'I sat on the bed, undid my shoes, took off my socks, and waited for what seemed an age. I was beginning to wonder if she'd changed her mind, when the bathroom door opened, and she stepped out. She'd shaken her hair loose so that it cascaded over her shoulders and upper chest. All she had on was a bra and a thong. She was stunning.'

Mayhew leaned forward, biro poised. 'Can you describe her underwear? It may be important?'

Rob nodded. 'It was red satin – the same shade as her dress – but trimmed in black lace. The thong was high sided, the satin came down in a V shape, and the lace was scalloped where it met her thighs. There was a small black bow in the centre of the bra, and another on the back of the thong. I remember thinking they looked like butterflies.'

'How did you come to see the one on the back of her thong, if she was facing you?'

'Because she turned to close the bathroom door. It was all part of the seduction. She looked over her shoulder, watched me looking at her, and wiggled her bum.'

That's a very clear description. That's good. It helps to confirm the fact that you were still reasonably sober.'

Rob shook his head. 'To tell you the truth, if I'd been blind drunk I don't think I would have forgotten what she looked like when she came out of that bathroom.'

'That's just the kind of remark I hope you are going to refrain from making when they question you. Familiarity doesn't only breed contempt, it breeds complacency as well. Just remember, this is not a game, and they are no longer on your side. And just because you know that you're innocent, it doesn't mean you don't have to prove the fact.'

Rob pushed himself away from the table, and folded his arms again. 'Don't you think I know that Henry? In here, it's just you and me. I'm being completely honest with you, because you need me to be. With them, it'll be strictly need to know. No codicils, no silly remarks. Trust me.'

Henry stared straight at his client, pausing for added gravitas. 'Good. Because when it comes down to it, it won't be about me trusting you, but about you being able to trust yourself. Now, as you very well know, this is the most important part. I'm sorry, but you are going to have to give me chapter and verse. No bullshitting. No modest skating over the details. Just tell it exactly how it happened. I'm unshockable, and my lips are sealed. And don't take too long about it. They're not going to wait for ever.'

Rob poured himself a drink of water. He downed half of it, set the plastic cup on the table, and stared at the desk, studiously avoiding Henry's eyes as he began.

'I started to stand up as she came towards me. She pushed me back down on the bed, and knelt in front of me. She began to undo the remaining buttons on my shirt. When she came to the last two she lost her patience and tugged at them. I think one of them broke. She pulled the shirt roughly over my shoulders and waited for me to shrug the sleeves from off my arms. Then she took my hands in hers and placed them behind her back, on the straps of the bra. As I undid the clasp, and eased them over her shoulders, she undid the buttons on my jeans, pulled them over my thighs, and down my legs. I had to lean back so that she could tug them off my feet. Then she leaned forward again, and I slid the bra straps down, and over her arms. She held the cups against her breasts and lifted her face, eyes closed, inviting me to kiss her.

We kissed for perhaps a minute or so, then I eased her hands away, and cupped her breasts. Her nipples were hard, her breasts as soft as the satin she had been wearing. She slipped her hand inside my briefs, and began to stroke me. I thought I was going to come there and then. I put my hand on hers. Said something like *not yet...too fast*. She stood up, pulled me to my feet, and then shoved me hard so that I fell back across the middle of the bed. She tugged my briefs off, and straddled me, her knees on either side of my waist. She put her hands on my shoulders and began to kiss me again. '

He picked up the cup, had another drink, and refilled it. 'This is a damn sight harder than I thought it would be,' he said. 'It's not just having to say it in front of you, it's knowing that all the time she was doing this...she was...planning to hang me out to dry.'

'We don't know that Robert.' Mayhew said gently. 'We have no idea what was going through her head at that point, or what may have happened to her after you left. Let's just get this over with, shall we?'

Rob pushed the cup away, and took up where he had left off. 'All the while we were kissing she was teasing me with her stomach and those satin thongs. Back and forth, back and forth. When she could tell I could barely stand it any longer she slid her briefs down around her ankles, and mounted me.'

'She was on top. Not the other way round?'

'Absolutely. She was really up for it. Like a wild animal. Her hair was waving from side to side, her breasts and stomach covered in sweat. She started yelling in what I assumed was Spanish, making guttural noises, thumping my shoulders and arms with her fists. At one point she gripped my hair and rocked my head back and forth in tandem with every thrust of her hips. Finally, she wrapped her arms around my back, leant her cheek alongside mine, and came. As she did so, her fingers dug into my back…'

He stopped mid flow, felt with his left hand between his shoulder blades, and winced. 'So that's what it was,' he said. I'd begun to think I was going mad.'

'What happened then?' Mayhew asked, a little too eagerly.

'I think she must have realised I hadn't come. She lay there, moaning quietly, making little pelvic thrusts until she felt my body tense, my back arch, and my stomach spasm. As soon as I was still, she disengaged, rolled off the bed, picked up her bra and thong, and disappeared into the bathroom.'

'As quick as that? Nothing said?'

'Just like that. Like I was suddenly a bed of hot coals. No post coital cigarette. No sweet nothings. Just, wham, bang, thank you Sam, and away. Not that I was complaining.'

'Until now.'

Rob nodded. The seriousness of the situation bearing down on him.

Mayhew looked at his watch. 'What happened next?'

'I lay there for a while, waiting for her to come out of the bathroom. She didn't. Nor was there any sound. No shower, no toilet flush, no crying. Nothing. I climbed off the bed, put my underpants on, and went over to the bathroom. I knocked on it, and called out her name.

Please go. She said. *Just go.*

I said something like, *Are you alright?*

She said. *Yes, I'm fine. Please just go now.*

I think I said, *Was it good for you?*

He grinned sheepishly. 'Typical male pride.'

She said.' *Yes it was good for me...now just go.*

'I asked if I could have her number. Give her a ring tomorrow. She didn't want to give it to me. I got the message loud and clear. I dressed, and got out of there.'

'Did anyone see you leave?'

'Somebody must have done. Although by then most of them were either smashed or otherwise engaged. I did say thanks to Vince on my way out. He was standing in one of the windows talking to the two East European guys. He should remember. They all looked pretty sober. In fact as I left he said, *'Glad you could come Rob. See you again I hope.'* Then as he turned away, I heard him say to the others. *That Angel, she's a piece of work, isn't she?*

'What did you think he meant by that?'

'I have no idea?'

'And now?'

'Your guess is as good as mine.'

'How did you get home?'

'I walked. It was ten to two when I got in. I just stripped off, and crawled into bed. Next thing I knew there was this ringing in my head, and thumping on the door.'

'Did you have anything else to drink before you left, or when you got home?'

Rob shook his head. Just a couple of glasses of water.'

'Before you stripped off?'

'Before I crawled into bed.'

Henry put down his biro and flicked through the pages of notes. 'That's it then,' he said. 'You are admitting to consensual sex. Your defence is an honest belief that her agreement to engage in sex with you was freely given. Free from coercion, self-induced intoxication, or otherwise recklessly taken. Your word against hers.'

Rob nodded his agreement. Then he looked up at his colleague. 'I'm not so sure about the reckless part,' he said. 'It felt pretty reckless to me.'

3

'How do you like your coffee?'

'Like my men; dark and strong.'

It wasn't the reply DI Holmes had been expecting. Not from someone who worked in the Sexual Crimes Team. And not at the start of a rape investigation. But then DS Beth Hale was not your average female officer, and dark humour was the standard way they all came to terms with the cesspit of human cruelty through which they waded on a daily basis. He filled the cup, picked up two tiny cartons of milk, and carried them to the desk.

'How much longer do you think we should give them?'

She glanced at her watch, and opened one of the cartons; tipping the milk into the mug, and blowing across its surface. 'Until we're ready. There's no rush anyway. They don't have the faintest idea what we've got. If he's innocent, then the truth is his best defence. If he's not, then it doesn't matter what he comes up with. The more he tries to fabricate, the worse it will become.' She took a sip, and put the mug down. 'Perfect. You can come and work for my team any time you like. We could do with a male who's housetrained.'

Holmes had never worked with DS Hale before, but he was warming to her. At five foot one inches tall, and at a guess size ten, she was a pocket battleship. Her hair was a mass of short loose curls; black, shot through with purple highlights. He didn't know if there was such a thing as a messy look, but if there was, this was it. Her eyes were hazel, intelligent, serious, except when she smiled; then they seemed to sparkle. She wore no make up, and didn't need to. Her lips were naturally pink, and her complexion pale, in stark contrast to her hair. He realised that she had caught him staring at her. 'I was just wondering,' he bumbled. 'If you were being serious. I was thinking about a transfer.'

She looked up at him; aghast. 'Transfer out of FMIT? You must be off your trolley. People are queuing up to get in. I wouldn't mind a spell in here I can tell you. Murder and major mayhem. Now that's what I call detection.' She turned back to papers spread across the desk, and shook her head. 'Rob Thornton. I find it hard to believe. It's only two months since he helped us to secure a conviction against a two time rapist. In the end it all came down to the quality of his cross examination. He was like a bull terrier. Grabbed the defendant by the scruff of his neck, tied him up in knots, and wouldn't let go until he'd forced a change of plea. Brilliant. Crusading, was how our Boss described it.' She shook her head. Three curls fell low across her forehead. 'But you can never tell. Especially when the demon drink's involved.' She turned to look up at him. 'How much had Thornton had?'

Holmes pulled up a chair, and sat down beside her. 'When we took the samples this morning, at six twenty four, he had a reading of ninety milligrams. Twelve percent over the legal driving limit. If we assume he's got a normal metabolism, that means that between one am, which is when we're told the alleged rape took place, and six thirty am when we took the sample, his liver processed about three units of alcohol.'

He pulled a calculator from the desk door and did the maths. 'That means he would have been between one and a half, and two times, over the drink drive limit. But sober enough to know if she had given her consent, or not.'

Hale shook her head. 'Even if he'd been blind drunk, self-induced drunkenness is no defence.' She reeled it off. 'Fotheringham; Regina versus CA 1989.'

'That's true,' Gordon agreed.' 'But what if she claims she was too drunk to give her consent?'

'That's wishful thinking Gordon. Remember, the Bill hasn't gone through Parliament yet. Unfortunately, Section 74 of the Sexual Offences Act 2003 made the assumption that even if she was drunk she would not have lost the capacity to consent; which you and I know is a load of bollocks. And look at that case in Swansea in 2005. The judge stopped the trial because the prosecution admitted that the victim said she was too drunk to recall whether she had given her consent or not. Apparently it's still impossible to be so drunk, that you're incapable of withdrawing consent.'

'Tell that to all those weekend binge drinkers tottering around on their high heels, wearing pelmet mini skirts, and see through blouses,' Holmes said. 'See if it makes a blind bit of difference.'

'It won't. *But it still makes them victims. Entitled to our very best efforts to secure justice on their behalf.* Do you know who said that? Robert Thornton. At a lecture I heard him give at Sedgeley Park. Anyway, it's all irrelevant.' She selected a sheet of paper, and held it up for him to see. 'She'd had even less than he had. But she had been taking cocaine.'

'You're joking?'

'No. We haven't got the lab results back on the various specimens we took, but there were clear traces in her nostrils, and on her dress.'

'You're not suggesting he gave it to her?'

'It's not beyond the realms of possibility is it? I'm prepared to bet half the people at that party were on the stuff. Barristers aren't immune. One's just been jailed down South, for seven years for possession, and seven years for possession with intent to deal. They caught him in the middle of cutting the stuff, and bulking it up.'

'Well we haven't found anything on him, or at his place. And he wasn't showing any of the usual signs.'

Hale looked at her watch again, and then picked up the video cassette in the middle of the desk. 'Look, Gordon, we'd better speed this up. I'll show you my initial interview with her, and then we can agree our strategy.'

Holmes pushed his chair away from the desk and stood. 'Fine. But tell me. Right now, from what she's told you, and what you've seen, what's your gut instinct?'

She stood up, the top of her head level with his shoulder, lifted her dimpled chin, and fixed him with a steely gaze. 'I don't believe in gut instincts. Not when it comes down to rape. Do you know that in 1977 thirty three percent of reported cases resulted in a conviction? By 2005 it was down to just over five percent. Fifty thousand women are raped every year. Those are the ones we know about. And the number of girls under twenty who are raped is growing at an alarming rate. Nationally, less than twenty percent of reported cases go to trial, because the dice is loaded against the victim. It doesn't matter what my gut tells me; what the jury is likely to believe is all that counts in the end.' She tossed him the videotape. 'You make your own mind up. Then we'll see what Mr Thornton has to say for himself.'

Rob was finding it difficult to gauge. Normally he could tell straight away if the police felt they had a strong case; if they believed the accused, or not. Sitting on this side of the table for the first time, as the alleged perpetrator, put a totally different slant on it. There was a part of his brain that was not functioning as it should. Emotion was getting in the way of reason. His reptilian brain swamping the receptors that might have told him where he stood. He had told his story without embroidery or excessive detail. It had gone almost exactly as Henry Mayhew had predicted. DI Holmes and DS Hale had listened dispassionately. Their questions had been few, and primarily for clarification. They had let him tell his story his way; watching and listening for the signs that he might be lying. The uncontrolled muscle contractions, perspiration, eyes cast down, low voice tone, speech unnaturally fast, or slow. Just as he had watched them; trying to read their reactions. And now they sat opposite him, their bodies turned away, whispering to each other; agreeing the next steps. Like a time-out huddle in a basketball match. They straightened up, and turned back to face him.

'So let's be clear about this Mr Thornton,' DI Holmes began. 'You admit that you had sexual congress with Ms Covas. And you are claiming that it was entirely consensual.'

'Absolutely.'

'At no time did she tell you, or attempt to make it clear to you by her actions, that she did not want to have sex with you?'

'That is correct.'

'So you are also saying that there was no reason why you would have to force yourself upon her?'

'That is correct.'

'No need to hold her down, force her legs apart, for example?'

'Absolutely not,'

'You said earlier that she initiated the union,' he looked at his notes,' Mounted me...' were the words you used.'

'That is correct.'

DS Hale leaned forward. 'Were you comfortable with that Mr Thornton?' she said. It was a simple question; matter of fact.

'Yes. It took me by surprise, but it was a pleasant surprise.'

'You didn't feel disempowered, unmanned?'

They were trying to rile him. He found himself leaning back, controlling himself, distancing himself from them.

'No, quite the reverse. I felt flattered.'

Henry Mayhew put his hand on Rob's arm, alarmed by the change in his client's manner. He whispered in his ear. 'You're starting to play the game. Stop now. Don't rise to the bait.'

Holmes and Hale looked put out by this intervention, just as they'd begun to get Thornton going, but let it go. It wasn't as though he'd been charged. Not yet. Only cautioned.

'Flattered?' Holmes said. 'That she found you so irresistible? So there really was no need to force yourself on her, knock her around a bit, anything like that?'

Rob sat up a little straighter. This line of questioning was ominous, unnecessary. He'd had enough experience to know where it was leading. He wanted it over with. Right now.

'No. Absolutely not,' he said. 'She initiated everything. She was a willing partner. Her consent was never in doubt.'

DI Holmes flipped open the brown manila folder on the table in front of him, took out a series of photographs, and set them down, one after the other so that Mayhew and his client could see them. 'Then perhaps you can explain these photographs to us.' he said, without a flicker of sarcasm.

Rob stared at them in horror and disbelief. The first showed the red satin dress ripped almost in half; the second, livid bruises across the upper arms and shoulders of a naked torso, whose head had been kept out of shot, but whose long black hair hung limp on either side. The final photo showed purple bruises on the inside of the upper thighs of a woman whom he had no doubt was Anjelita Covas, but whose most private parts had been discretely hidden by a piece of card. He continued to stare, his head spinning, as Henry Mayhew calmly picked each one up in turn, and studied them closely, before placing them back on the table.

'We will of course need at some stage to see the face that accompanies these photographs,' he said. 'So that we may verify that it is indeed the person who introduced herself to my client as Anjelita Covas.'

'Of course,' Holmes said. 'Well Mr Thornton? Can you explain how Ms Covas came by these injuries?'

'I am advising my client, that he does not have to answer any more questions.' Henry Mayhew said.

Rob turned on him, more aggressively than he intended, and far more than was good for his defence. 'Of course I bloody well have to answer that question,' he said. 'It's the most important of the lot. And I have some questions of my own.' He spun back to face his accusers. 'I have no idea how Ms Covas came by those injuries, nor how her dress came to be torn. When I left the room, she was fine. She was calm, she had no injuries, and since she removed her dress herself when she was in bathroom, I was never in a position to tear it. I can only assume that either someone else entered that room after I left, or those injuries were self-inflicted.'

DS Hale slowly gathered the photos, and passed them back to DI Holmes. 'Someone did enter that room after you left.' she said, calmly. 'A couple looking for the same kind of privacy you sought. Ms Covas, was sitting on the edge of the bed. She had a sheet wrapped around her. There was blood on it, and on her face, which was also bruised. She was crying. When I got there, at the same time as the ambulance, she was shaking and sobbing. At the hospital, when we finally prised the sheet away from her, she was still wearing her dress. It had been ripped almost in half across the right side of her body, and her bra – which you say you removed for her – had also been wrenched down on that side, exposing her breast.'

Rob was a loss to know how to respond. 'That is terrible,' he said at last. 'Firstly, because it just is. Secondly, because if what you say is true, about nobody else having had access to that room...then she must have done it to herself.'

'A possibility which has not escaped us,' DI Holmes said. 'But which I'm sure you will agree seems unlikely. Unless of course you can think of any reason why she, a complete stranger to you, would go to these lengths to get you into trouble?'

Rob shook his head. 'I had never laid eyes on her before. Nothing in her demeanour throughout the evening, nothing she said in the hours that we were together, gave the slightest hint that she was anything other than attracted to me. I'm sorry, but I can't believe any of this, let alone explain it.'

They chose that point to call a break. Ten minutes later they returned, and DI Holmes had a surprise for him.

'Mr Thornton. You will be aware that we have the power, if we wish, to hold you for a further twenty nine hours without charge. I've spoken with my commanding officer, and we are prepared to release you on police bail, pending further enquiries. There are two conditions to this bail. Firstly, that you report daily to a police station of your choice. Secondly, that you stay away from, and do not attempt to make any form of contact – directly or indirectly - with Ms Covas. Do you accept these conditions?'

They sat in the corner of the Old Nag's Head, away from the jukebox, and the fruit machines, just a street across from the station on Bootle Street were he had been held. Henry was nursing a brandy, Rob swirled the remains of a Virgin Mary around his glass.

'I don't know how you can drink that without the vodka,' Henry said in desperation. His client had not spoken a word since they'd sat down.

Rob lifted his glass, drained it, and slammed it back down on the table. The men at the pool table turned and stared for a moment, before returning to their game. 'Don't think I'm not tempted,' he replied, his voice close to a growl. 'Why would she do that? And how could I be such an idiot?'

Henry seized the opportunity. 'As to your second question, it's a bit late to concern yourself with that. The key lies with your first. Why would she falsely accuse you? If we find the answer to that, you'll be home and clear.'

Rob glared at him 'When, Henry. When we find out, not if.'

The solicitor's tone was now conciliatory. 'You're right. When we find out.' He sipped the brandy, marshalling his thoughts. 'There were no witnesses, or they would have charged you straight away. It's still her word against yours. Granted, those injuries look bad; especially hers. Far worse than they really are, I suspect. And I don't know what you thought, but at first sight I would have to question whether they were consistent with what little we know of her account.'

For the first time since they had left the police station he had really grabbed his client's attention. Rob's brow furrowed as he tried to recall the images he had pushed to the back of his mind. 'What do you mean, not consistent?'

'Come on Robert. Think about it. Just for a moment forget that you are the accused. Put yourself in your normal role. Let's start with the easy one. Your injuries; what, and where, are they?'

'On my chest, shoulders and upper arms. And the scratches on my back.'

'So how did she deliver those do you suppose?'

'I told you, with her fists.'

'When exactly?'

'When she was on top of me.'

'Ah, but that's your account. How do suppose she might have explained them? Remember what the detective said. You are supposed to have forced yourself upon her.'

'Well then, when I first came on to her perhaps.'

The Mathew shook his head. 'That might explain her injuries, but not yours. Firstly, you would be up close. Giving her no room to punch repeatedly with such ferocity. If she'd broken away, or begun to deliver blows, what do you think that you would have done?'

'Grab her wrists, or her arms.'

'Precisely.'

'All right then, she did it when I was on top of her, on the bed.'

'But surely you would have pinioned her arms?'

'Possibly.

'And then, there are the scratches on your back. If you were fighting desperately to save your honour, possibly your life, where would you go for?'

'The face, the eyes; the arms if they were holding me down.'

Henry smiled. His client's eyes had recovered their

spark. A corner had been turned. 'And I think we can assume that traces of your skin will have been found beneath Ms Covas' nails. Was the back of your shirt torn at all?'

'I don't think so. No, I'm pretty sure it wasn't.'

'Which tells us that your shirt had been removed before she scratched you. Why was Ms Covas not yelling blue murder at the point at which you were taking it off? Unless of course she was comfortable with seeing you half naked?'

Rob leant against the wall. 'Carter and Hale must been having this same conversation. Perhaps that's why they let me go so quickly.'

'Or perhaps it's because you are a barrister, and they're not going to act in haste. Certainly not without the say so of the Crown Prosecution Service. Ultimately they may feel that it still has to be tested in court. If you were acting for the prosecution, what would you do?'

'Double check her story. Look into her background. See if I could find any possible motive for her to make it up. Forestall the defence making out such a case.'

'And what causation might you expect to find?'

'You know the list: attention seeking; self disgust; to avoid admitting to other significant persons – family, husband, lover – that she had consented to sex with another man, whether drunk or otherwise; revenge; there was even a case where it was used to create an alibi. *I was being raped at the time.* How bizarre was that?'

'But we're only talking about a tiny minority of reported cases here.' Henry cautioned him.

Rob dismissed the empty glass with a flick of his hand, sending it scudding across the table where Mayhew stopped it with the palm of his hand. 'Don't you think I know that Henry?' he said. 'I've seen the effect that rape has on the victims. I think it's the vilest of crimes, save only child abuse. If I had to have a single reason to be a barrister it would be to find these women redress. It makes me sick to the stomach that so many are put off from reporting the crime because they're going to have their motives questioned in open court; cast in the role of perpetrator. That's why I've never accepted a brief for the defence in a case of rape. You know that.'

Henry reached out and put his hand on his client's arm. 'Well I'm afraid you don't have a choice my friend. This time, it's her, or you.'

4

It was gone two pm when Rob opened the door to his apartment. Although he knew what to expect it still came as a shock. Every cupboard and shelf had been emptied. Every piece of furniture upturned. Cushion and sofa covers had been removed, and thrown into the middle of the room. His precious collections of books, CDs and DVDs were at least in separate piles, and no attempt had been made to lift the wooden flooring. An hour and half later some semblance of order had been restored, and he felt a desperate need to get out in the fresh air.

The sky was clear. A bitter cold wind had swept in from the Urals, threatening snow on the Pennine heights, and sleet down here in centre of the city. Oblivious, he started walking aimlessly, up past the Bridgewater Hall, straight across Oxford Street, into Portland Street. At the junction with Princess Street he turned left, and walked the short distance to the Manchester Art Gallery. For almost an hour he wandered through the galleries, losing himself in familiar paintings, barely aware of his surroundings. He stopped before a painting by Valette that had always seemed to him to epitomise the historic soul of the city. In the foreground, a cellar man trundled his barrow across a fog bathed Albert Square. In the middle ground the Albert Memorial, and the statues of Oliver Heywood – banker, philanthropist and first

Freeman of the city - and Victorian Prime Minister William Gladstone, looked down upon the scene. In the middle distance, horse drawn cabs and motor cars vied with each other, and with the perilous tram lines. Soot-blackened, the town hall loomed above them all. When Rob took part in his first moot in Greys Inn of Court he had opened the debate with the words that Gladstone had used in his acceptance speech, here in Albert Square, when he was returned as Member of Parliament for South Lancashire. *"At last, my friends, I come amongst you. And I am come... unmuzzled."* After years having to represent the interests of those who had sponsored him for Parliament, Gladstone was finally free to speak for his electorate without fear or favour. It had become Rob's touchstone.

His ruminations were interrupted as a party of Spanish teenagers, their minders dressed in distinctive blue denim jackets, invaded the gallery, and hemmed him in. His heart began to race. He found himself short of breath. On the verge of panic. He pushed his way roughly through the crowd, ignoring the shouts and squeals of annoyance. A member of the Gallery staff rose from his chair beside the doorway as he passed, and raised his walkie talkie to his mouth. Only when Rob made it to the exit, and had began to breathe slowly and deeply, did his pulse slow down, and the tightness in his chest recede. He sat on the cold stone steps for a moment, oblivious to the people stepping around him. It was the first time in his life that he had experienced panic. It left him feeling tired and concerned in equal measure. Eventually he rose, recognised the pang in his stomach as hunger, and headed towards Albert Square.

Tampopo had become a resting post for shoppers exhausted from their Christmas shopping, taking refuge from the hordes around the Christmas Market. The long wooden refectory style tables in the basement were full. As he turned to go a group of four rose noisily, and left a welcoming space in the furthest corner. He ordered from memory. Gyoza, five small dumplings filled with minced pork, bamboo shoots, and spring onion, with a soy dip; and a selection of tempura vegetables with a plum dip; Seafood Ramen noodles with mussels, prawns and squid as the main; a bottle of golden Kirin beer, to wash it all down. At least, he reflected, there's nothing wrong with my appetite. Despite the proximity of his fellow diners on the table, the lively atmosphere, and passers by at street level who paused to peer through the semicircular windows down into the basement, he felt the same sense of isolation he had experienced in the gallery.

Rather than face the crowds beneath the Christmas lights strung across Deansgate, he retraced his steps, and reached the apartment shortly before six. There were no messages on his answer phone; none on his mobile. This was a first. He wondered how the news had spread so fast. Not even curiosity had overcome their embarrassment. To be fair, he wondered how he would begin a conversation with a friend accused of rape.

'How are you?'

Stupid question.

'I was really sorry to hear…'

Well nobody's died, and in any case is there a presumption of guilt here?

'I've just heard…is it true?

That I was arrested, or that I'm guilty?

'I've just heard…didn't believe it for a moment…'

Methinks he doth protest too much.

He was beginning to understand how difficult that might be. How do you approach a leper, without betraying fear, prejudice, or embarrassment? The phone rang. It was Henry Mayhew.

'Robert,' he said without preamble. Have you got the television on?'

'Yes.'

'Are you watching the news?'

A knot formed in Rob's stomach, pushing like a fist into his diaphragm. 'No.'

'Well switch over. You're on.'

A roving reporter was busy interviewing shoppers in St Ann's Square.

'Have I missed it?' he asked.

'No. They headlined it at the start of the programme. It'll come up shortly.'

He had to endure five nail biting minutes of inconsequential chatter about retail patterns; Christmas on credit; a feature on Man City's resurgence and the forthcoming derby game. Finally they returned to the studio. The presenters had on their serious faces. The man stepped forward.

'And now, to our main story this evening. We have just learned that in the early hours of this morning one of Manchester's up and coming barristers was arrested by the police, and questioned regarding an alleged serious sexual assault on a young woman.'

The female presenter stepped forward to join him. She held an expression fixed between surprise and grave concern. 'Robert Thornton, a leading junior counsel, who has appeared on this channel on a number of occasions, and has some impressive successes behind him, both for the defence, and the prosecution, was arrested this morning at his apartment, and taken to Bootle Street Police Station where he was questioned for several hours. We can now go live to Libby Adamovski, at St Mary's Hospital.'

'Thank you Kerry. Yes, I have just learned that in the early hours of this morning a young woman, in her twenties, was brought by the police, here, to the Sexual Assault Referral Centre, as a victim of serious sexual assault. Three hours later Robert Thornton, a Manchester barrister, was arrested by the police at his apartment in the centre of the city, and taken to Bootle Street Police Station, where he was questioned. I have to emphasise that he was not charged with any offence, but was released at midday, on police bail, pending further enquiries. I have been told that a condition of the bail is that he to report to Bootle Street Station on a daily basis.'

'Libby, do you have any information about the nature of the alleged assault, or the condition of the young woman?'

'Well as to the condition of the victim, whose name the police will not release of course, I understand that she is comfortable. As to the nature of the assault – sorry the alleged assault – I have no further on that, other than a suggestion – not corroborated either by the police or the hospital – that it may have involved an allegation of rape. This is Libby Adamovski, reporting for ITN.'

Back in the studio the male presenter turned

inwards towards the backdrop screen on which appeared a picture Rob recognised as having been taken of him on the steps outside Manchester Crown Court. He was standing behind his client, and her solicitor, smiling smugly.

'It is ironic that Robert Thornton should find himself being questioned in this case, not least because of his fearless reputation for prosecuting perpetrators of rape, and serious sexual assault. This photograph was taken earlier this year following one such successful prosecution, during which the victim, Ms Cranby, insisted on waving her right to anonymity so that she could speak publicly to highlight the devastating effects of these crimes.' He turned to his colleague. 'Kerry.'

Thank you Patrick,' she beamed. 'And now, let's see what the weather has in store for us, with Amy Potter.'

Angry, and shaken, Rob switched the television off and stood looking at the blank screen;.

'Robert…Robert. Are you still there?'

He lifted the phone to his ear. 'Yes Henry, I'm here.'

'Well it was pretty standard stuff. Could have been worse.'

Rob exploded. 'Worse? How the bloody hell could it have been worse? They went as far as they could without risking libel. And it could have been a bloody sight better. They could have said that a man had been arrested, and then released without charge. They didn't have to give my name. And what was that impressive successes behind him all about? Implying that I'm finished already.'

'Calm down Robert. You're being paranoid.'

'Paranoid?! Paranoid? You know what they say. Just because you're paranoid it doesn't mean they're not out to get you!'

'You're not the first high profile person to find himself in this position. You'll be surprised how quickly it will all blow over.'

'Not if it goes to trial it won't. Then it'll be a bloody circus.'

'Then we'll have to make sure it doesn't go to trial. And that, Robert, will require you to sort your head out, and cease acting like a complete moron. Now I'm going to put this phone down. I'll ring you in the morning in the hope that a good night's sleep will have restored a modicum of commonsense.'

Rob stood there for a moment listening to the high pitched tone, then he flung the phone onto the sofa, and stormed into the wet room where he splashed his face with water. The telephone rang again. He retrieved it from the sofa. It wasn't Henry's voice that he heard, but his mother's.

'Oh, Robert...'

The one opening gambit for which he had not prepared.

'Hi mum. You've seen the news then?'

'Oh Robert...'

He didn't want her to go on. Dreading what her next line might be he pulled himself together, and made it easy for her.

'It's all right mum, really it is. It's just a mistake, a misunderstanding. You don't need to worry, I'm going to sort it out.'

He heard her sigh with relief, wanting to believe

him. His mother was no shrinking violet even if it was his father's affair that had led to the break up of their marriage. She might not want to believe this of her son, but she would be perfectly able to envisage how it might just happen.

'Thank God,' she said. 'That's exactly what I told Marjorie'

Marjorie, her best friend and poker partner. They would all be ringing his mother now, offering their concern, wanting to hear the details. She didn't deserve this.

'Look mum. I can't tell you anymore at this stage – it's sub judice - but Henry Mayhew's on the case, and let's face it, no one is better placed than him and me to sort this out. So don't worry, and don't listen to any of the gossip mongers. As soon as it's done and dusted, you'll be the first to know.'

'If you say so Robert. Will you tell your father? I wouldn't want him to read it in the papers without hearing it from you.'

He had forgotten about his father. Now that he lived in France with his new wife he never listened to the radio, and relied on a single copy of the Sunday Times, delivered on a Monday, to catch up with news back home. That gave Rob little more than twenty four hours. Always assuming some nosey parker didn't take it into their head to give him a ring. Better to get it over with.

'You're right mum,' he said. 'I'll do it now. Now don't you worry. I'll speak to you later in the week, I'm sure it will have blown over by then.'

'We'll if you're certain there's nothing I can do?'

'I'm certain. Good night mum. Thanks for ringing.'

'Good night Robert. I'll pray for you.'

He switched the phone off and stared at it. God how he hated it when she did that. And what exactly would she be praying for? His freedom from false accusation, or forgiveness for his guilty soul?

The conversation with his father proved much easier. He was able to tell a slimmed down version. Party, attractive young woman, got on really well, had a bit to drink, she came on to me, one thing led to another, next morning the police are at the door saying she's claiming that I raped her. His father told him that he was bloody idiot. That of course it could happen to anyone, but that he should have known better. Glad he was told like this on the phone rather than had to read it in the papers. Good luck, and let him know when it was all over. And that was that. The sum total of the calls he received that night. Except for the text on his mobile he discovered when he went to bed, from Donald Weir QC, his Head of Chambers, telling him he would be in his office at eight am on Monday morning. He was not to ring back, because he was visiting relations.

He switched the television on, and sat there flicking aimlessly through the channels. There was nothing he could bear to watch. He dug out The Devil Wears Prada DVD, and put it on. Halfway through, he made himself a cheese sandwich with a couple of giant sized gherkins, and a glass of milk. When the film ended, he left everything where it was, and went to bed, exhausted.

On Sunday morning Rob woke refreshed. It was only when he went to the wet room, and caught sight of himself in the mirror, that the nightmare came flooding back. He made up a bacon and egg barm, and a pot of coffee, and scoured the papers. There was no mention of him, either because the news had broken too late for the first edition, or more probably because they were waiting to see how it might develop. Mid-morning, Harry Richmond finally plucked up enough courage to call. He was trying to sound cool, and failing; mainly because he wasn't pausing long enough for Rob to get a word in edgeways.

'Hi mate,' he said. 'How are you doing? I would have called earlier but I only just heard. You must be feeling gutted. What the hell happened there? You two seemed to be getting on just fine, the last time I looked. I couldn't believe it, but Stanley said he'd seen it on the news. What the hell's she playing at...'

'Whoaa Harry,' Rob interrupted. 'Slow down, take a breather. Give me chance to tell you.' He told the tale, in greater detail than with his father, and significantly less than with the police. 'So there you are,' he said. 'Unless she withdraws her complaint, or the CPS chicken out, I'm guilty until proved innocent.'

'Come on,' Harry said, with as much confidence as he could muster, which was far too little for Rob's liking. 'They're never going to take her word against yours. You're a respected barrister, what is she?'

'An overseas aid worker, over here to improve her English prior to going out to help with the reconstruction of flood damaged areas in Marharashtra.'

Harry was unable to help himself. 'Bloody Hell,' he said. 'A Mother Teresa.'

'Exactly. Always assuming that she didn't lie about that as well.'

'Well you'd better hope she did. Because a jury would love that.'

'Thanks. Don't you think I know that?'

'Sorry. Doesn't help to state the obvious.'

'No it doesn't.'

'Well, if there's anything I can do. I could put some feelers out about her through Vince if you like.'

'No. Leave that to Henry. I don't want anyone suggesting that I was using you to put pressure on her. One thing you can do though is be prepared to tell the police how she was behaving towards me on Friday night. Can you do that?'

'No problem. I mean I left before you went upstairs, but I saw her chatting you up. And she was sitting on the stairs with you when I went to the loo. And she was all over you on the dance floor as I was leaving.'

'Well make sure you do tell them. They'll be going through the list of guests, so they'll get to you eventually.'

'Do you want me to go in and volunteer to make a statement?'

'Better not at this stage. You can give one to Henry, but I'd wait for the police to come to you. They're bound to find out that you're not only a colleague in Chambers, but my best friend too. 'Whatever you say they'll take with a pinch of salt. Best not to seem too keen.'

'True. Look, why don't I come round this evening with some beers and a curry. We can watch a DVD. Take your mind off it.'

'If it's all the same to you Harry, I'd rather not. I'm not good company at the moment, not even for myself, let alone anyone else. But I appreciate that you called… eventually. I'll do the same for you one day.'

'Not if I can help it.' Harry said, displaying yet again his unerring lack of tact.

5

It was a frosty Monday morning; inside as well as out. Marion Riley, fifteen years on reception, had seen it all. But this was definitely a first.

'Mr Weir is in his office,' she said without looking up. 'He's expecting you.'

Rob had never failed to win a smile, until today. 'Thank you Marion,' he replied, as close to unruffled as he could get. Before leaving the apartment he had practised the voice, and the look, in the mirror. Relaxed, composed, light hearted, undismayed, quietly confident; and totally lacking authenticity. If the eyes were truly the window to the soul, his soul was in trouble. He was beginning to wonder if it would be better to stop trying, and allow his true feelings to show, but he doubted that people would be able to stomach pained, angry, and embarrassed, for long. He knocked on the sturdy wooden door. The shiny brass plaque was unequivocal: Donald Weir QC. Head of Chambers. The Headmaster's study.

'Come in.'

The voice fitted perfectly. Perhaps he too had been practising. Donald Weir, sixty four, silver haired without a trace of baldness, corpulent in face and figure having finally succumbed, in the twilight of his career, to long lunches and fine wines, sat erect in the

57

thick red leather chair behind the desk his grandfather had brought with him when he founded these Chambers a hundred and one years ago. Grandfather, father, and son, stared gravely down from the wood panelled walls. Three just men: disappointed, disenchanted, and betrayed. Donald waved his arm towards the pair of red leather Chesterfield club chairs.

'Ah, Robert. Do sit down.'

'Are you sure you wouldn't prefer me to stand?' Rob asked. As much to test the waters as to lighten the atmosphere.

Weir rose from behind his desk, and moved towards the second chair. 'Don't be daft man,' he said. 'This isn't a hanging.'

Rob waited for Donald to sink into his chair before joining him. 'More of a flogging perhaps?' That at least brought the hint of a smile.

'I can't pretend that I'm happy about this,' Donald told him. 'But you don't flog a man for stupidity. And you shouldn't start indulging in self-flagellation either. Come to think of it, next time you might want to try that instead. Damn sight less risky.'

This time it was Rob's turn to smile wryly. 'Might not be such a bad idea. Look I'm sorry Donald, I really am. Yes, I had sex with this woman. Almost entirely at her prompting I might add. But it was one hundred percent consensual. I wasn't drunk, and I have no idea why she would want to accuse me of rape. It doesn't make sense. I am guilty. Of stupidity. But that's all.'

Donald nodded his head wearily. 'I know,' he said. 'You may be brash, over confident, a bit full of yourself, but that's why I hired you. I don't believe you have it in you to behave like that. Even if you are drunk. Could have happened to any of us. Just unfortunate that it happened to you.' He paused for a moment and picked nervously at the buttons on the arm of his chair. 'What are you going to do about your briefs?' he asked.

It was an obvious question, but for some reason Rob had not seen it coming, never considered it, and was completely unprepared.

'Carry on with them,' he replied.

Donald Weir's face clouded over. 'You can't be serious? It stands to reason that you'll have to surrender them. At least until all this has blown over; been resolved.'

Rob's fingers dug into to the leather armrests. 'You do know I've not been charged?'

'Yes. But that's not the point. Did you see the news? Have you seen this morning's Manchester Evening News? How do you think this reflects on the Chambers? What must your clients think? Who in their right mind is going to want you to represent them until this is sorted?'

All questions Rob had been asking himself, and neatly avoiding. Now there was nowhere to hide. 'If I stop working now it will look like an admission of guilt. There will be people who may be reluctant to seek my advice, but I'll just have to see how that turns out. As for my present clients, I'll speak to them, and their solicitors, and tell them exactly what the situation is. They can decide for themselves.'

It was not what Donald wanted to hear. 'Well, you are only a tenant here,' he said. 'So I can't force you to take my advice, but I would urge to consider taking a back seat for the time being. You could concentrate on advocacy work. That way you wouldn't need to make any court appearances. If it's the fees you're worried about, I am sure that the rest of the tenants would rally round. They could pick up your current briefs, and share the proceeds with you. I'll be happy to suspend your rent until it's sorted.'

Rob levered himself to his feet. 'Thank you Donald. But no thank you. As far as I'm concerned it's going to be work as usual. I have no intention of skulking away like a naughty schoolboy. I'm sorry if that makes people feel uncomfortable, but it's nowhere as uncomfortable as I'm feeling I can assure you. In the unlikely event that I am charged, I shall be happy to follow your advice. It may even be that the Bar will seek to suspend me, although as their rules relate to professional misconduct, rather than personal misconduct, I think that improbable.'

Donald Weir rose, with a great deal more difficulty, to join him. They stood less than a yard apart, eye to eye. 'Is that you final word Robert?'

'I am afraid it is.'

'Very well. I rely on you to avoid doing or say anything which might affect the reputation of these Chambers.'

'Of course.' he said, and turned to go. Donald called after him.

'Oh, I nearly forgot. Apparently your pupil has come in early. She's eager to see you. I hope your new found notoriety isn't going to act like an aphrodisiac.'

It was a stupid thing to say. Rob turned, saw the awkward grin on Donald's face, and realised that he was simply embarrassed. It was a feeble attempt at humour, because the reality was so hard to comprehend. It was the kind of reaction to which he was going to have to get used.

There were three of them in a huddle around the reception desk as he came out. The thin, gaunt figure of Stanley Bollington, the Head Clerk, with twenty years experience beneath his belt; the ever efficient, and starchy, Sylvia Franklin, the Fees Clerk, forty going on sixty; and Marion Riley. They made a bad job of pretending not to notice as he passed them on his way to the stairs. He waited until he had begun to ascend before calling out to them.

'Morning everyone. Bit chilly today, but I think the sun's going to come out later.'

Through the corner of his eye he glimpsed them turning, frozen surprise thawing into nervous smiles.

Anna Gardener was waiting in his room. She leapt from her chair like a startled rabbit; concern and apprehension etched across her face. Twenty three years old, mouse brown hair gathered in a pony tail, slim, hardworking, very bright, and eager to please. She had a Double First from Exeter, had won the Hardwicke Scholarship to Lincoln's Inn, and was a third of the way through her pupillage. She was the third apprentice barrister for whom he had been the pupil master, and by far the most promising.

'Mr Thornton,' she stuttered, 'I'm sorry, you startled me.'

'I can't imagine why,' he said with a disarming smile intended to put her at her ease. 'The last time I checked this was my room.'

A crimson flush worked its way upwards from her neck and began to suffuse her cheeks.

'And how many times do I have to tell you, it's Rob.' He was about to take her gently by the arm to lower her back onto her chair when he thought better of it. 'Sit down Anna,' he said instead. 'And, while I make us a drink, tell me why you came in at this ungodly hour.' He moved to the small sink area, and switched on the kettle.

'Well…' she began, nervously. 'I just felt that I had to tell you how sorry I was to hear…well you know, what that woman is accusing you of. And if there is anything I can do to help…well, you only have to ask.'

He opened the cupboard door. 'The usual? Coffee? Or do you want to try a breakfast tea?'

'Oh, thanks, no, just a coffee please.'

'Well I must say that I'm really touched,' he said. 'I would have thought you'd have wanted to get as much distance between us as possible. Find a new pupil master. I didn't suppose you'd want to put me down as a referee at the end of the year.'

He handed her the coffee, and sat down opposite. She squirmed on her chair in fractious protest, creating a miniature wave across the surface of her coffee that threatened her trouser suit. She clamped the mug with her free hand, and waited until the surface stilled.

'How can you say that? I was over the moon when you agreed to take me on, and I haven't regretted a moment of it. I've learned so much. You've been patient, and you've set me challenges that have really stretched me. I shall count myself privileged to be able to tell people that you were my pupil master, and fortunate to have you as a referee.'

He blew on the surface of his mug. 'I'm duly flattered. I assume that means that you either believe that I'm innocent, or you don't mind whether I am or not?'

The wave threatened to erupt again. 'Of course you're innocent! You could *never* do anything like that.'

'Not even if I was drunk, drugged, high on cocaine or ecstasy?'

'You never get really drunk, you don't take drugs, and if you were drugged by someone else, you would have been incapable.'

'Would you consider defending me?' he asked. 'I think I'm going to have trouble finding someone able to combine a razor sharp intellect and the blind faith you appear to have in me.'

'I'm not blind, even if justice is supposed to be,' she saw him smile, and bristled. 'And please don't patronise me.'

'Fair enough,' he said. 'I take it you know where the concept of blind justice comes from?'

She nodded. 'From the code of King Hammurabi of Babylon. Once guilt had been determined – or even strongly presumed – the accused would be sat behind a screen, or blind, so that the presiding official – who had not been party to the proceedings, could hand down the prescribed punishment without fear or favour. The Romans coined the phrase lex talionis; the law of retaliation.'

'Exactly. An eye for an eye, a tooth for a tooth. Retribution, without taking any account of the circumstances or the status of either the accuser or the accused. In common parlance, let the punishment fit the crime. He paused to take a sip of tea. 'That, if I were to be found guilty, is precisely what would happen when the body builders cornered me in the prison showers.'

She gave an involuntary shudder at the thought. 'This is precisely why it must never come to trial. And that's how I can help.'

'How exactly?'

She put her mug down on the wooden floor, and leant forward excitedly. 'Your accuser is clearly lying. If, as it usually does, it comes down to her word against yours…' She waited for him to nod. '…then we have to find a way of discrediting her story. To reveal her motive. Expose her as a liar.'

'And what if she's simply delusional?'

'Is that what you suspect?'

'To be honest, I don't have the faintest idea.'

'Well if she is, we just have to be able to prove it.'

Her enthusiasm lifted his spirit momentarily. 'Your logic Anna, as always, is impeccable. But there's nothing we can do right now except wait. Unless I've been charged, any intrusion into her life will be come across as harassment, and weaken my case. In fact staying away from her is part of my bail conditions.'

'I know that. But there are two things we can do. Firstly, we can put a strategy together, just in case they do the unthinkable and want to take you to court. Secondly, I can do some basic research – from a distance. Just background stuff. It's what I do all the time. I don't have to go anywhere near her. Nobody will know. Trust me.'

Rob studied her closely. This was the second young woman in as many days asking him to trust her. Her intellect and loyalty were never in doubt, but her naivety still troubled him. On the other hand, she had been with him for four months and never put a foot wrong. And his instinct told him this was going all the way.

'You're on,' he said. 'But you do it my way; softly, softly.'

By ten o'clock, he had done some work on his most troublesome brief, spent ten minutes enduring Harry Richmond's well intentioned attempts to cheer him up, and had courtesy visits from two of his fellow tenants, Jonathan Barker-Smyth, and Timothy Swain, neither of whom, to his great relief, lingered more than a minute or so. But at least they had gone to the trouble of showing their faces and offering their support, which was more than the rest of them had done. It was time to report to Bootle Street, so he put on his coat and set off. He bumped into Henry Mayhew at the lights on the corner of Quay Street and Deansgate.

'Oh, good. I thought I'd come with you Robert, and get the lie of the land,' the solicitor said. 'You've saved me the trouble of coming round to your Chambers.'

They walked in silence up Peter Street and turned left into Southmill Street. Only when they reached the entrance to the police station did Henry try again. 'How are you holding up?' he asked.

'Ask me again in half an hour,' Rob replied.

Within two minutes of their arrival they were shown though to an interview room. DI Holmes was waiting for them.

'I'll keep this short,' he said. 'Forensics have confirmed Mr Thornton that you indeed had, as you freely admitted, sexual relations with Ms Covas. They have also eliminated the possibility that Ms Covas had had sex with anybody else that evening, or subsequently. The papers on the case are being prepared, and will be submitted in due course to the Crown Prosecution Service for a decision on whether or not you will be charged with the offence for which you were arrested and questioned.'

'Would it be possible to see the forensic evidence relating to the injuries evident in the photographs you showed us of Ms Covas?' Asked Mayhew pointedly.

It was obvious from the look on the detective's face that he knew what was being implied here. He shook his head slowly. 'I'm sorry sir, 'he said. 'You will of course have total access to all of the evidence, including the forensic reports, if your client is actually charged with an offence. But not until then.' He turned towards Rob. 'Is there anything Mr Thornton you would wish to add to your statement at this time that may help the Crown Prosecution Service arrive at a decision?'

Henry Mayhew answered for him. 'My client has nothing to add other than to protest his complete innocence of any wrongdoing.'

Holmes nodded and made a note. 'In that case it only remains for me to remind you that the conditions of your bail remain in place. Do you have any questions?'

'Now do you want to ask me how I feel?' Rob said as they headed back down Bootle Street. 'Well I'll tell you anyway. I feel trapped. Completely powerless. And thoroughly pissed off!'

He spent the afternoon going over the papers for an appearance at the Crown Court in the morning. It concerned a case of grievous bodily harm to which the accused had foolishly elected to plead not guilty, despite the fact that there were four witnesses to the assault, and a conveniently placed CCTV camera in the bar where it had occurred. Rob felt confident that by lunch time the defence would have finally persuaded him to change his plea; a little too late to influence the sentence that he would inevitably receive. When the time came to leave he found himself drawn, against his better judgement, towards the search engines. He entered the name of his accuser. Ten minutes later his trawl consisted of a Doretea Covas in the Bastrop County USA Marriage Index for 1924, a Dora Anjelita Mendez in 1961, an Anjelita Silva and Anjelita Comonech, even a barrister called Cancio Covas, and the actress Sara Covas with several Portuguese films to her credit. After half an hour he'd uncovered numerous marine biologists, engineers, sociologists with the name Covas; a Maria Isabel Covas, and a Maria Merces Covas. But not a single Anjelita Covas.

He turned his attention to the social networks, starting with Facebook, Bibo, MySpace, and Yahoo 360, but each of them required him to register. He realised that if he did there was always the possibility that the police would discover what he had been doing, and suspect his motives. He was sufficiently computer literate to realise that even if he used a false name his email address would give him away. He decided to leave it to his pupil. If her blog was anything to go by, Anna was probably a social network junkie anyway. He sensed a migraine coming on. Something he had not experienced since his school days. The walls felt as though they were closing in. He logged off, locked up, and left.

6

There was no way he could face cooking for himself. And the way things were shaping up, eating out would mean eating alone. Even Harry Richmond had made himself scarce during the afternoon, and had left Chambers conspicuously early. Home alone was preferable every time. At the moment it was the only option. It was bad enough people avoiding him at work, but to take a table at one of his favourite haunts, and then find acquaintances scurrying past, or turning their backs to avoid catching his eye, would hardly be conducive to good digestion. He could imagine the pained or pitying expressions in the eyes of the maitre d' and the waitresses.

He entered the Tesco Express on Quay Street underneath Overseas House, just two blocks from his Chambers. A regular here, he found himself browsing the shelves head down, avoiding eye contact. Exactly the behaviour he had promised himself he would avoid. He pulled himself together, and chose a *Finest Steak and Ale with Cheddar Mash* for this evening, a *Chicken, Chorizo, Cheese and Potato Bake,* and an *Aberdeen Angus Cottage Pie* for later in the week. Two cartons of milk, a carton of fresh orange juice, and a multi pack of crisps completed his mental list but there was a tempting special offer at the end of the aisle by the cash out; two 750ml bottles of Leffe Brune for the price of one. Perfect with the pie. He surveyed the contents of the basket. Northern metro man. He walked back down the aisle, picked up a small bag of apples, and placed them in the basket. He watched them settle themselves around the bottles of beer, amused that he could worry about healthy eating at a time like this. The girl at the till was new, and barely gave him a second glance.

He stripped off and had a shower. Cocooned in his wet room, lathered in foaming gel, he felt the tension leaching away. He switched off the steaming jets, and stood there for a minute or two in the up draught from the extractor fan. Still conscious of the newly formed scabs in the middle of his back he left his body to drip dry rather than risk the towel.

Twenty minutes later, he pushed aside the remains of the steak and ale pie – a few crumbs in a swirl of gravy – and changed channels on the television. He had no stomach for any of it. He tried the music system. Far from calming, it made him increasingly restless. Incapable of relaxing, he gave in, and took and apple and the beer to his work desk. He switched on the angle poise lamp, selected a notepad and a biro, wrote down the heading - *Motives* – and underlined it twice. He started with the ones that he and Henry had discussed: *self disgust; to avoid admitting to others that she had had sex with another man; revenge; creating an alibi.* He added *attention seeking, paranoid schizophrenia,* and *bi-polar disorder.* He went over each of them in turn, holding them up in his mind like a mirror against his recollections of her that night. One by one he eliminated them on the grounds that that there had been nothing in her behaviour to validate them. That left just three. Notwithstanding his legal training, and several related cases under his belt, he had to admit that he knew too little about paranoid schizophrenia or bi-polar disorder to decide one way or the other. If either was the explanation, he felt confident that psychiatric reports called for by the defence would reveal the fact. That left him with just one. He circled the word *Revenge*, and began another list.

There were, he supposed, two categories of possibility. She wanted revenge on him, personally. Or she sought revenge on men in general. Any man would do. The latter seemed so bizarre and ill-fated – that he should be the random victim – and clearly indicative of serious mental disturbance, that he decided to leave that for the experts. Her life and medical history would surely throw that up. He decided to concentrate on the former. He, and he alone, was the focus of her revenge. He remembered the handkerchief fluttering innocently to the floor. Was that the opening gambit in a meticulous game plan? He recognised the signs of anger welling up, and took a swig of beer. A cool head was called for. Like never before.

For the life of him he could think of no one in his personal life he had knowingly injured. And there was the rub. Saint Rob would never have set out to hurt anyone, physically, financially, or emotionally. But that wasn't the point was it? How was he to know who he may have hurt unintentionally? Someone who perceived a hurt, where none was intended? And if he had, how the hell was he going to find out? He wracked his brains for a full hour. He revisited every relationship that he had had that either ended acrimoniously, or where promises to continue as good friends had never come to fruition. It wasn't that there were so many, rather that he found himself dissecting each of them with the care and precision of a surgeon. He began to recall, and almost experience, some of the positive emotions associated with the early stages of those relationships; and something of the pain of hopes unfulfilled, and joyless, guilty separation. In none of them could he see the face of Anjelita Covas, or any link, or possible connection.

He turned his attention to his professional career, albeit relatively short. Here there were many more possibilities. There were those clients he had defended unsuccessfully. Any one of them - presupposing they were not currently in jail - or family, friends or partners in crime, if they were, might harbour a bitter resentment. Any one of them might seek this means of ruining his personal and private reputation, and bringing his career to an ignominious end. He shuddered as it occurred to him that if the instigator were still inside, then that revenge might well be intended to escalate once Rob found the prison gates closing behind him. He took another swig of beer, and thought about the other permutations. There were those he had successfully prosecuted. The victims and family of perpetrators he had successfully defended, or failed to get convicted. There were even witnesses he had subpoenaed, whose marriages, reputations or businesses had been ruined as a direct result. Especially those he had been warned not to call. For the first time it dawned on him just how many people's lives his professional interventions impinged upon.

On his home computer he had a log of every brief he had accepted. Only the salient details were recorded. The dates, names of the acting solicitor and rest of the legal team, the opposing team, the judge, the charges, relevant points of law that arose during the trial, and - most importantly – the result. He decided to begin with the three most recent years. Given that he had no idea what he was looking for, he started with the obvious; sexually related crimes. He would eliminate these first.

There were a total of fifteen cases; ten wins, four losses, one no contest in which the prosecution had withdrawn the charges before it came to trial. At the time he had been loath to chalk that up as a win. As far as he could tell, none of the fifteen cases had involved anyone – either as victim or alleged perpetrator - with the name Covas, nor with any Latin sounding name. Nor did he recall any witnesses who might have fallen into that category. There were always the jurors of course, but that would take for ever to check. If Anjelita Covas had been on any of the juries herself, he was certain that he would have remembered.

He began to work methodically through the rest of the logs. This was a truly motley crew. There were moving traffic offences such as speeding, drunk driving, leaving the scene of an accident, causing death by dangerous driving. Cases involving possession of Class A drugs, possession with intent to deal, dealing, and even one memorable case involving drug trafficking. There were several involving robbery, one of counterfeiting, two of extortion, and one of conspiracy to pervert the course of justice. By far the majority were those involving assault; grievous and actual bodily harm. There were three of manslaughter, and two memorable cases of murder; both successful convictions. It was almost ten o'clock by the time he had worked his way through them all. Not the slightest glimmer of a connection had emerged. He felt really tired, and was trying to decide whether to pack in it, or start to have a look at his current briefs. There was one in particular that had the potential to make a lot of people unhappy. It involved him defending a major gang leader, who dealt in the importation and distribution of drugs, extortion, and who was suspected of – although not yet charged with – multiple murders. He pushed the computer keyboard to one side to make room, and opened the drawer in which the case file lay. He was about to begin when the door bell rang. He couldn't imagine who would be calling on him this late, and crossed to the intercom rather than going immediately to the door.

'Hi,' he said.

'Mr Thornton…Robert,' He had to strain to hear the almost conspiratorial whisper. 'It's me, Anna. Let me in. I've got something I think you'll want to see.'

It was, Rob decided, her excitement, rather than the stairs that had left her breathless. He let her in.

'Why didn't you use the lift?' he asked as he took her coat and hung it in the wet room to dry.

'Because I hate lifts – especially ones in high rise buildings. If you'd ever been trapped for two hours in a twenty floor concrete block of council flats you would be too.'

He came back into the lounge. 'On your own?'

'No. I was surrounded by pizza cartons, fag packets, needles, and a pool of urine.'

Rob could see her point. 'These apartments are six months old,' he said as he joined her on the sofa. 'They're exclusively owner occupied, except for the penthouses and suites owned by the Aparthotel. And I think you'll find the toilets are sufficient, and attractive enough, not to require the lifts to be used as public urinals.'

'Even so,' she said. 'I don't think I'm going to be able to trust lifts again. Anyway, it's healthier to use the stairs,' she grinned endearingly. 'You should try it.'

'Can I get you a drink?' he asked.

'No. Look, I'm sorry to burst in on you like this, but I just had to show you. You're not going to believe it.' She held up her laptop like a trophy. 'I've been working on it all day, and just when I thought it was going nowhere, up this popped.'

'All day? Have you had anything to eat?'

She had to think about it, which told him all he needed to know. 'Look,' he said. 'I'm going to pop something in the microwave. You set your computer up, or you can do it on mine if you think it'll be quicker. Just make sure you save the file that's open first.'

When he returned from the kitchen, Anna had found the relevant site on the internet, and was waiting for it to recognise her password.

'Come over here and have this,' he said. 'I don't want you spluttering cottage pie all over the key board.'

While she tucked in Rob sat and watched, drinking from a can of Coco Cola. Between mouthfuls she filled him in on the background.

'I started with the normal search engines, and then I went into the major social networks. I couldn't find a trace of an Anjelita Rosa Covas anywhere. It was as though she didn't exist – either in the real world, or the virtual world. There were Anjelitas, Rosas, and Covas, and even a couple of Rosa Covas's, but none were her; all too old, or too young. I kept a record of every one of them though, just in case there's some kind of family link.'

As she stopped to fork a mouthful in, and wash it down with some water, he reflected that they must have been trawling through some of the same genealogy sites at the same time.

'Until,' she said wiping away a smear of brown sauce with the back of her hand. 'I started to trawl through some of the more specialist social networks. I came across this particular one. It's a small British self help network for female victims of domestic violence and sexual assault. Just like all of the others, I had to register and choose a password. There were real time conversations going on between counsellors, other members, and new members recounting their experiences or asking for help and advice. I went into the archives and started trawling through some of the exchanges stored there.'

'Why would they do that?' he wanted to know. 'Store all of these presumably harrowing accounts?'

'A number of reasons I suppose. So that people can see the scale of the problem? So that they'll know that they're not alone? So they can find out how other people have managed to cope, and maybe even get on with their lives? Anyway, I found this woman calling herself Angel. In a series of exchanges Angel described how she and her older sister Rose were raped by a gang of young men. She was too frightened to go into the witness box but her sister did. And guess what? The defending barrister destroyed her in the witness box, and the rapist walked free. Her sister committed suicide.' She jabbed the air with her fork. 'How's that for a motive? And come on, Angel and Rose? How much of a coincidence is that?'

He could see her point, but it was stretching it a bit to make a connection. Even if she was right, the same questions remained. Was it random, or had she targeted him? And if so, why him? Why not the barrister who'd been involved?

'And it gets even better,' she told him. 'I did the obvious. Entered Rosa, suicide, into one search engine after another. I struck lucky with Alta Vista. And guess what? '

He shook his head, unwillingly to even try to second guess her. It was simply too bizarre.

'According to the Portuguese regional newspaper, A Voz des Tras-O-Montes, five years ago, in Ribeira de Pena, Rosa Andrades committed suicide whilst staying with her sister at a friend's house. She had been giving evidence against a group of local youths 'suspeita de rapto' – suspected of rape - when she broke down, and the trial collapsed. And what do you suppose her sister's name was?'

'Anjelita?'

'How did you guess?'

'And her sister has waited five years to take her

revenge on a perfect stranger in another country hundreds of miles away?'

'Stranger things have happened.' She handed him her plate. 'Thanks, that was terrific.' She could see him trying to make sense of it. 'Look,' she said. 'You've got to admit this is too much of a coincidence. It has to be her.'

He took the plate out into the kitchen, to give himself time to think. 'So she wasn't Spanish at all, she was Portuguese?'

'Yep.'

'And all of this was in Portuguese?

'Yep.'

'I didn't know you could speak it?'

'I can't. But I can speak Spanish and Italian, so it's not that difficult to make out,' she grinned cheekily. 'Anyway, I cheated. I just put the entire text it into Babel Fish.'

Rob sat down beside her. 'It doesn't make sense though, does it? Even if it is her; why me?'

'Why not? If half the stuff in the story she tells is true, she has every right to be very bitter, not to mention seriously disturbed. And if it isn't, then her sanity is even more in doubt. Either way, I wouldn't rule out the potential for indiscriminate revenge.' She got up walked over to his computer desk. 'Come and see for yourself.'

7

Anna spent a minute or so introducing him to the site. From the outset he felt like an intruder, a peeping tom, spying on these distressed and deeply wounded young women. Not just young women either. He shouldn't have been surprised, or shocked, to find one in her seventies, and another in her eighties; but he was. He watched as she entered the archives, and typed in the name Angel. It struck him for the first time that this was his sister's name – Angela. A dialogue box appeared, containing a reminder that this site was protected. This was followed by another, with a date, and an introductory statement about how the network had been set up by a small group of British women who had been victims themselves, and wanted to use their experience to help others to overcome the psychological, social, and emotional impact of sexual assault. It also told him that this particular piece of dialogue was just over four years old.

'This is it,' she said as she handed him the mouse. 'Here. You take over. You can read it at your own pace.'

He settled into his chair, and began to scroll slowly down.

'Hi. My name is Moira…would you like to tell me yours?'

'Angel.'

'Hi Angel. I work as a volunteer counsellor in this network...am I right in thinking that you wanted to speak with a counsellor?'

'Yes.'

'And you've read the home page...and know something of what this network is for?'

'Yes.'

'Have you read any of the other accounts that women have been willing to share on this site?'

'Yes.'

'OK. That's good Angel...so you know that there are a lot of women and girls who have experienced uninvited and unprovoked attacks, and that talking about their experiences has helped them...in one way or another...to move on with their lives?'

'Yes.'

'And is that why you've joined this network?'

'Yes.'

'That's very good Angel. So what is it you'd like to talk with me about?'

Rob had to scroll down almost a complete page to locate the next part of the dialogue.

'That's because Angel didn't reply immediately,' Anna explained. 'Because it happened real time, those gaps are silences. I think it's to do with the software, or they might do that so that the counsellors can analyse it afterwards.'

He nodded and carried on reading. Moira had decided to provide a little prompt.

'Is it about something that has happened to you...or to some one else?'

'Both'.

'To you...and to someone else?'

'Yes'.

'OK Angel. Well, before we talk anymore...it's very important that I remind you that nothing you share with me...nothing that we talk about...will be shared outside this network. Nor will it be shared within this network without your permission. You do understand that?'

'Yes.'

'This conversation is completely confidential?'

'Yes, I understand.'

'Good. And just in case you do decide later that you would like to share our conversations within the network... to help other women or girls like you...I suggest that you change the names of those involved in your story... including your own. Is that alright with you Angel?'

'Yes.'

'Angel is not your real name'

There was a brief pause.

'No.'

'OK. Well let's get started shall we Angel? I have all the time in the world...so...just take your time. Start only when you're ready.'

There was a long silence. About thirty seconds he estimated. Then Moira gave another prompt.

'I'm still here Angel.'

Ten seconds passed.

'This is very hard Moira...'

'I do know Angel...take as long as you need.'

'I don't...think I can do this...'

'Yes you can. You are stronger than you think...and I promise you that talking about it is going to help.'

This time the pause was shorter.

'It was a really hot day. Even in the evening it was too

hot to stay in doors. Our parents were away, visiting our relatives. My brother said that he and some of his friends were going down to the river to have a picnic and a swim to cool off. He asked if we would like to go with them.'

'I'm sorry to interrupt you Angel, you said "we".

'My sister Rosa...and me.'

'OK. Thank you Angel. Please go on.'

'It seemed like a good idea. We knew everyone, and it was something we'd done a few times before. My parents would not have approved, but they were not to know...and it had always been safe before. When we got there Rosa and me went into the bushes and put our swimming costumes on...the boys already had theirs on under their jeans. We had a swim and messed about...it was a good time...we enjoyed ourselves. The boys brought a portable barbecue... we had some barbecued chicken and pork...and corn bread...and some wine...not a lot... just a little bit. We were beginning to get cold. I said we should start back. The boys wanted to stay a bit longer. Then a group of seven or eight older boys...young men... turned up.... on motorbikes...

There was a long silence. He could picture the counsellor leaning forward, willing her to continue, waiting patiently.

'I had seen them before. Always stayed clear of them... they had a reputation for causing trouble. They had weapons with them... bastão... how do you say...for baseball?'

'A baseball bat?'

'Yes...baseball bats. And some of them had knives. Three of them came and stood over Rosa and me. My brother Emilio tried to get between them and us, but two of the others hit him on his legs, and on his arms, with their bats... and then they chased my brother and his friends away. Rosa and me, we put our arms around each other...pleaded with them to leave us alone. Rosa told them our parents were coming to pick us up... but they just laughed. They found the bottles of wine and began taking it in turns to drink what was left. Then...

Perhaps twenty seconds passed before Moira intervened.

'It's alright Angel. Try taking deep breaths if you need to. Take as long as you need. I'm not going anywhere.'

More time passed, and just when it seemed to Rob that Angel was unable to go on another dialogue box appeared.

'They pulled us apart and dragged us by our arms...and by our hair...into the bushes. We were screaming...they put their hands over our mouths and pushed us to the ground. They ripped our costumes off, held us down...and then...they took it in turns... to...'

This time the counsellor did not wait.

'To rape you Angel. Is that what they did? Force themselves upon you?'

'Yes.'

'They did not have sex with you and your sister ...this was not making love. They raped you. Against your will. None of this was your fault Angel, you know that don't you?'

Another pause.

'Yes.'

'Good...And then what happened?'

'They went back down towards the beach. They were laughing and joking...saying terrible things. One of them came back and threatened us. He said if we told anyone what had happened they would find us and kill us, and our family too. When he had gone I found my costume and tried to get it on…but it was impossible. Then Rosa put her arms around me and we hugged. I was crying, but she was silent. She just kept stroking my hair. Then we heard them start up their motorbikes, and ride away. We waited and waited, fearing they would come back. Then we crept down to the beach. Rosa took me by the hand and led me into the river. The water was cold, but we didn't care. We scrubbed and scrubbed with our bare hands trying to wash ourselves clean of their filth and sweat. Then I lay back in the river with my eyes closed. I just wanted the water to swallow me up…to drown it all away…as though it had never happened. I would have let the river take me, then and there, but Rosa grabbed my arm, slapped my face…pulled me from the water. We found our clothes, and had just got dressed when my brother came back with one of his friends. They took us home.'

'To your parents?'

'They were not due back for another two days.'

'So did you tell anyone else?'

'No…we were too scared…and embarrassed. And we were both hurting. We had pains in our stomachs, and our arms and legs were really sore. We just stayed in doors, and hugged each other. We tried to pretend nothing had happened.'

'And when your parents came home?'

'We didn't say anything. They had left me in charge while they were away. I knew they would blame me…my mother…I knew she would never forgive me. But they knew something was wrong. They could tell. In the end Rosa blurted it out. She was really angry…she wanted those boys to pay for what they had done.'

'How did your parents react?'

'They went louco…crazy. They blamed me as I knew

84

*they would. My father slapped me over and over again...
my mother screamed at me to get out of the house. She said
Rosa and me...we are both finished.'*

'Finished?'

*'Ruined...my mother, she is a cigano...gypsy...in her
culture virginity is not just expected...it is required. She
said no one would marry either of us.'*

'But this was not your fault. You were both blameless...'

*'She said it makes no difference. She threw us both out.
We went to stay with the family of my best friend. They had
a spare room they let us share.'*

'How old were you Angel...when this happened?'

'Seventeen.'

'And Rosa?'

'She was fifteen.'

This time the silence was on Moira's side. Rob
could sense her fighting to keep in check the
overwhelming instinct to express her sympathy with
this desperate young women.

'What happened next Angel?'

*'Rosa went to the police. She told them what had
happened. She told them the name of one of the boys. The
police were reluctant to believe her. They said there was no
evidence...we should have called them right away. She
insisted...she had kept her costume...she showed them it...
told them how it had been torn from her. They wanted to
know why I had not come to them with her, or our brother,
or our parents. She tried to explain, but they were not
listening. She pleaded with me to go back to the police with
her.'*

'And did you?'

*'Yes. They made me tell my story separately, then they
had a doctor examine us. He said there was clear evidence*

of…'

'Take your time Angel.'

'Of sexual activity…he said there was also… "Evidência do trauma compatível com penetração múltipla e forçada."

'Multiple forced penetration?'

'Si…yes.'

'So then they had to believe you?'

'Yes.'

'And these men were arrested?'

'Yes.'

'And?'

'Rosa and me, we gave statements and signed them. A trial was arranged…but when the time came I could not go into the witness box. It all came back. I was scared… shaking…I could barely breathe…'

'I understand Angel. Many women in your position experience those feelings.'

'But you don't understand…Rosa…she felt the same but her anger helped her overcome it…at least at first. She went into the witness box…she held up her head, looked into the eyes of those boys…told her story…'

'You must have been so proud of her?'

'Yes…and so ashamed of myself…'

Whoops, thought Rob. Moira's first slip, and she had been doing so well.

'And then the time came for their advogado to question her.'

'I'm sorry Angel, advogado. Is that an advocate?'

'Yes, you say barrister.'

'I see. Thank you. Go on.'

'It was terrible. He began to tear her story to pieces. He told her she was making it up because she had had sex with some other boys, and was frightened of what her parents

would say when they found out. That these boys we had accused had nothing to do with it. That it was obvious... because neither her...sister...nor her brother were willing to come into the witness box and back her story up. She was a hysterical girl trying to excuse her own wickedness. Had her own parents not thrown her out? And what of the other boys who had been at the picnic...why had they not come forward? Was it because it was them that she had had sex with...willingly?'

'Why did they not come forward Angel?'

'Because they had been threatened too...and because their parents forbade them to get involved.'

'And perhaps because they were ashamed of their cowardice in running off and leaving you. Not even going for help?'

There was a twenty second pause.

'They had less reason to be ashamed of their cowardice than me. Rosa was my sister.'

'What happened Angel?'

'The judge dismissed the case. He said the evidence was only circunstancial...'

'Circumstantial?'

'Yes...and proven to be unreliable...'

'And how did that make you feel Angel?'

'I was just numb inside. But it wasn't important how I felt. I had always known that they would get away with it. But Rosa...she really believed she would see them sent to prison. It destroyed her to see them laughing and joking on the steps of the courts, shaking hands with their advogado. He turned and looked over his shoulder towards us...the smile frozen on his lips. And I knew... in that moment... that he knew they were guilty...and he knew what he had done to us...done to my little Rosa...'

This time the silence went on and on. Rob could almost see her, head in hands, weeping uncontrollably. It was only when Anna tentatively handed him a handkerchief that he realised that there were tears in his own eyes, and on his cheeks. It was Moira who broke the silence.

'That must have been so hard for you, Angel.'

'But you don't understand Moira. This was not...the end. After the trial Rosa went...um...escudo...you say... into a shell? She never spoke, hardly eat or drank. I tried everything. Nothing worked. One evening, five weeks later, I arrive back at my friends house...I had a job in a restaurant to help pay my way into university...and Rosa was gone. I search everywhere...I ring everyone...but there is no sign...'

Twenty seconds went by. He imagined her steeling herself for what he already knew would be the conclusion to her story.

'The police came at six o'clock in the morning. They had found the body of a young woman, and wanted me to identify her. She had been found washed up on the banks of the river Tâmega. The waters are calm along that stretch... but deep. They think she had taken some pills... and then... simply walked out into the river. She was lying there in this cold bare room, on a blue plastic sheet. She looked so small, and frail...her hair was straggly and in knots... speckled with pieces of duck weed...like little emeralds. My little Rosa...she looked so peaceful...and I...I felt sick to my stomach. Completely empty...lost...alone.'

8

It ended abruptly. There was no response to Moira's appeals. It looked as though Angel had walked away. Anna pointed to the cursor, still pulsing on the screen.

'She's still on line,' she said. 'Keep scrolling down, and you'll find her again.'

'I'm not sure I can take any more of this,' Rob said. 'I feel like a wrung out dishcloth.'

'Just think what *she* must have been feeling like.' Anna reminded him.

'But that's the point, I am doing, and it's killing me. You forget, I've held this woman, talked with her, looked deep into her eyes, danced with her, made love to her. I should have had some sense of all of this.'

'Well you didn't. So stop feeling sorry for yourself, and read what happened next.' She pointed to the screen. Angel was back on line.

'I'm sorry. This is so hard.'

'Please Angel, you must never feel you have to apologise. I can't pretend to imagine how all that must have felt...or how you feel right now. If you want to call it a day, and come back again later, that's fine by me. We can even agree a time if you like?'

'No...it's alright. I'd like to get it over with.'

'That's fine. Perhaps it will help if I ask you some questions now. Not about what happened, but about you... about your feelings. Would that be OK?'

'Yes.'

'Thank you Angel. OK then. Can you begin by telling me how long ago this happened?'

'A year ago…next Saturday…'

'Is that why you have contacted us…because you think the anniversary will remind you of what happened?'

'Yes.'

'So you must eighteen now. What are you doing in your life?'

'I am at university…studying English and Sociology.'

'That sounds really good. Perhaps we can talk about that later; perhaps on another day. But for now, can you begin by telling me how you were feeling in the first few weeks after you were assaulted, and how you found yourself behaving?'

'I was very afraid. I would start shaking without any reason. I found it hard to leave the house of my friend. The first time I did…I was in the local grocery shop and my chest began to tighten up…and there were these pains… and I couldn't…get my breath. People in the shop came to help me. It was very frightening. I did not know what was happening to me.'

'You had a panic attack Angel. Did that happen at any other time?'

'A few times. One night…I woke up in the night. Rosa was having a nightmare. I lay down beside her…held her… till she calmed down. Then when I sat up to get back in bed the pains came …and I couldn't breathe…I truly thought I was going to die.'

'Who do you think you were frightened of Angel?'

'The ones who attacked us, they said they would be watching us. I was scared they might…kill us. And I didn't know how Rosa and me were going to manage…

without our family. And I missed our brother so much. I knew he would be blaming himself...and I wanted to tell him it was alright...it was not his fault.'

'Whose fault do you think it was Angel?'

Ten seconds into the silence the counsellor repeated her question.

'Angel. Whose fault do you think it was?'

Five seconds passed.

'The boys who attacked us...'

'Exactly. So long as you are sure about that?'

'Yes.'

'Apart from the panic attacks, did you have any other sensations? Were you ill at all?'

'I had difficulty sleeping. I would get cramps that woke me up... in my stomach, and in my leg,. My friend said that I would often shout in my sleep, but I don't remember that. I hardly ate or drank at all for months.'

'Why was that Angel?'

'I don't know...I just seemed to lose my appetite.'

'How is your appetite these days?'

'It's a bit better, but I don't seem to take any pleasure in eating anymore.'

'And how are you sleeping?'

'Not very well...I still wake up in the night, and sometimes when I do I find that I'm shivering...even though it isn't cold.'

'Do you still have panic attacks?'

'No...but I can't get in a lift. I always use the stairs. The first time I got in a lift here at the university it felt as though the walls were closing in, and the ceiling pressing down on me.'

'Apart from feeling frightened, have you experienced any other emotions Angel?'

'For a long time I felt…I still feel…ashamed. I mean, I know it wasn't our fault…but I still feel ashamed…and humiliated. Even now, I can't go in the student bar because I think that people are…looking at me…talking about me… because they know what happened to me.'

'Have you ever tried to block it out Angel? Tried to pretend that it never happened?'

'Only the first two days…before our parents came home. After that it was impossible…especially with the trial. Everybody knew what happened…I knew. And those boys were still around…just the other side of the mountain. That's why…after Rosa died…I had to move away. My father asked me to come back home, but I knew that it was only because of Rosa. And my mother still looked at me as though I was…dirty…''

'Has all of this ever made you feel angry Angel? You haven't mentioned feeling angry…'

'I did not at first…but I do now.'

'Who do you feel angry at Angel?'

'At God. Why did he let it happen to us? What had we done to deserve it? At those boys…At the advogado who got them off…who destroyed and killed my Rosa…at her advogado, who sat there and let him do it…and most of all I am angry at myself.'

'Why are you angry at yourself Angel?'

'Because if we hadn't gone to the river it would never have happened…it was me who persuaded Rosa to come with us…If I'd tried harder…fought back harder…I should have protected her.'

'You have every right to feel angry Angel. You want justice. You deserve justice. Unfortunately life is not just. Bad things can happen to good people. Tell me Angel…have you ever spoken to anyone else about these feelings?'

'I didn't want to talk to anybody about it. I thought that if I didn't talk about it I could forget it. It would fade away...'

'But it hasn't?'

'No.'

'Which is why you decided to join the network...to talk with me?'

'Yes.'

'Well you've done the right thing. Doing this today has been a really important first step on your road to coming to terms with this. And you have to do that Angel, so that you can move on with your life. You do understand that?'

'Yes.'

'Good, well you have been really brave it making this step. You should feel very proud of yourself.'

Ten seconds passed.

'Angel?'

'Yes.'

'Unless there is anything else you want to say to me right now, I think it's probably best if we take a break now. You can come back anytime that is convenient for you, providing that I am on line. You'll be able to tell as soon as you log on. If I am free to talk you'll see my name, alongside others on the left of the page, below the page menu. Will you do that...come back, and carry on our conversation?'

'Yes.'

'Everything you've told me about your feelings is completely normal Angel...it's important that you understand that.'

'Yes.'

'You have suffered two bereavements. Firstly your own innocence...and then your sister Rosa. The feelings you have shared with me are those we all have to go through *before we can come to terms with loss, and move on with our lives. It sounds as though you have reached a stage that we call depression. Having the courage to come on line and speak with me shows that your are fighting that. Well the good news is that the next stage is one where you will be able to accept that life can go on, and you will be ready to do that, without ever looking back. From what you have told me... you are well down that road... although it may not feel like it right now. I would be honoured if you wanted me to walk the rest of the way alongside you...Angel? Are you still there?'*

'Yes Moira...I would like that.'

'Good. Then I look forward to hearing from you again soon. Goodbye Angel.'

'Goodbye Moira...and...thank you.'

Rob continued to scroll down in the hope that he would find some more.

'That's it,' Anna told him. 'They both logged off.'

'I'm not surprised,' he said. 'They must both be exhausted. I know I am. I feel emotionally drained.' He turned back to the screen. Is that it then?' That's all there is?'

She leaned over his shoulder, and took control of the mouse. 'No actually. She does come back. About a week later. It's all here in the archive. But prepare yourself. It's not good news.' She brought up the relevant file and pushed the mouse back towards him.

'Angel. It's good to hear from you again. How have you been?'

'Not good Moira...not good.'

'I'm sorry to hear that. Do you want to tell me about it?'

There was a long silence, broken finally by Angel.

'Yes.'

'OK Angel...I'm listening.'

'I have been having flashbacks...I never had them before.'

'Of the assault itself?'

'Yes...and of the courtroom.'

'Do these flashbacks come during the day or night?'

'At night...they wake me up... and I can still see them until I put the light on.'

'Do you want to tell me about them?'

'I am at the beach, looking down on what's happening to us... and I start shouting at myself to fight, and I wake up and I'm still shouting...and then I'm in the river splashing myself...and I can hear them laughing as they leave the beach.'

'And in court?'

'I am in the witness box telling the judge what happened...and then I see them being led down into the cells...they have handcuffs on...and everyone is cheering... and Rosa...she is there...and she's smiling at me...'

'You realise that this is happening now because it is exactly a year ago since you were attacked?'

'Yes...but I want it to go away. I can't stand it. I feel it like a pain, a physical pain inside my soul.'

'Angel, listen carefully. These feelings surfacing now, is all part of the healing process. If you can harness them, and make sense of them, they will help you to move on.'

'But I feel dirty, useless...I can't concentrate in lectures...I can't study...I can't do this anymore...I don't know why I came back...'

'Angel...listen. Now more than ever, it's important that you do continue to speak with someone. You are so close to *resolving this. If not me, then there will be a counsellor at the University you can speak to in confidence. Will you promise me that you will do that?...Angel?...Angel!*

Rob scrolled down with increasing desperation.

'She's logged off,' Anna told him starkly. 'And there's no use searching. I tried. She doesn't come back to this site; not ever.'

'What I don't understand,' Rob said, standing up and stretching to ease the tension in his neck and back. 'Is how come this is available in the archive if she didn't come back?'

'Good question. I assume that Angel must have ticked the box giving permission at the beginning – or more probably at the end of the first session.'

'You'd think either Moira or the site manager would have made the decision to hide it. It's not exactly an example of a successful outcome.'

Possibly. But they might have decided to leave it open just in case she came back. In any case, there's still a lot for others to learn from it.'

'Remind me. How long ago did this exchange take place?'

'Four years ago. A year after she and her sister were raped.'

'So if it is my Anjelita Rosa Covas, that makes her twenty two.'

'And does that fit?'

'Oh yes,' he said his voice heavy with regret. 'Significantly more sophisticated, apparently confident, and slightly more world weary than your average twenty two year old, but yes, it would fit.'

He insisted on walking her to her car. Not just because she was carrying her laptop. They were both aware that it was probably not something he would have done before tonight.

Back in the apartment he paced the lounge restlessly before sitting down again in front of the computer screen. He revisited the site, but found he was unable to enter beyond the home page without registering. Instead, he followed a link on the page entitled The Rape Trauma Syndrome. This led him to a succession of sites where he learnt more than he really wanted to know about the multiple impacts of violent sexual assault, and the often lifelong effects on both female and male victims. It did little to ease the troubled emotions he was experiencing. Not least because, by the time he finally gave up, and went to bed at two in the morning, it was only too clear that Angel - Anjelita Andrades, alias Anjelita Rosa Covas – was highly unlikely to have reached the stage where she had accepted and assimilated the experience into her life, and moved positively on. He had no idea if he, Robert Thornton, had become part of her tortured search for resolution, or simply an object of revenge. Was he therapy or retribution? Or had he simply made her feel even worse? He doubted that was possible.

9

Tuesday 19th December

The morning began with disappointment. Henry Mayhew rang to say that one of Rob's clients was insisting that he find her a new barrister. It was a domestic violence case that Rob had taken on through the Bar Pro Bono Unit simply because he felt so strongly about it. It was a difficult case the local Law Centre had asked Henry to look into. The client was in real fear of her own life, and that of her three children. She was seeking a non-molestation order against her partner, together with an order covering maintenance, and strictly supervised contact on his part. Under normal circumstances the withdrawal of his client's confidence would not have been a bitter disappointment. He had done all the ground work, and was confident that anyone could now pick it up, and see it through to a successful conclusion. As a pro bono case there was no fee involved. But this was not a normal circumstance. He had built up a good relationship with his client. Had found himself empathising strongly with her plight. She was genuinely grateful, and more than happy to put her trust in him; until now. The reason was self evident. Why would a woman at risk want to be near, let alone depend upon, Robert Thornton, suspected rapist?

Although it hurt, he didn't dwell on it for long. He was too busy trying to process what he had learned the night before. It left him with a dilemma. How much, if anything, should he share with Henry Mayhew, or the police? He had been warned to steer clear of Anjelita Rosa Covas, directly and indirectly. And he was clear that even if it could be confirmed that Angel was indeed Anjelita Andrades, and she his accuser, that only provided a possible explanation as to why she might lie. From the point of view of the police it would not exclude the possibility, however remote, that her life had collided, by some cruel trick of fate, with yet another rapist. Robert Thornton; a drunken barrister who did not understand the meaning of the word no. He could imagine the closing speech to the jury. A tragic young woman trying to make a new life for herself, destroyed for a second time. Her physical and emotional scars ripped open, by a man whose profession made him uniquely aware of the imperative to elicit clear consent, and the consequences of not doing so. And of the consequences of allowing himself to be consumed by selfish lust. It was the speech he would make for the prosecution. He decided not to tell Henry just yet, and certainly not the police.

He arrived early at Bootle Street, a little before ten. They had both agreed, in the absence of any new developments, that it was not necessary for Mayhew to join him. In any case, if need be, Henry's offices were literally three minutes away. DI Holmes and DS Hale were waiting for him. He had difficulty reading their faces. But something had definitely changed.

'You'd better come through to the interview room,' DI Holmes said, holding the door open.'

Rob hung back. 'Then perhaps I should call Mr Mayhew?'

DS Hale shook her head. 'I really don't think that will be necessary Mr Thornton. You can decide for yourself when we tell you why we want to speak with you. But best not to do that here.'

He followed them down the corridor, and into the room. They waited until he had settled himself, then Holmes said. 'We don't intend to tape this conversation, and it's not under caution. If anything you say leads us to believe that we should change that, then I'll tell you, and then you can decide if you want to call Mr Mayhew. Is that alright with you?'

Perplexed, he nodded. In his experience, this was not uncommon, but he had difficulty in understanding why they would want to do it at such an early stage in their investigation.

DI Holmes steepled his fingers. 'Perhaps I could begin by asking where you were yesterday evening. Say between nine pm and midnight?'

'I was at home.'

'On your own?'

He paused before he replied. Wondering how this would look. How to explain it.

'No. I was with Anna Gardener.'

They glanced at each other. Surprise on both their faces. He read their minds. A man accused of rape. Alone in his own apartment with a woman so soon after the event. Was he addicted to sex?

'I see,' Holmes said in a voice loaded with disapproval. 'And Anna Gardener is…?'

'My pupil. She is attached to me for the first and second six of her pupillage.'

'Six?' DS Hale wanted to know.

'It's work-based training – apprenticeship if you like - divided into two six month periods, or sixes, during which the pupils assist and observe an experienced barrister. Successful completion of the year usually ends in them being called to the Bar, and becoming a fully fledged barrister.'

'And is that what Ms Gardener was doing? Observing and assisting you?' It was a loaded question.

'Yes Detective Inspector Holmes, she was sharing some research she had completed for me, relevant to a brief I have to complete this afternoon.' He realised that it was the first lie he had told them since this nightmare had begun. He wondered if it showed. But their minds were elsewhere.

'Have you had, or attempted to make, any contact with Ms Covas, Mr Thornton?' DS Hale asked.

'Contact?'

'Phoned her, sent her a text message, an email, written her a note or a letter, sent her a fax. Accosted her in the street, or in her hotel?'

'I didn't know she was staying in a hotel.'

DI Holmes leant forward adding weight to his request. 'Please answer the question Mr Thornton.'

'No. I haven't seen, spoken to, or approached her in any way since that night.'

Holmes let out a heavy sigh. Exchanged meaningful but inscrutable looks with DS Hale, and sat back in his chair.

'Ms Covas has gone missing,' he said. 'She left the

hotel in which she was staying at around half past ten yesterday evening. The room was prepaid. She paid for a few extras with cash, and simply left. It was a strange time to be leaving don't you think? And according to the concierge, she did not take a taxi. Just set off down the street wheeling her case behind her.'

Concierge, Rob was thinking. That narrows it down to a handful of hotels in the city centre. What Holmes had to say next recaptured his attention.

'When she didn't turn up for an interview first thing this morning DS Hale went round there, and discovered that she had checked out. Not only that, but the hotel cleaning staff had reported traces of blood on her bed linen, and on the bathroom towels. Not necessarily suspicious of course, could have been to do with her original injuries, or the time of the month...' He sensed his colleague's disapproving stare, and lost his thread.

'And the duty manager,' Beth Hale said, taking up the narrative. 'Handed me a note addressed to me she'd left at the desk. In it, she said that she wanted to withdraw her accusation. She apologised for the trouble she'd caused. She said whatever happened she would not go into the witness box. She signed it. Anjelita Rosa Covas. So, I hope that you can appreciate why it was that we needed to know if you had had any contact with her?'

Rob barely heard the question. He should have been feeling as though a weight had been removed from his shoulders, but he did not. This was not how it was supposed to end. He needed to know why she had chosen to do it to him. Was it calculated, or an act of sudden – in the circumstances, understandable -

madness? Was she in fact Anjelita Andrades, and if so how must she be feeling at this moment? He wanted to see her. To tell her that he forgave her. That she must forgive herself. That he would like to help her to move on. And at the same time he wanted to shake her, shout at her, ask her if she realised what she had done. Anger and empathy vied with each other to fill the space that relief should have occupied.

Above the roar and thunder of his own thoughts, He heard, as though in slow motion, the voice of DI Holmes.

'Under the circumstances,' Holmes was saying. 'Would you mind if we spoke to Ms Gardener, and checked your mobile phone and emails at home, and at the office? Just to be absolutely sure.'

Rob had to force himself to think about that. He took his time replying, staring down at the table top. 'Providing that it is in my presence, and restricted to my emails, sent and received texts, calls and messages for the last two days.' He looked up. 'Actually, I am also prepared to show you my most recent letter and document files by date order. Just to get this over with. But only one of you if you don't mind. I have had enough of my privacy being invaded to last me a lifetime.' He took his mobile phone from his pocket, and placed it down on the table. 'Perhaps you could check this now. I am expecting some calls shortly.'

It took just two minutes for them to check his phone. It was agreed that DS Hale would go with him; first to his office, and then to his apartment.

Fellow tenant barristers, Lamiah Nasir and Jonathan Walker Smyth, were deep in conversation in the centre of the foyer with Sylvia Franklin, the practice fees clerk. They had to step aside to let Rob Thornton and Beth Hale pass. Jonathan managed a polite if curious smile, but the others looked studiously away. Lamiah, in behaviour entirely out of character, pretended to adjust her headscarf. Rob knew it was to avoid having to look him in the eyes. He couldn't blame her. She more than the others would feel that his behaviour – whatever the truth or otherwise of the allegations – was a kind of betrayal. They had worked together to prevent the deportation of two Ethiopian asylum seekers; women who had fled here as a refuge and place of healing following the destruction of their village, rape, and torture. It would not be enough for her to learn that his accuser had walked away; withdrawn her accusation. Just as it was not enough for him.

They were in his office for the five minutes it took for him to call up his email log and current document files. DS Hale had left her car at the station. They walked the half a mile to his apartment in an uneasy silence. Once there they repeated the exercise he had gone through in Chambers; bringing up the list of recent incoming and outgoing calls on his land line; opening up his email and document files. He made sure she went nowhere near his recent internet history. Only when the permutations had been exhausted did she seem to thaw.

'Do you think I could have a drink?' she said quite unexpectedly. 'I'm really parched.'

He took that as a positive sign; an olive branch, and seized it with a feeling of relief that took him by surprise. 'Is that a hot or a cold drink?'

'She smiled. On a day like to day? It's got to be hot. Coffee would be great if you've got it.'

As he switched the kettle on, and put the beans in the electric grinder, she walked across to the windows in the lounge. 'It's a fabulous view from up here. Do you ever get used to it?'

'Not so far. I don't think I'm likely to either. Would you like anything with this? A piece of toast? Some crisps? It's all I've got in I'm afraid.'

She shook her head, and he noticed for the first time the way the sunlight caught the purple highlights in her hair. She turned as he walked across to join her, took the mug, and raised it to her lips, blowing gently across the surface.

'It's not the Beetham Tower,' he said. 'But I can see clear across to the Pennines. There's the City of Manchester Stadium down there, and the B of the Bang, and beyond it you can just make out the ribbon of the M60 motorway. You wouldn't believe the sunrise across those hills. I don't think I've seen any two alike.'

'You're lucky,' she said. 'I look straight out onto the side of a block just like this one. That's when I do get a chance to look out of the window. These days I seem to be up at the crack of dawn, and back just before lights out. I can't even see the stars. The nearest I get is night lights on other people's balconies.' She turned to face him. 'Look, do you mind if we sit down for a moment?'

Rob pointed to the sofa. 'Be my guest.' Unsure of where this was leading, he chose to sit on the bean bag rather than beside her.

'Is it alright to put this down on here?' she asked

holding up her mug.

He got up, and brought two beer mats across from his desk.

She put her mug down, and placed her hands on her knees. An open position, he noted; neither defensive nor aggressive. 'Look Rob...can I call you that?'

He nodded.

'I think you deserve to know exactly where you stand.'

He wasn't sure he liked the sound of that. When people said things like that it generally meant that you were not standing where you thought you were; nor where you wanted to be.

'You see, we always had some concerns about Ms Covas' story.' She began.

'Concerns?'

'Her story was convincingly told,' she said. 'And believe me, I've heard a lot. But there were some inconsistencies. Her injuries for example. They were real enough, and some of them were what you might expect to find; but not all of them. And they were not consistent with each other, or with the story she told. It was almost as though there were two different attacks. The one she was describing, and another one. And some of them were much more likely to have been self-inflicted. They were far too superficial, and evidently produced by smaller fingers, and a smaller fist than yours.'

She stopped for a moment, and searched his face for signs of surprise, of relief, of anything. But he was too busy trying to imagine how she must have punched and torn at herself, and what difference she must have imagined that would make.

'Are you alright?' she asked, mistaking his blank expression for shock.

'No I'm fine,' he said. 'Really. Please go on.'

'And then there was the fact that no one who was at that party seemed to know who she had come with. Who had invited her. Either she walked in off the street, or someone was distancing himself...herself from Ms Covas.'

'She must have had an explanation of her own?'

She shook her head. 'She claimed she was with a man she met in her hotel bar. He invited her along. In her shock she couldn't remember his name. Her description of him was so hazy as to be useless.'

'What was she doing in the hotel? Does she live in Manchester?'

'She said she was just visiting the city. Thinking of moving up here. Wanted to see if it was really as cool as people said it was.'

'Doesn't sound very likely. So she lives down South?'

She folded her arms. 'I'm sorry. I can't you tell where she said she lived. It wouldn't be... appropriate; even if I could. In any case, that was another thing. We've not been able to verify the details she gave us. Not only that, but there is no record of anyone with her name having a national insurance number, or a driving licence, or a passport. Nor does she appear in any immigration records – although if she really is a European national we wouldn't expect her to. We have to assume that she is using an alias, but we have no idea why.'

Rob could have told her, but this wasn't the time.

He was not supposed to know anything about her. He'd had the opportunity to tell them both what he'd learned, and had failed to do so. And now she'd vanished. Blurting it out now was only going to feed any lingering suspicion they might have.

'Where do you think she's gone?' he asked.

'We have no idea. We'll have a look at the CCTVs around the hotel; at the station and the airport. But it's unlikely she'll have been catching any trains or planes at that time of night; leastways, not internal flights. But she left of her own volition. It's not our job to go chasing after her.'

'But what about the blood...in the hotel?'

'Unfortunately, the hotel staff had bundled up the linen, and put it down the laundry chute. They'd also mopped it up in the bathroom by the time we found out about it. Health and safety reasons apparently. From what we could gather there wasn't that much... like someone had cut themselves shaving. And we know that she seemed all right when she walked away from the hotel.'

'I really appreciate you telling me all this,' Rob said. 'Aren't you going out on a limb? I am still on bail.'

'Technically, yes. But you won't be by tomorrow morning. The CPS has already been informed, and as soon as I report back it will only be a formality. You must know that. Without her evidence there's no case.'

'But surely, you would want to find her. Try to get her to change her mind. Give her an opportunity to reconsider?'

'Ordinarily, yes. But given that her accusation was

always shaky for the reasons I've shared with you, and especially the fact that she's lied about her identity, it would be a waste of time. In any case, why would you want us keep the case open?'

She picked up her mug, and was about to have a drink, when she stopped, the mug suspended in mid air, and fixed him with a cool appraising stare. 'Tell me you're not thinking of taking this further? Making a complaint...taking out a civil suit for defamation... something like that?'

He shook his head. 'No. To be honest, I'm just concerned about her.'

She drained the coffee, placed the mug back down on the mat, and stood up. 'Well don't be. Like you, I have no idea what must have been going on in her head. And yes, I would like to know. But right know I have ongoing cases to attend to involving three other young women. And two new ones; a girl, and a young man, each of whom has suffered a genuine attack. They have a right to my undivided attention. Ms Covas, whoever she is, does not.

She crossed to the doorway, and then turned to face him. 'Look Rob, these last few days must have been something of a nightmare, but it's over now. You'll be hearing from us before the day is out. The Press office will issue a statement confirming that no charges will be forthcoming, and the case is closed. Your solicitor will want to make a statement of his own I guess, on your behalf. Then you can get on with your life.'

He led the way down the hall. 'Easier said than done, ' he said. 'Mud sticks.' He opened the door for her, and stood back. 'But thanks anyway...for taking the trouble to tell me like this; off the record.'

She smiled. 'You're welcome. You've already built up quite a reputation for prosecuting cases like this. I hope you're not going to let this change all that?'

Rob smiled back. 'I hope not. We'll see.' As she turned to go he called after her. 'The hotel...was she staying there on her own? Did she pay for the room, or did someone else?'

She stopped and looked back at him. She suddenly looked weary in the artificial light from the stairway. 'It was a double room, booked in her name. It was paid for with a prepaid credit card. Nigh on impossible to trace. We are assuming that she was there alone, but she may have had visitors. Anyway, that's irrelevant now. There is no investigation. Case closed. Take my advice Mr Thornton. Do yourself a favour. Let it go.'

10

DS Hale proved as good as her word. He had a call late in the afternoon asking if he could attend Bootle Street, together with his solicitor. Holmes was polite and formal. He even expressed his commiserations for the trouble to which he, Mr Thornton, had been put. Well short of an apology. It left Rob feeling that that he'd deserved all he'd got. Beth Hale remained silent throughout. Just the ghost of a smile betrayed the fact that she had forewarned him.

Afterwards, he agreed a statement with Henry that missed the late edition of the Manchester Evening News but would figure in the morning edition. DI Holmes popped up on the North West tea time news, confirming that the investigation had been completed, and no action would be taken. The reporter tried to draw him on precisely why the investigation was closed. The detective attempted to prevaricate, which only made matters worse. Finally he gave in, and admitted that the complaint had been withdrawn, and there were no grounds for pursuing the case. When asked if Mr Robert Thornton had therefore been exonerated, he appeared flustered, and replied that the case was closed. When the point was pressed, his minder from the police press office drew him expertly away. Rob switched off in disgust. Holmes's inexperience had shown. They should never have let him do it. The overwhelming impression he had created, deliberately or otherwise, was that something unsavoury had gone on. Rob cursed, and threw the remote control on the sofa. His current ambition was to keep winning his briefs. Becoming a Queen's Counsel, perhaps a judge one day, had always been on his radar. Thanks to Anjelita Covas, and DI Holmes, he felt certain that was now nothing more than a pipe dream.

Henry's piece appeared on page two, together with another unrelated photograph of Rob, taken from their archives, and a short quote from DS Hale. He had to read it through several times before he could convince himself that some of the damage had been repaired. He now had a second reason to be grateful to Beth Hale. Presumably annoyed by Holmes's performance, she had gone out of her way to use the phrase "completely exonerated". He wondered if she had gone through their press office, or out on a limb for the second time in as many days. He fancied it was the latter, in which case she would no doubt get some flack from the upper echelons at Chester House.

Eye contact was still a little on the scarce side when he walked into Chambers that morning. But at least people acknowledged him. Harry Richmond's greeting, on the other hand, was effusive. His friend insisted on shepherding him into his office, eager to hear all.

'Well done, mate,' he said. 'What a result!'

'It's not a bloody game Harry,' Rob told him.

'I know, I know, but even so. What the hell happened?'

Now Rob was really irritated. 'I was innocent,

that's what happened. What the hell do you think happened?'

'They saw through her story? She fessed up? She got cold feet and dropped the charges?' Harry must have spotted the glint in his friend's eye, and the hard set of his chin. 'Don't get me wrong Rob. I meant she got cold feet because she could see the police knew she was lying.'

Rob rounded his desk, and slumped down in his chair.

' Well it was both. They saw through her story, and she walked away. She withdrew her complaint.'

'That's brilliant.'

Rob looked up at Harry's beaming face. 'Is it?'

'Of course it bloody well is! The bitch was going to screw you for a second time.'

Rob's stomach tightened, his hands balled into tight fists. He felt that he should be defending her. Protecting her reputation. He could hear those youths on the beach in the mountain valley, using the very same phrase as they hitched up their jeans, and swaggered manfully from the bushes. "She's a bitch. She deserved it. They both did. The bitches got what was coming!" He felt an urge to leap to his feet. To yell at Harry Richmond. To tell him what she had endured. To make him understand. But he knew that it would be futile, and impossible, to try to communicate what he felt, what he had experienced. Even more difficult to explain that, in some strange way, he was bound to her.

'Whatever.' He said. 'I don't want to talk about it.'

'Fair enough,' his friend conceded. 'I can understand that. Fancy coming for a drink this evening to celebrate?' He saw Rob's hand move towards the solid crystal paper weight, and moved nimbly to the door. He placed one hand on the door knob, and held the other out in front of him; part apology, part defence. 'Alright. I get the idea. You want to be left alone. I'm sorry.' He opened the door to go, and then turned back momentarily. 'Oh, I nearly forgot. Weir wants to see you in his office. Soon as.'

Donald Weir was not alone. Stanley Bollington, was already seated as Rob walked in. The two of them rose, smiling, to greet him. Weir waved his hand imperiously, inviting him to take the other seat.

'Robert. Good to see you. Thank you for dropping in,' he waited until Rob had settled himself. 'So how are you feeling? Relieved no doubt?'

'Fine thank you.'

Donald beamed. It was evident to Rob that it was his Head of Chambers who was most relieved. 'Good, good. Of course the outcome was never in doubt. Even so…it must have been a trying few days for you,' He waited for a response, and receiving none, plunged on. 'Stanley here has just brought me a new brief. Rather an interesting one as it happens, and very lucrative. I thought you might like to lead on it.' He nodded to Stanley who passed across a manilla file. Rob took it, and read the first page.

Barry Moss, twenty nine years of age, had been arrested, and charged, with conspiracy to evade the prohibition and importation of a controlled drug; conspiracy to supply drugs; conspiracy to pervert the course of justice, and conspiracy to commit murder.

The charge followed months of covert customs investigation, and the involvement of the recently formed National Crime Squad. If convicted, he would be looking at a minimum of thirty years.

'According to the police,' Donald told him. 'Moss heads a drugs network without parallel in UK drugs law enforcement. They also suspect that he not only supplies the major drug distribution gangs in the north, but is the mastermind mind behind a recent amalgamation of several of the largest gangs. The charges relating to conspiracy to commit murder, stem from the recent deaths of gang leaders who allegedly stood in his way. Unfortunately for the police, despite their undercover and covert operations, their case hangs, and falls, on the evidence of an informer. I happen to know that the CPS very nearly refused to support the case going to trial.'

'According to Mr. Moss's solicitor,' Stanley Bollington chipped in. 'In addition to certain inducements offered by the police, the informer has a personal score to settle with Mr. Moss.'

'So you see Robert,' Donald continued. 'This has the considerable virtue of being high profile, lucrative, and eminently winnable. Something of a full house.'

Rob closed the folder, and placed it on the desk. 'Why me?' he asked. Am I being welcomed back into the fold? Or is this your way of letting the world know that my Chambers are one hundred per cent behind me?'

Donald and Stanley exchanged glances of surprise and concern. Responses that had been all too frequent in recent days.

'Now that's hardly fair Robert,' Donald told him.

'Stanley tells me that you've had one brief withdrawn, so I know you are in a position to pick this one up. And I am also confident that you will do a splendid job on it. As for welcoming you back…as far as I am concerned, you never left our fold. And even if it does have the effect of reminding people that you have done nothing to be ashamed off, what harm is there in that?'

Up until that final sentence, Rob reflected, Donald had been doing well. But he had an annoying habit these days of adding codicil's that let him down; revealed his true intent. Nevertheless, he had a point. If he was to move on, put this behind him, he had to swallow his pride, stop being paranoid, and accept people's clumsy attempts to make him feel better – and make themselves feel better - as graciously as possible.

'I'm sorry Donald,' he said. 'You're right of course. Thank you. '

Anna was waiting outside his office. Her cheeks flushed with excitement.

'I'm so pleased for you,' she burbled as he ushered her into the room. 'What happened? Did you show them the web site? Did they confront her? Did she confess?'

He lobbed the file that contained the brief onto his desk, sat down in an easy chair, and invited her to do the same.

'None of those, as it happens,' he said.

She frowned. He couldn't help noticing how when she did that her eyebrows almost met in the centre of her forehead.

'What do you mean?' she said. 'You didn't show them?'

'I didn't need to. She booked out of her hotel, leaving a note for the police in which she withdrew her complaint.'

The eyebrows leapt apart. Her smile, he decided, really did light up her face.

'That's brilliant...' she caught the expression on his face. '...isn't it ?'

'Not really. She said that she was withdrawing her complaint, not that she'd made it all up. Worse still, she said that whatever happened she would not go into the witness box. How do you think that makes me feel?'

'But that's because of what happened to her sister. It has nothing whatsoever to do with you. And the police don't know anything about that anyway. They're just going to assume she's frightened of committing perjury.'

'Or that I am guilty, and she can't face being cross examined?'

'And is that what they think?'

He shook his head. 'As it happens, no. There were problems with her story and some of the physical evidence. No. They don't think I raped her.'

'There you go then. We know you're innocent, they know you're innocent. Case closed.'

'That's what Detective Sergeant Hale said.'

'What did you say to that?'

'There was nothing I could say. It's just that it doesn't feel closed. I don't feel any closure. Don't ask me why...I can't explain it. I just don't.' He reached across to his desk and pulled the file towards him.

'Look, I'm really grateful for the work you did for me yesterday, and I suppose I'm relieved that I didn't end up having to tell the police about it. But if you don't mind, I'd rather not talk about it anymore.' He held up the file. 'I've just been handed this brief. I think you'll find it interesting. How would you like to come and meet the client, and his solicitor? I don't think you've been inside Her Majesty's Prison, Strangeways?

They decided to walk the one and a quarter miles, past the Cathedral, Chetham's School of Music and the Nynex Arena, onto Great Ducie Street. As they set off the sun was sharp in a cloudless sky. Reflected shafts of silver from the aluminium chairs and tables outside the bars and restaurants on Deansgate played counterpoint to the Christmas lights above. Northern spirit shone forth in the scores of people braving the winter chill to breathe life into a pavement café society on this, the eve of the winter solstice.

'What do you know about Strangeways?' Rob asked as they shouldered their way through the mass of shoppers and hopeful diners blocking the pavement in front of La Tasca.

'Not a lot. The Smiths, and Emily Wilding Davison.'

'Come again?'

'The Smiths' Album - *Strangeways Here We Come* – wasn't it one of their last records before they broke up?'

He could see it now. Morrissey's face in silhouette on a yellow background. He had to shout as a couple with a push chair, standing resolute in the centre of the pavement, forced them apart. 'I thought they were before your time?'

She shouted back. 'First time round maybe, but not since he came back in 2004. I've got his latest CD, *Torment of the Ringleaders*. Wouldn't mind seeing him in concert.'

'What about Emily Wilding Davison?' he said as they came together again. 'She wasn't one of the Smiths. Wasn't she the suffragette who threw herself under the King's horse at the Derby?'

'Stepped out more likely. Anyway, six years before that, she was sentenced to nine months hard labour in Strangeways for throwing rocks at David Lloyd George when he came to Manchester. Like a lot of the suffragettes, she tried to starve herself. When they tried to force-feed her she blockaded herself in her cell. So one of the warders decided to shove a hose into the room and drown her out. Nearly managed it too. Apparently, she sued the prison governor, and was awarded 40 shillings in compensation.'

'How come you know all this?' he asked as they waited at the lights opposite the towering glass frame of No 1 Deansgate.

'I did the Suffragettes for my GCSE History Project. I thought they were probably quite a ballsy lot. I wasn't wrong.'

Five minutes later they were staring up at the sleek modern wall around the prison perimeter, and the imposing prison Victorian cell blocks beyond. Renamed Manchester Prison, aka Strangeways, this was Alfred Waterhouses's gothic Victorian monument to law and order.

'Waterhouse designed Manchester Town Hall as well,' Rob told her. 'Appropriate when you think about it. One building for the city worthies, and another for the city worthless. This one became a template for prisons at that time. The wings containing the cells radiate from the centre like the spokes of a wheel. It's called a radial Panopticon. The massive chimney at the centre was used for ventilation, heating, and as a look out.'

'I'm not usually into architecture,' she said, staring up at the curiously erotic chimney. 'But have you noticed the tower's looking distinctly priapic.'

'That,' he said, with a grin. 'Is probably because it's a penal institution.'

They were still laughing as they reached the first checkpoint, a fact not lost on the security guard who took his time checking their credentials before accompanying them to the administration block on F Wing. The walls of the waiting room were covered with photographs and framed documents recounting the history of the prison.

'These were taken during the riots in 1990,' he told her, pointing out a series showing groups of men - some hooded - standing and sitting on the leaden roofs of the chapel. 'The prison was so badly damaged, physically and morally, that it didn't open again until 1994.'

'What sparked them off?'

'Overcrowding; beatings; forced injections to tranquilize some of the prisoners.'

Blimey,' she said, wide eyed. 'Doesn't sound like they'd made much progress since Emily Davison's time.'

Barry Moss looked a good deal older than his twenty nine years. He was short and stocky, and even here - on remand - he exuded a confident air that bordered on arrogance. His hair was dark and short, with the beginnings of a widow's peak. His eyebrows, wide and high, long, and weirdly far apart, gave his face a look of permanent disappointment. His chin was prominent and bullish, his mouth thin and tight, and his nose – broken some years before - had reset itself off centre. But it was the eyes that grabbed you. The right one almost square, the left an oval shape that sloped carelessly downwards. The irises were uniform pools of dark grey glass; obsidian, with a cold hard stare to match. Rob could feel Anna shrinking back as Moss tilted his head, and cast those eyes insolently across her face and body.

'Pupil?' he said in the gravely voice of a smoker, 'And what are you teaching her exactly, Mr Thornton?'

'The importance of choosing one's clients with care.' Rob replied in the confident knowledge that he didn't need this; that he could walk away right now.

Moss switched his gaze to the barrister. His mouth formed the hint of a sneer. 'That works both ways Mr Thornton. From what I hear, you've recently had a bit of bother yourself. Maybe I should be careful who I pay to represent me?'

Rob picked up his briefcase and made to push back his chair. Moss leant back and raised a hand in submission.

'Hold your horses,' he said. 'I was only joking. To be honest, I'd prefer a brief who knows what it's like to find himself on the wrong side of the law. To be innocently accused.'

Rob was tempted to keep going all the way to the door. If Anna had not been there he might well have done, but he knew it would be a cop out. If he rejected every client he took an instant dislike to, his income and his reputation would plummet. Besides, what he needed right now was a challenge, and he had handled nastier pieces of work than Barry Moss. He put the briefcase down on the table, opened it, and withdrew the brief, and a small legal notebook.

'So you're innocent?' he said, watching his client closely.

'Of course.' Moss replied. His eyes never wavered, the facial muscles remained fixed.

A very accomplished liar Rob decided. The result of years of practice. He had seen it a hundred times before. Too polished to be plausible, but impossible to detect. As was so often the case, it was his solicitor who gave it away. The anxious glance at his client to see how he would handle it; the embarrassed dropping of the head to focus on an imaginary spot on the surface of the table. Rob passed the notebook to Anna sitting nervously beside him, and opened the file.

'OK,' he said. 'Let's see if I've got this right. The police have charged you with four counts of conspiracy related to the importation and supply of drugs, murder, and perversion of the course of justice. Given that all of the charges relate to conspiracy, am I right in assuming that you were never caught in the commission of any of the acts of smuggling, dealing, or murder?'

Moss linked his hands together and placed them behind his head. 'Dead right I wasn't.' he said. 'That's because it's all bollocks.'

'That's as maybe,' Rob told him. 'But I'm sure you're aware that you'll need a little more than that to convince the jury.'

Moss smiled thinly. 'It's the police that are going to have to do the convincing. Their so called evidence is as thin as the ice that weasel Tommo is skating on.'

Rob turned the pages. 'Ah yes,' he said. 'Michael John Thomas, their principle witness.'

'Their only witness,' Moss pointed out. 'The rest are all bizzies, and everything they've got to say rests on what he's supposed to have told them. It's a fit up.'

Rob couldn't fault his argument. The evidence consisted of transcripts of telephone conversations between Moss and his associates. The prosecution would be claiming that they related to dates and times of drops and pick ups of drug consignments off the Essex Coast, the removal of rival gang leaders by force, and bribes and threats, in equal measure, made to customs officers and East coast port officials. The critical weakness in the case was that all of the conversations were in loose coded form. The interpretation of the code had been provided by one Michael John Thomas, allegedly one of Moss's own lieutenants. Donald had been right, and so had Moss. Shake Thomas, and the case would collapse like a house of cards.

'Why would Thomas lie? Put his life on the line?' he asked.

Moss shook his head from side to side. 'Now then Mr Thornton. That's not very nice is it? Implying that I might be a threat to him. Tommo was a friend. Why would I want to kill him, even if he is saying these wicked things about me?'

'More to the point, Mr Moss,' Rob said. 'Why would he lie about you?'

Barry Moss unclasped his hands, sat up, and placed them on the table in front of him. 'That's easy,' he said. 'I was shagging his missus.'

11

The weather had changed dramatically. An icy drizzle came slanting out of a leaden sky. The sloping pavement was treacherous. They had no option but to take a taxi.

'So you are going to represent him then?' Anna asked as the cab set off. Rob leant forward, and closed the sliding glass window in the partition between them and the driver.

'Of course. Why wouldn't I?' He said.

'Is he guilty?'

'I don't know. Probably.'

'Don't you want to know?'

He knew that she was being deliberately provocative. It was part of the ritual they played as pupil, and pupil master. A verbal contest testing, in the real world, all the legal ethics theory taught in dusty academe.

'No,' he replied, 'Because that would present me with a dilemma. I would either have to persuade him to change his plea to guilty, or cease to represent him.'

'Don't you have another option? Even if you know he's guilty, if he continues to maintain his innocence you could continue to represent him on the basis that the prosecution cannot provide the necessary evidence to achieve a guilty verdict.'

'Which is the precisely the case I believe we have here. But actually, I would have a further option; to show that the prosecution case is wrong in fact, or in law.'

She turned towards him, straining at her seat belt; completely caught up in the debate.

'But what happens then if the prosecution comes up with a vital piece of evidence? Say they find another, more reliable, witness who can corroborate what Thomas says?'

'Then I would have to advise him to change his plea. If he didn't – and assuming that he had already admitted his guilt to me - I would withdraw from the case on grounds of professional embarrassment.'

'Which is the same as telling the court you know for a fact that he is guilty?'

'Exactly. But that's not going to happen is it? There's no way Moss is going to admit his guilt to me, or anyone else.

She settled back in her seat. 'Has he a good chance?'

'I'd say so. All of the evidence is circumstantial, and the bulk of it is based on hearsay. The only real witness they have is a paid informer. But it's the personal dimension that will clinch it. Any jury is going to understand the humiliation of losing your partner to your boss, and supposed friend. It's a hell of a motive for committing perjury, especially when you've been offered police protection, a change of name, some kind of immunity from the charges they could probably throw at him, and a completely new life.'

'Doesn't it ever get to you? Knowing that you've helped a guilty person to walk away? That he's going to carry on harming tens of thousands of people's lives?'

'It's not our responsibility to carry that burden. Our job is to defend our client to the best of our ability, within the bounds of the law as it exists. Justice is about justification. If the prosecution can't justify the charges, then the accused has to walk free. Otherwise it makes a mockery of the system. In any case, if Moss were to go inside, his place would simply be taken by someone equally nasty; possibly nastier. As long as there's a demand, someone will step in to supply.'

'So you're content to be a hired gun?'

'If you want to put it like that. But I try to do my job competently. I am as zealous in the pursuit of...' he almost said truth, but managed to check himself in time. '...Justice for those I defend, as for those I prosecute. In the end if someone whom I believe to be guilty walks away through my efforts, then at least I will have exposed flaws in the justice system. Maybe helped in some small way to improve it.'

The taxi pulled up outside their Chambers, and the window slid open. 'That's three fifty.' The driver told them.

'That's a bit steep isn't it?' Anna couldn't help remarking as Rob paid, and waited for a receipt.

'Blame the traffic on Deansgate,' shouted the driver as he pulled away. 'I just read the meter.'

She chose to ignore him. 'What if someone you know to be innocent gets put away?' she said as he opened the door to the Chambers for her.

'That's a different matter entirely,' he said. 'That's when I have sleepless nights.'

Which was not strictly true, he reflected as he closed the door to his office. It wasn't the only time. Last night, for example, he had slept fitfully; tossing and turning until the early hours. Images of Anjelita Covas haunted him, alternating between imagined scenes on the banks of the river Tamega, and their evening together in Vince's penthouse apartment. He could see her face even now, smell her perfume, and sense her presence in this room. He knew that it was madness, but he felt a weight of guilt, of responsibility. So many questions spun round in his head. What had happened in that hotel room? Come to that who paid for it, and why did they use a prepaid credit card? Had she been forced to get him to make love to her, to mutilate herself, and then accuse him of rape? What had prompted her to withdraw her complaint? Her account on that website had disturbed him more deeply than he'd first realised.. He needed to know where she was now. That she was safe. He sat behind his desk and put his head in his hands; pushing the images away, preparing to focus on the work in hand. The phone rang. It was Tasha on reception.

'Mr Thornton, there's a call for you. It's your mother.'

'Thank you Tash. Please put her through.'

'Robert! It's me. Your Mother.' Her tone was much changed from the last time she had rung him; high as a kite, and without the aid of alcohol. He knew that for a fact because she hadn't touched a drop since his father had left in an alcoholic haze of self-recrimination. 'Why didn't you ring and tell me?' she said. 'I've just seen it in the papers. They've let you go.'

'They didn't let me go mother, I wasn't actually in custody.'

'Don't quibble Robert, you know how it annoys me. That woman's finally seen sense, and admitted that she lied.'

'Well, it wasn't quite like that,' he began, but she struck like viper.

'There you go again; splitting hairs. Anyway, it doesn't matter does it? It's all over, that's the important thing. So when are you coming down? Friday or Saturday?'

According to his desk calendar today was the twenty first; Saturday was Christmas Eve. It felt like he'd lost a week of his life. 'I don't know,' he said. I need to check my diary. It's got a bit messed up with one thing and another.'

'With that woman more like,' she said bitterly. 'Well I've got a lovely fresh turkey on order, and your favourite Christmas pudding, so you'd better not let me down.'

He smiled at the memory of the early days, when his parents were struggling to establish themselves. Going up to the old Smithfield market with her on Christmas Eve to get a bargain; damaged turkeys, half price or even less. 'How many legs has it got Mum?' he said. Her laugh made him feel good. It wasn't something she did a lot these days.

'It's got two of everything, except for the parson's nose. If you're really good, you can have that yourself. Just let me know as soon as you can. And don't let me down. If you're not here on Christmas Eve, you'll be the one with something missing.'

The remainder of the day passed without incident. He had enough emails and work piled up to take his mind off Anjelita Andrades, aka Covas, until his mobile told him he had text. He flipped it open, and had to read it several times before it registered.

> *My gift I hope your thanks has won,*
> *Now there's no need for you to run!*

It made no sense. He tried without success to return the call. The sender had switched off. But at least the number came up. It had to be from her. Who else could it be? And then it occurred to him that if someone had put her up to it, then it could be from them. He was still trying to decide what to do about it when the door opened, and Harry Richmond breezed in.

'What's up Robbo?' He said. 'You look like death warmed up.'

Rob was more distracted than irritated. 'Don't you ever knock Harry,' he said unconvincingly. 'I could have been with a client.'

Harry sat down in one of the easy chairs. 'Well you aren't. Anyway, I checked first with Tasha. Come on what's up?'

Rob showed him the text.

'Probably a nutter,' Harry told him. 'Brought up on Rupert Bear cartoons. Someone who's seen it on the tele, on the internet, or read about it in the papers.'

'So how did they get my mobile number?'

'OK. So how many nutters have you given your number to?'

Rob retrieved his phone. 'You're not taking this seriously,' he said.

'And you are?'

'Yes. I'm worried it might be from her.'

'Bloody hell, that would be a worry. First she seduces you, then she accuses you of rape, now she's stalking you. What next?'

'I need to trace that number,' he said toying with his phone. 'But that means going to the police. I've had enough of them for the time being, and I get the impression they've had enough of me.'

'You don't have to go to the police. There's always Burnmoor.'

Rob wondered why he hadn't thought of it. Peter Burnmoor. The private investigator they used for most of their work. He could track that number down in no time, no questions asked. While he was at it, he could also try and find out who paid for her hotel room. 'Peter, you're a genius,' he said as he reached for the phone.

It took Burnmoor less than an hour and a half. 'I've got a name, an address, and a credit rating,' he said. 'Which do you want first?'

'Give me all of them,' Rob said, 'In that order.'

'The phone belongs to an Angela Andrews. She gave her address as Number Three, Back Green Lanes, Stoke Newington, London, N16. And her credit rating is good. If she wanted a mortgage up to £350,000, that wouldn't be a problem. While I was about it, I checked to see if she's got a land line. She hasn't. And before you ask, she lives in flat, and it's rented. The landlord is Church Street Estates, Church Street, Stoke Newington. I've got their number if you want it? I've got someone working on the hotel bill. I'll get back to you as soon as I've got something on that.'

Rob stared in disbelief at the details he had scribbled on the pad. Back Green Lanes, Stoke Newington. If he was right, she was living within a half a mile of where he had been brought up. He made himself a cup of coffee while he let it sink in. Angela Andrews; Anjelita Rosa Covas; Angel. It was a lot of aliases for one so young. Her credit rating implied an annual income of up to £70,000 a year. At her age, that was some going. But at least he now knew that the text was from her. Or from someone using her phone. He sat there for several minutes, sipping his coffee, thinking it through. He was still thinking when the phone rang again. It was Burnmoor.

'Which do you want first?' he said. 'The good news or the bad news?'

'Give me the bad news.' He said.

'Couldn't get a name on the credit card. Like you said, it's one of those new prepaid ones. Anyone can buy one over the counter, no questions asked, and use it till the money they've put on it has run out. Just like a phone card.

'And the good news?'

'My colleague sweet talked a girl on the reception who remembered the transaction. They don't get many of those after all. She says it was a man. In his late forties, early fifties. Very well dressed. She couldn't understand why he wasn't using a normal credit card, until she saw the woman who came to book in, and collect the key. She says he was definitely Russian.'

'Russian? How could she be that definite?'

'Because she's Ukrainian, and has good reason to recognise her erstwhile masters.'

'Did she ever see them together?'

'No. But she did see him again. The evening the girl checked out, he walked past reception, on his way out of the hotel,

'What time was this?'

'She wasn't sure, but she thought about an hour before the girl left herself.'

'Thanks Peter,' Rob said. 'I owe you.'

'Don't worry,' Burnmoor replied. My invoice is in the post.'

Rob put the phone down, pushed his mug aside, and made his way to Harry's room.

He slammed his hand down on the desk, causing the computer keyboard to jump. 'It was that bloody Russian,' he said. 'It must have been. I want you to get on the phone right now, and ask Vince what the hell is going on.'

Harry backed away, both hands raised defensively. 'Hang on Rob. You don't know that it was him. You can't expect me to go charging in there making accusations.'

'I think I can; given the kind of accusations that have been made against me. By a guest at your friend's party, aided by one of his other *special* guests.'

'Look, think about it. Why would Vince want to get involved with anything that was going to go down in his apartment; on his own doorstep? In any case, he didn't know I was going to ask you to come along. Even I didn't. It was spur of the moment wasn't it?'

That pulled Rob up short. He had a fair point. Two fair points. On the other hand, it was his only lead. 'Even so,' he said. 'Either you ask him, or I do.'

Harry shook his head. 'Well then I'm afraid it's going to have to be you. You don't know Vince. He's not only stinking rich, he's also well connected. I don't want to get on the wrong side of him, not over this.'

Rob reached across, picked up the post-it-notes pad from the side of the phone, and threw it down in front of Harry. 'All you have to do is write down his office address.'

Vincent Varden's offices were in a recently renovated mill, on Jersey Street, in Ancoats; another district of Manchester rising like a phoenix from the ashes of twentieth century neglect. The hard faced blonde on reception had begun by claiming that Mr Varden was out. When Rob pointed out that Vince's distinctive gold coloured Mercedes, with its V1 licence plate, was sitting out there in the car park, she checked again. Mr Varden, it transpired, must have slipped back in while she was otherwise engaged. Unfortunately it was him that was now engaged; all afternoon.

'Tell him it's Robert Thornton,' he said. 'And that if I have to sit on the bonnet of his car until he leaves for home, so be it. And tell him that just in case he's thinking of calling security, that car park is technically a public place. And so long as I am not doing any damage to his car, anyone laying so much as a finger on me will be committing common assault under both common law and statute, and I shall not hesitate to report it as such.'

Vince Varden was all sweetness and light. 'Rob,' he said as he advanced across the massive corner office, arm extended in greeting. 'How are you? I was so pleased to hear that all charges had been dropped.'

'Charges were never brought,' Rob told him brusquely as his reluctant hand was gripped, and squeezed, a little harder than was really necessary.

'Of course not, slip of the tongue.' Vince placed an arm around his shoulders and steered him to a leather sofa between two of the original iron pillars supporting the intricate red brick cathedral roof. 'Can I get you a drink?'

Caught slightly of guard, Rob sat down; more out of politeness than in anticipation that he would be staying long. 'No thank you. This isn't a social visit.'

Vince sat at the opposite end of the sofa, his arm resting casually along the top. 'I never got a chance to apologise for what happened in my apartment,' he said. 'So I'll do it now. Should never have happened. I don't have friends who would do that sort of thing.'

'So Anjelita Rosa Covas was not one of your friends, nor one of your guests.'

'That's right. She wasn't'

'But you knew who she was?' Vince gave no indication that he was going to reply. 'As I left that night,' Rob reminded him. You said, "That Angel, she's a piece of work, isn't she?"

Vince's smile was lizard like; cold and thin, with a hint of tongue. 'Did I? I don't really remember. But I could have done. After all, she was, wasn't she? But you'd know more about that than any of us.'

He ignored the jibe. 'You told the police that you had no idea how she came to be at your party. That she was not invited.'

'That's right, because it was true.'

'But she came with your Russian friend, didn't she?' In the space of a second, he saw the pupils in Vince's eyes widen, then shrink to pinpoints.

'Very good, Rob.' His tone was condescending. 'She did indeed come as a guest of Dimitri, but he never informed me he would be bringing her. We were in the middle of rather a substantial deal involving property here, in Bosnia, and in Montenegro. I had no intention of embarrassing him by involving him with the police; or drawing him into a pile of shit that was not of his making.'

'But you were happy to let me wallow in it?'

Vince removed his hand from the back of the sofa, and folded his arms. 'But you see Mr Thornton, I had no way of knowing what you'd got up to in that room. Put yourself in my position. You go into one of my bedrooms, without so much as a by or a leave. Next thing, you come out, and rush off. Then she appears, wrapped in a sheet, bruised, smeared with blood, and yelling rape. What was I to think? What were any of us to think? I didn't know you any more than I knew her. If it had been down to me there's no way the police would have been called, but some tosser rang them on their mobile phone. So I don't think you're in any position to come here lecturing me, do you?'

Put like that, Rob could see his point. It softened his approach, but not his resolve. 'You're right, he said. I owe you an apology. But it doesn't change the fact that I need to find Ms Covas. I need to know that she is alright. And I'm not going to rest until I do.'

Vince's expression started out incredulous, and softened to pity. 'My, my,' he said. 'She has got under your skin. One minute she's hanging you out to dry, the next, you want to be her guardian angel.'

Angel, that's ironic Rob was thinking; or is there more to it than that?

Vince got up, thrust his hands into his pockets, and walked over to the window. 'What is it you want from me?' he said, staring out over the canal.

'The name and address of your Russian associate.'

'The deal never went through you know.'

'I'm sorry to hear that. It really was not my fault though.'

'You're right, it wasn't.' Vince turned to face him. 'I pulled out at the eleventh hour. I had a feeling I might be biting off more than I could chew. What is it they say about eating with the devil?'

Rob smiled. 'Therfor bihoveth him a ful long spoon, that shal ete with a feend.' He said. 'It's from Chaucer's The Squire's Tale.'

Vince nodded. 'Well then, he knew a thing or two that Chaucer. But I doubt there's a spoon that's long enough when it comes to Dimitri.' He moved to his desk, picked up his chrome and gold leaf roller ball, and scribbled on his message pad. He tore off the top sheet, and held it out. As Rob took hold of it Vince hung on, looked him squarely in the eyes, and said. 'I mean it. This is one mean bastard. He wasn't best pleased when I pulled out of that deal. My guess is he'll be even less happy about renewing his acquaintance with you.' He let go, and watched as Rob read it, folded it, and placed it in his pocket.

'Thank you,' Rob said. 'And I'm sorry about what happened…at your apartment.'

Vince nodded, and watched silently until Rob

reached the door. Then he called after him. This time his voice was charged with menace. 'I mean it. The best thing you can do is forget about Ms Covas. If you can't, you'd better watch your back. And you didn't get that name and address from me. So I suggest you memorise it, and flush it down the toilet. Because if this comes back to haunt me, you're going to need a bloody sight more than a long spoon when I catch up with you.'

12

Rob caught the earliest available train from Piccadilly. First Class, with the full Virgin Great British Breakfast. A far cry from the tiny flat on the fourth floor of the five storey Millington House council flats, just off Stoke Newington Church Street. His mother had just started teaching at Highbury Grove School where, two weeks short of his twelfth birthday, he would join her as a pupil. This was the first time, apart from a visit to the Emirates Stadium courtesy of a grateful client, he had been back.

He was impressed that the Left Luggage office at Euston required him to open up his case to search for noxious chemicals, guns, or a miniaturised nuclear bomb. He wondered what unusual and embarrassing objects they might come across on an average working day. It probably explained why they looked so happy in their work. That, and the six pound fifty pence charge. He could have taken a taxi, but time was not an imperative, and the roads would be heavily congested on this Friday before Christmas. He crossed the concourse, and took the escalator to the Underground. His destination was more or less equidistant from three stations: Finsbury Park, Highbury and Islington, and The Arsenal. For purely

139

emotional reasons, he opted for the latter.

Fifteen minutes later he emerged onto Gillespie Road, and the familiar sight of the solid, stately, Victorian terraces, with their bold bay windows supported by stone pillars, and pretentious Grecian pediments. Across the road, it was absence of the familiar that caused his heart to sink. Gone was the great North stand. Through the broad gap between houses, where he and his father had been swept along by the crowds pouring into the stadium precinct, he could see that the South stand had also disappeared, to make way for mews developments, and social housing. Huge earth movers lumbered across the hallowed turf; now a massive scar of clay and stone. Bright red scaffolding, over which soared lofty cranes, cocooned the remaining stands; including the one to the East with its famous art deco frontage, and the iconic artillery piece above the entrance. According to the monthly newsletter, to which he still subscribed, flats and apartments costing up to £750,000 would fill the old East stand. There would be no shortage of takers. He had even considered an apartment as an occasional pied-à-terre, and an investment for his pension portfolio.

He set off, his back to the omnipresent Emirates Stadium that had replaced his beloved Highbury, turned right down Blackstock Road, and around the south side of Highbury Quadrant. Opposite the eponymous White House pub he realised he had overshot, and carried on until came out opposite Clissold Park. He turned right here, and within a minute was standing outside a brand new block of flats where once, he recalled, had stood an allotment.

Back Green Lanes. A bland three storey construction squeezed onto a corner plot. There were six flats in all, accessed through a buzzer beside each name plate. Only there were no names; only numbers. This was the inner city after all. There was also a brass security lock, with a set of numbers, set into the door itself. Several times he buzzed number three. He was about to give up, when he spotted a silhouette through the frosted glass of the hallway entrance. He stood back as the door opened, and held it as a large woman in a green overall, jeans, and white sweat shirt, clutching a mop, a bucket, and a box of cleaning materials, struggled out. Despite the freezing cold, droplets of sweat glistened in her hair, and on her forehead. As she passed him, murmuring her thanks, an overpowering body odour assaulted his nostrils. Rob slipped inside.

As the door clicked shut behind him he took stock. The walls were plain magnolia. Six aluminium letter boxes, each with a numbered security tumbler, had been built into the wall just inside the door, which presupposed that whoever delivered the mail had the access code for the door. Not much use if you were expecting a courier, or a supermarket delivery, he reflected, unless you arranged a time to be in. The door to flat one was on his immediate left; the one to flat two, on his right. Ahead, a polished steel staircase climbed up to another landing, before turning back on itself. He climbed the stairs, each step echoing in the narrow stairwell. The door to flat three was immediately above flat one. Like all of the others, it was unremarkable. Just the number plate, another buzzer, and a security spy hole in the centre of the door. There was nobody in. Either that, or they chose, or were unable, to answer. He stood there for several minutes uncertain about what to do next. He heard a sound behind him, and turned to find the door to flat four open on its security chain.

'What do you want?' Said a disembodied female voice from behind the door; middle aged, at a guess.

He assumed that whoever came with that voice was watching him through the spy hole. 'I was hoping to speak with Angela,' he said. 'Angela Andrews.'

There was a pause.

'How do you know her?'

He decided a half truth was better than none. 'We met in Manchester last week. I said I'd be in London today. She asked me to look her up. But she hasn't been answering her mobile phone all week. I was worried about her.'

He heard the chain come off its hook. The door was pushed open far enough for him to see a woman considerably older than her voice had suggested; in her late sixties he supposed. Her hair was silver, permed in a style that aged, but her lilac top and skirt really suited her. Her face was lightly tanned which helped to soften the wrinkles around her eyes and mouth. She inspected him for a moment, pushed the door wide, and stepped out into the corridor. Her right hand, he noticed, hovered just inside the door; where the panic button would be located.

'You can't be too careful these days,' she said. 'Even with the buzzers and the security lock. Not to mention the cameras.' He followed her gaze to the tell tale glass sphere that he had mistaken for a ceiling light. 'You'd be surprised how many non residents manage to get in.' she said. Her brow furrowed. 'Come to that, how did you get in?'

'The cleaner I'm afraid. She was just leaving as I arrived.'

'Typical! Might as well put a sign on the door with the code on.' She stepped away from the door, and moved close to him, reassured by his honesty. 'You said you met Angela in Manchester? Where was that?'

'At a party,' he told her. 'She was with a colleague from work.'

'Ah yes,' she said with a smile that spoke of affection. 'She loves her parties does Angela. Gets away quite lot actually. Abroad even. Brings me back presents when she's been abroad. Never brings any of her friends or workmates back here though. Very quiet when she's at home is Angela.'

'Did you know she was going to be away this time?' he asked, before she had the chance to lapse into further reminiscences.

'Oh yes. She always let's me know. I keep an eye on the flat you see. I even have her spare key.'

He knew that he had to play this carefully. 'Look, I'm really worried about her,' he said. 'Did she give you any idea when she'd be back.'

Her brow furrowed again, and her cheeks and lips became pinched. 'Well, actually I was beginning to get worried myself. She did say she'd be back on Tuesday. That's four days ago. She's never gone over that long before without letting me know. And I never got a card.'

'A card?'

143

'It was my birthday yesterday. Last year, just after we both moved into these flats, she gave me some flowers and a card on my birthday. And she made a point of checking the date this time, just before she went away. It's not like her to forget something like that.'

'You don't think she might have come back too late to want to disturb you, and then had some kind of accident do you?' he suggested.

Her hands flew to her mouth. 'Oh my good God,' she cried, 'I hope not. I never thought of that.'

'Don't you think you should check?' he said. 'I can always wait outside.'

'No fear,' she replied. 'You're coming in with me. Just hang on. I'll get the key.'

A narrow hallway – more of a corridor - ran from the door to the lounge. On the right were a bathroom and toilet, and a small kitchen diner. On the left, were a small twin bedroom, and a marginally larger bedroom with a queen size bed. She insisted that that they inspect each room together, starting with the lounge. The walls were painted in a colour best described as buttermilk. There was a scattering of coloured abstract prints framed in black, a small flat screen television, a tiny wireless music centre with ipod speakers, a red two seater sofa, a matching bean bag, and a flat pack wooden bookcase crammed with books. As far as he could tell they were a mix of language books, travel books, and paperback novels; most in English, some in Portuguese. There was no table of any kind, and no fire place. The room was as neat as a new pin. Antiseptic. A little soulless. He could see her sitting here on her own, curled up on the sofa, a tray on her lap, watching television, reading a book. Not for the first time, he felt a protective impulse.

'Well she's not in here.' The woman said, as she led the way to the master bedroom.

A pale blue winter duvet covered a queen size bed too big for this room. At the top of the bed, on the bulge where the pillows were, a small teddy bear clutching a pale blue cushion had been perched. He thought he caught a faint trace of the perfume she had worn on the night he met her, but it could just as easily have been a trick of memory. On the bedside table were a travel clock, and a photo of the girl he knew as Anjelita Rosa Covas.

She had her arm around another girl. It had been taken some years ago, when she was in her late teens. The two girls were leaning against the wooden veranda rail of a mountain chalet. There was snow on the peaks behind them, and they were smiling. From the difference in their ages, and the unmistakeable resemblance, Rob knew with painful certainty that the other girl was Rosa. Taken perhaps the winter before a summer that had brought death to the younger sister, and a living death to the elder.

'Well she's not here.' Behind him, the woman had opened the doors of the two fitted wardrobes. 'And look at these would you!' Unable to help herself she began fingering costumes and opening drawers. Rob took the opportunity, while she was thus distracted, to snap the photo with his mobile phone.

He turned to find two identical closets with contents as far from each other as chalk from cheese.

145

In the left hand wardrobe were two pairs of faded high street brand jeans in blue and black, some chinos, and two mid length black skirts. Above them, hung loose fitting shirts and blouses. Beneath, were several pairs of trainers, two pairs of black patent shoes, and two pairs of plain calf length brown boots. A set of side shelves contained neat stacks of sweat shirts and plain T-shirts. Below them, a rack of drawers containing everyday briefs, bras, socks and tights, screamed bland, boring, sensible. The second closet was crammed with designer clothes; dresses, suits, skirts, and tops, arranged from left to right by category - evening wear, day wear, formal, informal and by length - each with its own accessories. These drawers were full of exotic, sensual underwear. It didn't take a genius to know that some of the shoes were Jimmy Choo. Or that the dressing table drawers would be similarly divided in terms of jewellery, make up and perfume. It was if two different people slept in this room.

The second bedroom showed no sign of ever having been used except that the wardrobes housed several up-market travel bags, and suit carriers, and served as an overflow for the designer clothes. The bathroom was clean and anodyne. Rob asked if he could possibly use the toilet – giving the excuse that he had been travelling all day.

'Well…I suppose,' she said. 'As long as you leave it as you find it.'

As soon as the door was locked he opened the cabinet above the sink. There were the usual suspects, but nothing to suggest that she was taking medicine; prescribed or otherwise. He flushed the chain, washed and dried his hands, and opened the door. She was waiting outside. Like a sentry.

'I don't even know your name.' She said, as though it had just occurred to her.

'Nor I yours,' Rob replied, playing for time. He was wondering whether to lie, until he remembered the camera on landing. 'My name is Robert. Robert Thornton. When you see Angela, Mrs…?

'My name is Marjory,' she said.

'Well, Marjory, will you tell her I'm sorry I turned up like this. But I was worried about her.'

Her forehead furrowed again, and she looked at him for the first time with a hint of suspicion 'I thought you said she was expecting you?'

'She was. But I promised I'd ring and let her know. Not just pitch up on her doorstep.'

'And you did ring, didn't you?'

'That's right, but her phone was off.' He was beginning to feel as though he was in the witness box. Marjory would make a pretty relentless inquisitor.

'Yes, well I tried to ring her too,' she said. 'She didn't take my calls either. Anyway, at least she's not had a nasty accident, and been lying here all on her own.'

He followed her into a galley kitchen equally devoid of character. Every surface was empty, except for a kettle, toaster, and a two cup coffee percolator. There was not so much as fridge magnet or a post-it-note. Exceptionally, a winter flowering orange cymbidium orchid perched on the window ledge, its clusters of perfect petals highlighting the intensely erotic lip and column in the centre. It struck him that this was the only indication of life in the entire flat.

147

He left his card with Marjory so that she could let him know if Angela Andrews turned up, or if she heard from her. It had already occurred to him that Anjelita – for he had now resolved to call her by her real name, at least in his own head – might go straight to the police. And if she didn't turn up, then Marjory would almost certainly contact them. He was past caring. In any case, he reasoned, if he was looking for her how could he possibly have had anything to do with her disappearance? His alter ego leapt in for the prosecution.

Come come, Mr Thornton. Isn't that what you would want us to think? A man of your intelligence might see it as a perfect ploy to put us off the scent. Kill the lady, and then pretend to be looking for her? Don't take us for fools. We weren't born yesterday.

He stood outside the Robinson Crusoe pub, at the junction with Green Lanes and Stoke Newington Church Street, waiting to cross over to the entrance to Clissold Park. Had he not been pondering on the fact that his alter ego - whether acting for prosecution or defence – always seemed to acknowledge the innate intelligence of Robert Thornton, Barrister at Law, he might have noticed the two men hurrying up Church Street, on the far side of the road. He might also have noticed one of them point towards him. But he did not. He crossed over, and entered the park.

They followed at a prudent distance, hanging back as he stopped by the animal enclosure, searching in vain for the wallabies he recalled from his youth, finding only deer, and goats, and rabbits in their winter coats. They followed as he crossed over the stretch of water known as New River, that once provided drinking water to the city, and paused as a third man hurried to join them from the Bridge Gate. They followed him up the slope, and into the café inside the imposing eighteen century Clissold Mansion, where yummy mummies in heavy hooded woollen jumpers, and zipped jackets, hand knitted by Tibetan refugees in Nepal, struggled spasmodically, and unconvincingly, to control their progeny. As he queued for a ham and cheese pannini, they decided to split. Two stayed in the front room, the third in the back. Both exits covered.

Fifteen minutes later, Rob resolved to follow his only other lead. The address Vince had given him was on the other side of the city, in fashionable South Kensington. He reckoned it would take about twenty five minutes travel time, plus the fifteen minutes walk to the station. This time he opted for Finsbury Park, on the basis that more trains would be likely to stop there. He skirted the pond, where ducks and swans waited patiently for the children to spill from the café and hurl pieces of scone in their direction, and turned to head North West towards the Lodge Gate.

Two men in black leather jackets fell into step on either side of him, and a third pressed something hard and sharp into his back. Just about where he suspected one of his kidneys to be.

'Don't do anything stupid.' The one on his right, hissed. 'Just keep walking.' His accent was foreign, most likely Turkish.

Rob cursed himself for a fool; for wandering around without his antennae up. For coming here without the spare wallet he carried abroad, stuffed with impressive looking cards for stores, and video shops, and the single five pound note for authenticity. He'd learned enough from countless court appearances to know that he was going to hand over whatever it was they wanted. Mobile phone, wallet, even his Burberry coat if they wanted it. But please God, not his kidney. They edged him along the left fork of the path, down behind the clubhouse of the Bowling Green, then left down the far side of the building, until he came face to face with a pair of tall green bins. They pushed him up against the wall and encircled him. Now he could see the knife. A cross between a stiletto and the one his fishmonger used for gutting fish at Thomson's in the Arndale Market. The blade hovered uncomfortably close to his neck. He know knew why it was that people wet themselves.

'Very sensible.' It was the one who had spoken before. Several inches shorter than Rob, moustached, a little overweight judging by the way his paunch strained to escape the jacket. 'Now where's your wallet?'

Rob lifted his arm slowly, intending to reach inside his coat pocket. His wrist was seized roughly by the one on his left. The knife came closer.

'I said, where is it? Not show me it.' The Moustache reached into Rob's coat, removed his wallet, and flipped it open. He checked each credit card in turn, before placing them back in their slots. He found the small clutch of business cards in the underneath compartment, extracted one, and held it close to his face, as though farsighted.

'So Mr Robert Thornton,' he said. 'What is your interest in Miss Andrews?'

'I'm a friend.' He said.'

'A friend from where? She doesn't have any friends.'

'From Manchester,' he said as firmly as possible, emboldened by the fact that they were asking questions, not carving tattoos. Questions were his stock in trade. 'I was with her a few days ago.'

'How few?' The Moustache had moved a little closer. His breath stank of something rancid. His clothes of tobacco.

'Last Saturday,' he said.

'And you have seen her since then?'

'No.'

'Why are you here now?'

Their eyes bored into his. He sensed that they were willing him to get the answers wrong. 'Because she suggested I contact her when I was in London. And here I am.'

'Why didn't you call her, on your phone? You do have a phone?'

'Yes I have. And I did...call her.'

Too late, Rob realised that they had only to check the dialled numbers on his phone to know that he was lying. The only London number he had called in days was his mother's, and if they knew the mobile number used by Angela Andrews, then their prayers were answered, and his unlikely ever to be heard.

'What did she say?'

'She didn't answer. Her phone was switched off. That's why I came to her flat. I was concerned.'

The three of them looked at each other. The Moustache nodded sagely. 'We also are concerned,' he said. 'You see Miss Andrews is one of our tenants.

We look out for our tenants. We become concerned when one of them is not around when we expect her to be. We become more concerned when strangers come poking their noses into her flat.'

'Especially when her rent has not been paid in the week of Christmas.' Said the one with the knife.

'Shut up, you fool.' Snapped Moustache.

The stupid grin on the face of the Knife was wiped away, which disappointed Rob because the tip of the blade was suddenly against his jaw.

'So you have no idea where she may be?'

'Rob shook his head. It was a bad mistake. He felt a sharp prick, and the sudden warmth of blood on his cold skin. Moustache seemed not to notice.

'Well Mr Thornton,' he said, flicking Rob's nose with the edge of the business card. 'We know where to get hold of you. And if you should hear from Miss Andrews, or discover her whereabouts, you will ring this number.' He took a biro from the inner zipped pocket of his jacket, and wrote it down on the right side of Rob's shirt collar. 'Just ask for Erkan. And stay away from her flat.' He stepped back, placed the card in his pocket, and threw the wallet at Rob's feet. 'And if you should think of trying to take this further, I suggest you think again. We never met. However, we do have CCTV of you gaining illegal entry to our property, and to the flat of a missing person.' He and his colleague turned, and walked away, leaving Rob alone with the Knife.

He read disappointment in his assailant's eyes, and closed his own. Three quarters of the way through an Act of Contrition he felt the pressure from the knife lift, and the blade withdraw, heard the footsteps retreating up the path, and sensed that he was alone. He opened his eyes, and took a handkerchief from his trouser pocket. He held it to his neck to stem the flow, bent to pick up his wallet, and found that his hand was shaking. He stood there for a full five minutes, waiting until the bleeding ceased. When he felt sufficiently recovered, he noted the direction in which his assailants had gone, and set off in the opposite direction, towards the White House Gate.

13

By the time the train reached Kings Cross there was standing room only. Rob sat silently, head down, squashed against the window by a large African lady doing her best to avoid contact with the people in the aisle. He turned up the collar of his coat to hide the phone number on his shirt, and the cut on his face. He was still in shock. His face was pale and clammy, and he knew that he still had the stench of fear about him. Twice the woman leaned closer to ask if he was sick, her ample bosom pinioning his arm. At Warren Street, she hauled her bulk from the seat, and forced her way through the crowd. A pretty young Muslim woman in a dark blue pinstriped suit, and pale blue hijab, took her place. She glanced across at him. The half smile on her face froze. She made to rise, but the gap she'd vacated had already been filled. Instead she angled herself away from him, and fixed her gaze on the floor. As the train entered the tunnel, Rob looked at his reflection in the window. A ghost stared back.

As the train pulled into Victoria the woman carved a path for him to the doors. He stood clutching the overhead strap as the train slowed down. Where the windows met the roof, a London Poem of the Month stared back at him.

Life is a moment in eternity - seize it, live it, love it, and let go. Marcus, aged 12, Paradise Street, Rotherhithe.

Rob grimaced. Doing precisely that explained the mess that he was now in. Except that he was unable to let go.

He couldn't face changing to the Piccadilly line to travel the single station to South Kensington, but he had underestimated the number of likeminded travellers queuing for taxis. He decided to grab a coffee while he took stock. It was a bad idea. The glossy exterior masked a set of miserable staff, and half inebriated customers. He made short shrift of his cappuccino, and visited the toilets to freshen up. The place stunk of sick, and urine. He splashed his eyes, ran his handkerchief under the tap, rinsed it out, and warily dabbed away the blood congealed around the wound. There was nothing to be done, he decided, about the bold blue numbers on the collar of his shirt. He looked around for a paper towel, and decided against the automatic dryer; the thought of blowing this much recycled fetid air over his face, a step too far. It was bad enough that he had just used water that had passed seven times through human bodies. He used the tail of his shirt to dry his face and hands, tucked it back in, and hurried out into the fresh air. According to his mini A-Z, it was less than a half a mile to his destination. He set off on foot.

Burton Mews, was on the southernmost fringe of Belgravia, just a stone's throw from Sloane Square. He had read that the Russians already owned a sizeable chunk of the French Riviera, and were now using the millions siphoned from oil revenues, and foreign aid, to establish a foothold in London. He ought not to have been surprised. The nouveau riche from just about every nation and niche of instant stardom had aspirations to own property here. Were it not for the Duke of Westminster, and the Crown and Church Estates, he doubted there would be more than a handful of British residents. Give it a couple of decades, and he expected the Chinese and Indians would have a sizeable foothold. Always assuming it wasn't under water by then.

A Lexus, a Mercedes, and a Humvee – all of them black - filled the spaces in front of Thurloe House. Rob checked his reflection in the tinted widows of the Humvee. He fingered his hair into shape, pulled the collars of his coat across his neck, crossed to the front door, and rang the bell. The voice on the intercom was female, pleasant, and polite, with just a hint of an East European accent.

'How may I help you?'

'Mr Robert Thornton. I would like to speak to Mr Izmailov, Dimitri Izmailov.'

'You wish to speak with Mr Izmailov?' She said. A gentle correction he felt, rather than a rebuke.

'That's correct. I wish to speak with Mr Izmailov.'

'I do not appear to have a record of your appointment Mr Thornton.'

She made it sound like an apology. She would, he decided, make a great receptionist at Weir Chambers.

'I am afraid that was my oversight,' he said. 'But I'm only in London for a few hours, and I would be most obliged if Mr Izmailov could spare me just a minute or two. It is most urgent.'

'Mr Izmailov is in conference at the moment,' she said. 'But I shall see if I can disturb him. Will he be aware of the nature of your business?'

'Tell him I have come from Manchester, regarding a mutual friend. From The Hilton Hotel.'

He paced up and down for several minutes, before the front door opened, and a tall and slender woman with smiling eyes, and long black hair, wearing an elegant two piece suit, beckoned.

'Mr Thornton,' she said as she ushered him in. I am sorry to have kept you waiting. It is cold today is it not? Mr Izmailov can spare you just five minutes.' In a voice intended to be amiably conspiratorial she added: 'And I must warn you, he is very precise in his appointments. Five minutes means exactly that.' She led him down a corridor to the door at the furthest end. She knocked, waited for the invitation to enter, opened the door, and stood aside to let him in. The door closed behind him.

Dimitri Izmailov, his face in shadow, was seated at the furthest end of an oval table of steel and glass. He made no attempt get up. Rob found himself flanked on either side by two large men; large in every sense. Not quite as broad as they were long, but not far short. One wore black trousers, and a black polar neck, the other, a charcoal suit with an open neck white shirt. Rob doubted there was an off the peg collar large enough to button around either of their necks.

'Come in Mr Thornton,' Izmailov said. 'Your time is running out.'

The double meaning of the phrase was not lost on Rob, but just in case it hadn't registered, one of them stepped behind him, seized his arms, and held them out at shoulder height while his companion patted him down with a firm and practised hand that could never have been mistaken for intimacy. Satisfied that he was clean, they each placed a hand behind his shoulder blades, and propelled him forwards until he reached the table. One of them pulled out a chair, the other shifted his grip to his shoulder and pushed him down onto the seat. They stepped back. He could sense them folding their arms behind him. Izmailov appraised him coolly.

'We have a saying, Mr Thornton. The man who walks into the cave of the bear is brave; but he who walks in unarmed is merely foolish.'

'I had no reason to fear you Mr Izmailov, since I am not here to threaten you.' Rob replied with considerably more conviction than he felt.

Izmailov smiled sagely. 'That is because you are in no position to threaten me, Mr Thornton. With respect to you however, I am.' He stood and walked around the table until there was just one chair between them. He pulled it out, and sat down. Rob felt the others move closer until their knuckles brushed his shoulders. Izmailov leaned forward and stared at him. 'And if I might say so, you are looking pretty shit today Robert. Perhaps I may call you Robert? And, since we have a mutual friend, you shall call me Dimitri?'

Before he could reply Izmailov raised his right hand to stop him. 'No, there is no need. You see Vince rang to tell me you were coming. That you had found out about me – not of course through him – and to expect you. Unlike you, Vince is afraid of me I think.' He leaned forward and turned back the collars of Rob's coat. 'Mo, mo,' he said lifting Rob's chin.

'What have we here Robert?' He undid the top two buttons and pushed back the coat flap revealing the trail of dried blood down the left side of the shirt front. 'You appear to making a habit of going where you are not welcome.' He pointed to the number on the collar. 'The people who did this...this is their number, no? Would you like that I send my boys over? Teach them a lesson?'

Rob straightened his coat, and did up the buttons. 'No thank you Dimitri,' he said. 'If you really would like to help I have just one question.'

Dimitri leant back in his chair. 'You want to know about the girl.'

'That's right. I want to find Anjelita Covas. I want to know where you met her.'

The surprise on the Russian's face was genuine. 'Anjelita Covas? And why would you want to do that? That bitch has caused enough trouble already Robert. For you, and for me.'

'Because she has disappeared.'

'Not your problem my friend. If I were in your shoes I would wish her disappeared.'

Rob was unable to help himself. 'And what about in yours?' he asked.

Each of his shoulders was seized in a vice like grip. Dimitri sat forward, his face close enough for the spittle to spray across his face. 'I'd paid the hotel bill. Told her I was very disappointed in her. Told her I hoped I'd never see her again. I left her in that hotel. I haven't seen her since. I don't care where the hell she is, and if you've any sense, neither will you, Mr Nosey Lawyer.'

The strain of the morning's events finally told on

Rob. 'Did letting her know how disappointed you were, involve beating her up?' He shouted, completely unaware that he was losing control.

He found himself hauled from his seat. His legs were like jelly, but it didn't matter. Suspended in mid air, he had no need of them.

'So I gave her a slap. She was lucky I didn't mark her.' Dimitri looked at his watch. 'Time's up,' he said. 'Get him out of here.'

His feet quite literally didn't touch the ground as they carried him towards the door.

'I'm not going to let this go,' Rob shouted. 'Whatever it takes.'

Dimitri said something in Russian. Rob was suddenly turned, and pinned against the wall beside the door. Insanely, it occurred to him that this must be how a butterfly felt in the grip of a lepidopterist. Dimitri rose, and walked slowly towards him. He stopped a few feet away, and put his hand inside his breast coat pocket. Rob's heart had taken a pounding already today. Now he felt like it was going to give up. Dimitri withdrew his hand. He was holding a business card. He took hold of Rob's chin with his left hand, forced it down until his mouth was open, stuck the card between his teeth, and pushed it roughly shut with the heel of his hand.

'This is what you want, I think,' he said coldly. 'I no longer have need of it. Soon I shall have an agency of my own. You are going to leave now, and I will never see or hear from you again. Because if I do, you will never be seen or heard of again.' He stared into Rob's eyes. 'Do you understand Mr Thornton?'

Rob had just enough time to nod before the door was flung open, and he was propelled through it. The young woman was standing by the front door, holding it open. 'Good afternoon, Mr Thornton. Lovely to see you. Do have a nice day.' She said breezily, as though this was a daily occurrence.

Perhaps it was, Rob reflected, as he leant on the bonnet of the Humvee, and threw up all over the front nearside tyre.

He had the presence of mind to retrieve the card from the gutter. And to buy two bottles of water from the first grocery store he passed on the way to the internet café. Now he sat on the low brick wall dousing his shoes and the bottom of his trousers. The business card lay on the wall beside him, drying. Behind him, in the middle of the green triangle at the centre of this cross roads, the elegant statue of Zoltan Godaly - almost golden in the sun - stared down disdainfully, reminding him of how confidently he had started out that day, and how far he had fallen. When he was sure that he no longer smelt like a vagrant, even if he did look like one, he took his life into his hands to dodge the traffic on the Old Brompton Road, to reach the Global Talk Internet café on the far side.

He bought himself an hour of time, and sat down at a terminal alongside the tourists, students, and the far from home for whom this was a lifeline. He began by checking his emails. Swiftly dispatched, since there were few this close to the Christmas weekend, he turned his attention to the card. The title was unambiguous.

Elite Executive Escorts – Home and Abroad.

He typed in the web address and was immediately surprised by the sophistication of the site. There were no scantily clad women, or girls; no smutty invitations; no glib descriptions full of double meanings. Just a series of menu options, and a very professional introduction. It told him that he would find a gallery of just 25 elite escorts, carefully selected for VIP members only.

Apparently, these members were people of sufficient wealth and discernment to appreciate the very best of everything. All of the escorts – in addition to being exceptionally beautiful, sophisticated, and multi talented - had been educated to degree level and beyond, and spoke at least two languages; including English and their own. The agency went to great pains to stress that this was an escorting service only. The fee structure shown was indicative of the sort of fee he could expect to pay as a member, although rates would vary according to the escort he chose, and his specific requirements. Fees paid to escorts were for companionship – time spent together – only. They did not constitute payment for any intimate or sexual services. Elite Executive Escorts would not accept any anonymous bookings. For every booking they required a credit card number, for verification purposes only. If he was interested in becoming a member, he had only to complete the online membership form. Membership, he was assured, was normally approved within two minutes from the point at which an application was received. Oh yes, he reflected, on the sole condition that your credit limit was bottomless.

He tried several times to get into the gallery without success. There was no way round it. If he wanted to see inside he would have to register as a member. He clicked the link, and read the disclaimer.

Please note. The details which you provide enable us to ensure that you receive the very best match to your requirements. They will remain entirely confidential within the terms of the Data Protection Act, will not be shared with any second party, and will be destroyed should you later decide to terminate your membership. [We are proud to say, that thanks to the exceptional calibre of the escorts who choose us to represent them, this is something which we have yet to experience.]

Whatever else, they had got themselves a good lawyer, and a literate web designer. The questions on the form were only to be expected. They wanted his name, age, ethnicity and country of origin, and any special interests; the examples included cultural, intellectual, sporting, gastronomic, and social. Not unreasonably they needed to know in which languages he was comfortable to converse. His credit number, he was assured, would be used for verification purposes only. All payments should be made to his escort in cash [British Sterling, American Dollars and Euros only]. Payment could be made by credit card, providing that it was the card with which he had registered his membership. And finally, they required his mobile phone number, in the event that either he, or his escort, was delayed or unable to make the appointment.

He decided to go ahead. This was not after all a

hard core porn site. There would be no Operation Ore coming to call. And it was no business of his bank what site he chose to visit. Nevertheless, he felt uneasy as he punched in the details. True to their word, within two minutes he was welcomed by name as their newest member. There on the member's page flashed the invitation to enter the gallery.

One name stared out him; Angel. When the link opened, his heart skipped a beat; not for the first time today, but for a very different reason. Angel was indeed Anjelita Rosa Covas, and, according to the photo on his mobile screen saver, Angela Andrews. She was every bit as beautiful as he remembered. There were four photographs of her: in a suit, in evening wear, a swimming costume, and in a casual silk sweater and tight fitting slacks. According to the promotional CV, Angel is an intelligent, well educated, independent escort based in West London, educated at universities in Portugal and London. She offers exclusive high end services in the UK; and also abroad should you wish a travelling companion, someone to accompany you to a conference, sales meeting or seminar, or with whom to enjoy a city break or short vacation. Her age was given as twenty six, her size as 10, her height as five feet eight, and her bust as 34F.

Rob clicked on the table of rates. He had to check them twice to make sure he hadn't made a mistake. A quick coffee and a chat would set him back two hundred and fifty pounds; a couple of hours, six hundred and fifty pounds. Overnight in London cost a cool three thousand pounds, and double that for a

Special Weekend whatever that might involve. There were higher rates for a trip to Europe, or a transatlantic break. A one week Getaway, would cost him twelve thousand pounds. And none of this, allegedly, included activities of a sexual nature. He didn't dare compute the notional cost of their evening together. Come to that, he didn't want to.

He tried, using the number provided, to book Angel for dinner the following evening, and was informed, with a courtesy matched only by Dimitri's receptionist, that she was unavailable. He wondered if she might be available next week, and was given the same reply, this time with a hint of unease. He was told that tomorrow was a particularly busy time as he might appreciate – it being Saturday the twenty third, the day before Christmas Eve - and only three of their escorts were available. She gave him the names, and suggested he check their details on the gallery, and get back to her.

He put his mobile away, and suddenly became aware that the woman on his left had not only overheard his conversation, but was staring at his screen with a distinct air of disapproval. The boy on his right, was similarly engaged, but with a smirk on his face. He pressed the button on the monitor that brought up the screen saver, and had a think. She was neither at home, nor available for work. He only had a few days here in London, and would have to head back no later than Wednesday; the day after Boxing Day. This looked like a dead end. He was damned if he was going to come all this way, get attacked and threatened twice in the space of two hours, and go back empty handed. Someone had to know something. In desperation he brought up the gallery again, checked the names he had been given, and made a booking. If she worked for the same agency she must know something, he reasoned, and anyway he could afford it. And it had to be better than staying in with mother.

14

By the time he reached Euston, rush hour was approaching its peak. Thousands of commuters jostled with those who had left work at midday and were now making their way out of the capital to spend Christmas with friends and family, or to head for the airport to jet off to warmer climes, and ski resorts.

Having reclaimed his case, he had to queue to get into the washroom in the First Class Lounge. Ignoring the disapproving glares of fellow travellers he shaved his face – carefully skirting the livid wound on his neck – changed his shirt, and combed his hair as best he could. The result, although a vast improvement, left a lot to be desired.

It was over an hour later that he walked out onto Station Approach in West Drayton, just seventeen miles to the West. Although he had the option to take a taxi, it was less than a quarter of a mile, and he felt he needed the chilly evening air to clear his head before he faced his mother. He set off down Station Road, turned right into Church Road, and right again down to the bottom of tree lined West Drayton Park Avenue. Even though he had not called ahead to warn her, his mother was standing in the huge bay window of the fine Edwardian semi to which she had been forced to downsize three years ago. He saw her wave, and recognised the familiar flutter of the curtain as she opened the door into the hallway. As he walked down the drive the front door was flung open, and she stood there with her arms open wide.

'Robert! You should have rung. I was so worried.' She threw her arms around him, and stood on tip toe to kiss his cheek. He bent to meet her.

'I'm sorry Mum. I wasn't sure how long it would take with it being rush hour, and I know how you worry if I promise a time, and then get delayed.'

'Well I worry even more if I don't hear from you at all. You said you were getting the ten fifty five from Manchester. That was over seven and a half hours ago. What was I to think?' She let go, took his free arm, and pulled him into the house. As soon as the door had closed behind him she made him put down his case, and turned him towards the light. 'Now,' she said. 'Let's have a look at you.' Eagle eyed as ever, she homed in on the cut beneath his chin. She fingered it gently. 'What have you done here?' He took her hand gently, and guided it away.

'It's nothing I just cut myself shaving. That's all.'

'Well you should be more careful. And you look terrible. You haven't been looking after yourself have you?' She picked up his case, ignored his protestations, and led the way up the staircase. 'Your bed is made up, and I've put the winter duvet on. There's a nice steak and kidney pudding in the oven, with creamy mashed potatoes, and garden peas. Apple pie and custard to follow; your favourites.'

Rob decided not tell her that they hadn't his been favourites since he'd left primary school. Besides, he was ravenous.

'I've put you a set of towels out in the bathroom,' she said, pushing open the door into the master bedroom. 'And while you're unpacking I'll run you a bath. It looks like you need one.'

'Hang on Mom, this is your bedroom,' Rob said.

'Well I've moved out while you're here. I'll be perfectly happy in the back room, it's quite cosy really. In fact I think I might stay there when you've gone. There's a nice view over the back garden. '

It was this mixture of self sacrifice, and the urge to control, Rob reflected, that had partly explained why his father had finally done the unthinkable, and had the affair that ended his parent's marriage of thirty years. It wasn't as simple as that, he knew, but it was a major part of it. It was also why he found it difficult himself to visit his mother for more than a couple of days at a time. But he couldn't fault her instincts, or her planning. As he unpacked, the seductive sound of the water tumbling into the bath was a whispered invitation to paradise.

He lay in the bath with his fingers in his ears, and his head beneath the surface, letting the warmth seep into every pore. Thus immersed, he failed to hear the ring tone of his mobile phone.

'Robert!'

The only reason that he was able to hear his mother was that she was standing over him, his phone in her outstretched hand.

'This is the second time they've rung,' she said as he wiped the water from his eyes. 'I thought it might be urgent.'

'Thanks Mom,' he said, suddenly, and awkwardly, aware that here he was, a grown man, naked in the presence of his mother. A mother had who never allowed her husband to watch her undress. Who insisted that he turn out the light while she put on her nightie. 'I'd better not get it wet,' he said. 'If you could just put it down on the stool, I'll answer it when I've dried off.'

She stood her ground. 'It might be important,' she said. 'This is the second time they've rung.'

'I know Mom. That's the second time you've told me.'

She turned and placed it on the stool, straightened up, and opened the door. 'There's no need to get shirty,' she said. 'I was only trying to help. And you'd better get a move on. Or you pie is going to burn.' She closed the door firmly; like a full stop.

He waited until he was dressed before he rang last number recall. The caller had not left their number. Nor was there a message on his answer phone. He was halfway down the stairs when it rang again. He sat on the step, and accepted the call.

'Hello?'

'Is that Robert?' It was pleasant young voice, with a touch of Australian sunshine.

'Yes, this is Robert.'

'Oh good. I thought I must have the wrong number. This is Sam.'

'Hello Sam,' he said, 'Sorry about that, I was in the bath.' Too much information, too soon, he reflected. Wrong signal. Definitely the wrong signal.

'Why not,' she replied cheerfully. 'Just what I like to do on a winter's evening, at the end of a hard week. Anyway, I understand we have a date; for lunch, tomorrow?'

'That's right...if that's OK with you?' God I'm beginning to sound like a total idiot, he decided. Of course it's alright with her, it's her job, her occupation. It's like asking the court stenographer if she'd mind recording the proceedings.

'That would be wonderful,' she said with as much enthusiasm as if it was a real first date. 'Where did you have in mind?'

That really threw him. He'd not given it a thought. The possibilities flooded in; Joe Allen, Browns, Bertorellis, The Ivy, Nobu, Hard Rock Café. He had no idea what would be most appropriate; most conducive to what he had mind. He wanted to impress, but not go over the top. He needed a degree of privacy, but definitely not intimacy. And all the time she was on the end of the line, waiting for an answer, firming up her initial suspicion that he was a patently inexperienced punter, with more money than sense.

'Why don't you choose?' he said. 'You must have a favourite?'

'If you'd like me to Robert?' she said, with just the smallest hint of surprise.

'Yes I really would. Anywhere at all.'

'In that case, why don't we make it The Ritz?'

'The Ritz?' He needn't have worried about going over the top. He recalled that he had taken his mother there for afternoon tea when he passed his finals and had to book four weeks in advance. 'Will we be able to get a table with such short notice?'

'No problem,' she said, with a confidence borne of experience. 'Just leave it with me.'

'OK, The Ritz it is,' he said. 'How about twelve

thirty, for one o'clock. We can have a drink in the bar first. '

'That would be splendid Robert.'

It was the first thing she had said that sounded out of character, part of a script.

'I'm really looking forward to meeting you.' She added.

That was the second. 'And me you, Sam. Oh, and by the way, I'm six foot one, with brown eyes and black hair. I'll be wearing a beige linen jacket with a blue check shirt, and a gold and blue tie.'

'Mmm…' she made it sound as though she had just bitten into a liqueur chocolate. 'You're going to be easy to find. Oh, and Robert; I'm sure you know, no jeans and no trainers. They are very particular. No exceptions.'

'Who was that Robert?' His mother asked as he walked into the kitchen.

'Just a friend from University,' he said. 'We agreed to meet for lunch tomorrow.'

'The Ritz,' she said as she lifted the casserole dish from the stove with her oven gloves. 'That's going to set you back a bit.'

He smiled to hide his annoyance that she had been listening in to his conversation, wondered if she'd been puzzled that he'd needed to provide a description, and then rebuked himself. The door to the kitchen had been open after all, and the hallway would act like a wind tunnel. And anyway, he'd developed a habit of speaking too loudly on his mobile. He feared it that it might become an affectation.

'Now sit yourself down,' she said, bringing the peas to the table. 'Do I know this Sam? I don't seem to remember him. Did he go on to the Inns of Court with you?'

'No Mom, she didn't,' he said. 'In fact I haven't seen her since I left Uni.'

She pulled up her chair and sat down opposite him, a smile suffusing her face. 'She. That's nice. After all that time…and at the Ritz.'

He cut into the pastry, and began to spoon the steaming chunks of steak and kidney onto his plate. They smelt fantastic. She had been right. It was one of those aromas from your youth that had the power to instantly transport you back; an olfactory time machine. 'We're just catching up Mom,' he said. 'It's nothing serious.'

'Pity,' she replied, watching with quiet satisfaction as he piled up his plate. 'It's time you found someone you could settle down with. Then you wouldn't find yourself getting into a spot of bother like you did last week. Besides, I think I'm about ready to become a grandmother.'

A spot of bother, Rob reflected. Just like she was commenting on the weather. Only a mother could pull off an understatement like that.

15

Saturday the 23rd of December.

'Wakey wakey, tea and cakey.'

Rob pulled the sheet up over his head, and turned over. His father's National Service refrain had come back to haunt him through his mother's voice.

'Come along Robert,' she said as she placed the cup and saucer on the bedside table. 'It's nine thirty. You haven't had your breakfast yet, and I'm sure you'll want to really spruce yourself up for your tete a tete with Sam.'

'I've told you Mom, it's not a tete-a-tete, it's a catch up,' he muttered; his obvious irritation giving the lie to his assurances. 'And I don't want any breakfast thanks.'

She turned and made for the door. 'Breakfast in fifteen minutes. Be there!'

Sausage, bacon, scrambled eggs, tomatoes, toast, and a pot of tea. It was pointless reminding her that he was having lunch at The Ritz. She hadn't forgotten, simply assumed that he still had the appetite of a rugby playing nineteen year old. He left as much as he could safely get away with; half a sausage, one slice of toast and some bacon rind.

As he set off down the drive her voice pursued him. 'While you're there, could you just pop across to

Neal's Yard in Covent Garden, and get me an Organic three seed loaf, a piece of Colston Bassett Stilton – Christmas just isn't the same without a nice piece of Stilton – and get yourself some Stinking Bishop; I know how you love to spread it thick and runny on your oat meal biscuits.'

On the train Rob tried to recall what Sam's CV had said on the website. He realised that he had registered absolutely nothing about her physical statistics. He seemed to recall that she was blond, Australian, and supposedly had a BA in International Business. He was firmly convinced that you couldn't believe a word they said on these sites. Caveat emptor – "Let the buyer beware." It was as true today as the day it was coined in the mists of time. There was one condition that offered the buyer redress, and that was if the seller had deliberately set out to deceive. Under modern commercial law of course the goods also had to be of merchantable quality. Somehow he rated the likelihood of getting his money back from an escort agency as somewhere between zero, and minus infinity.

He had left himself with plenty of time in hand, and called at Neal's Yard on his way to the hotel. He left the carrier bag with the porter, hopeful that the temperature in the luggage room would be cool enough to prevent the smell of the ripened cheese from impregnating every other piece of baggage. He made his way to the sumptuous splendour of the art deco Rivoli Bar. This was the third time he had been here. If anything, he was even more impressed by the way the designer had pulled off the combination of satinwood, alabaster, gold leaf, sparkling chandeliers beneath their golden shells, and up-lit Lalique glass. He fancied he could even detect the scent of the camphor wood. It could easily have been a complete disaster, yet it was a triumph. Whatever else, this Sam had style. Or at least she knew it when she saw it. The only element of which he was uncertain was the huge allegorical painting of an androgynous naked figure – possibly Pluto the God of Wealth, or his mother Dimeter - seated in the clouds, cradling an inverted cornucopian shell, beside a golden radiating sun that reminded him, bizarrely, of the solar monstrance in the Temple Church of the Inner and Middle Temple. The bar was already filling up, and the only table for two was beside, and beneath, the painting in the furthest corner. At precisely twelve thirty, she entered the bar.

Had he not seen her photos on the website he would instantly have known that it was her. She was blond. Five foot eight, without her three inch heels; chosen he guessed to complement his own stature as described over the phone. She had a strong, yet sensuous and athletic body, contained in a taupe three quarter length dress, tied with a long belt in the same material trimmed in pink. Over it, she wore a fitted silk shirt in a slightly darker shade, printed with swirling patterns of delicate pink and pale blue flowers. The sleeves gave the impression of having been rolled up to just above the elbow, and the scalloped collar was open just enough to reveal the promising swell of her breasts. Before he had time to rise she had waved discreetly, and was smiling as she came towards him, her hair swaying and tumbling in waves to her shoulders. She walked like a model. He wondered if that was part of the training or if it came natural to her. She placed a long and slender hand on his shoulder, and kissed him on the cheek.

'Robert,' she said. 'It's great to see you again.'

A nice touch, he thought, satisfying the curiosity of fellow diners who had followed her entrance with interest, and dismissing the need for awkward formal introductions.

Her eyes were cornflower blue; like the flowers on her shirt. For moment his heart swelled with pride and anticipation, as he forgot that this was not what it seemed.

'Sit down,' he said pulling out her chair. 'I've got champagne on ice. I thought we could drink it through the meal. I think it's so much lighter than wine at lunch time.'

He made to catch the attention of the bar waiter, and found that there was no need. The ice bucket, bottle, and glasses, were already on their way. He wondered if it had been a mistake. He was trying to appear masterful, stay in control. But perhaps she wasn't into champagne.

'Champers,' she said. 'Lovely.' When it was clear he didn't know how to respond she quickly added. 'I really love it here, don't you?'

'Absolutely,' he replied, acutely conscious of the waiter standing over the table, easing the cork out of the bottle with a sigh. He only just managed to avoid telling her that the last time he had been here was with his mother. Instead he waited for their glasses to be filled, and proposed a toast. 'To Lunch,' he said for want of anything better. 'And to Christmas.' As soon as the waiter had gone he slid the envelope across the space between them, and looked away as she discretely placed it into her Ballenciaga bag.

They filled the time before they went through to the restaurant with small talk, mainly about her. He discovered that following her BA she had worked for three years in a company importing a range of goods from Asia – Japan and China in particular. She got to travel a lot, and gained a great deal of experience, but could see a great big glass ceiling above her, so she decided to do an MBA. Much to her surprise, she was offered a place at the University of Southern Australia, on the Adelaide Campus. Because she had only been able to save half the fees, and a little towards her accommodation, she had asked if she could defer it for a year, and found it was actively encouraged. So she set off for Europe on the first leg of what she had intended as a back packing world tour, with some serious part time work along the way. In the event, a fellow Aussie she met in London told her about the agency, and here she was.

'To be honest,' she said, loosening up over her second glass of champagne. 'I've only been with the agency for four months, and I already have enough to cover the whole course, and some. In fact I'm beginning to wonder if I'll ever make as much when I've got my MBA – not the first five years or so at least.' She put her hand to her mouth, apprehension cloudy her pretty blue eyes. 'Bloody hell,' she whispered. 'You're not from the Revenue are you?'

Rob laughed. 'No I'm not. But if, as part of some undercover operation, they get to meet girls like you in places like this, at the tax payer's expense, I wouldn't mind signing up.'

She looked over the menu, leaned across the table, and lowered her voice.

'Look. I don't mean to be indelicate, but before I choose, you're not planning to go on anywhere else afterwards are you? You don't have anything else in mind?'

'No Sam,' he said. 'Much as I'm tempted to. Just lunch.'

She ordered the courgette flower filled with crab and ginger, and a lemon grass velouté; followed by braised fillet of brill with fresh linguine and sea food velouté. Rob went for the warm salad of pigeon, with foie gras, and pear and sesame vinaigrette, followed by the navarin of lamb.

By the time they had finished their starters she knew a little of his background; that he was a Barrister, single, and in London visiting his mother for Christmas.

'Look, I hope you don't mind my asking,' she said, sipping her fourth glass. 'But I'm really surprised that a single man as attractive, and intelligent, and obviously well off as you are, needs to pay for a little female company?'

It was a question rather than a statement. One that Rob knew he couldn't delay answering much longer. 'Alright,' he said. 'The fact is that I'm looking for someone.'

'A girl?' she asked, intrigued.

'Yes, a girl. Well a woman really.'

'Like me?'

It was evident that she had misunderstood. Got the wrong end of the stick. Assumed that he thought he had signed up to a dating agency, a glorified marriage bureau. 'Oh God, no!' he said, a little more loudly than he'd intended. Heads turned, and he heard a muted tut tut. 'I'm looking for someone who seems to have gone missing.'

'Wow,' she said, clearly intrigued. 'But what has that got to do with you meeting me like this?' She looked around conspiratorially. 'Did she disappear here? Oh no, of course she didn't. I chose The Ritz - because it's about close for refurbishment incidentally and it might be my last opportunity - so there's no way you could have known.'

'No it's not that,' he told her. He took a deep breath. 'She works for your agency. She works for Elite Executive Escorts.'

She sat back, her glass suspended in mid air. Then calmly, coolly, she set it down on the table, and stared at him. Her eyes had taken on a colder shade; ice blue. 'You're not stalking her are you?'

'No Sam,' he said, as convincingly as possible. 'I am not stalking her.

'Well it happens. They go out with you once, sometimes twice, get fixated; obsessed even. When you see that happening you either accept that you're getting in deep – he's going to want to set you up as an exclusive mistress, or want to marry you – or else you make sure you're unavailable to that client from then on. That's one of the advantages of being free lance.'

'Free lance? What does that mean?' He asked.

'I pay the agency a monthly rental that covers the booking service, and the website; and on a sliding scale, based on the length of each booking, for the use of a West End Apartment, protection, and the limousine. The agency can refuse to represent me at any time, and I can walk away whenever I want, on condition I give a month's notice, and pay two month's rental. Maybe that's what she did. The one you're looking for.'

'I doubt it,' he told her. 'It was very sudden, and she's still on the agency web site, but they're not taking bookings.'

They waited while their plates were removed and the order for dessert taken. When the waiter had gone he said. 'Look, Sam, I really need to find this woman. But if you don't want to help, I'll understand.'

'Can I be frank Robert?' She replied. 'I have clients who just want someone to look good on their arm, to impress business contacts or friends; ones who want to get their own back on their partner or make someone jealous; and ones who just want to shag the pants off me. But you, you're a first. All you want to do is pump me for information about another escort. Don't get me wrong. So long as you're paying, you're in the driving seat. But I have to say, it's really weird.'

'I know,' Rob said. 'To be perfectly honest, it's pretty weird for me too.'

'Well just because we both work for the same agency that doesn't mean I'll even know who she is, let alone where she might be now. It doesn't work like that. Like I said. We're free lance; free agents.'

'I understand. Her name in the Members Gallery is Angel.'

Her eyes widened. 'Angel. I know Angel. We did a couple of parties together. Nothing smutty. Just when there were going to be a number of single men, and they wanted to brighten the place up a bit. Bring

181

a bit of class. We also went on a double date. Same kind of thing. It was an Embassy party. South American. Angel speaks fluent Spanish and Portuguese. Came in handy a few times I can tell you. Avoided some serious misunderstandings,' she gave him a meaningful wink. 'If you know what I mean.'

'Tell me about her.'

'There's not a lot to tell. She's intelligent, very attractive. I take it you've met her?' Rob nodded. 'Sultry, dark, brooding, sexy, all of that.' She continued. 'Made me feel quite jealous really. She's been with the agency about a year or so. I think she lives somewhere up East; Islington, Hackney, somewhere like that, but I've never been there. She never talks about her family, or mentions friends. Not that that means anything. We all like to keep our professional and private lives separate.'

'Does she have any particular, regular, clients?' he asked.

She shook her head. 'I wouldn't know if she did. Nor would she know about mine.'

Rob was running out of questions. In desperation, he asked: 'Do you think she slept with her clients?'

She smiled. 'I'd be surprised if she didn't. From what I heard, she'd even do doubles and threesomes. But I was surprised. There is something reserved about her. You can always tell when the girls are up for it. They're really confident and bubbly on the outside – over extrovert if you know what I mean – but they actually build a kind of shell around them. You see it when they think nobody's looking at them. Especially when they're freshening up their make up in the ladies. It's like they're putting on another layer of protection between them, and the client; a mask. Angel was like that.'

'What about you, Sam?' he said without thinking. 'Given you're only in this to pay your way, do you sleep with your clients?' She wasn't the slightest bit phased by the question.

'Not really. I promised myself from the start that I would stick to the escort part. Quite a few of the girls do you know; draw a line. If I'm honest, I have slept with some of my clients – just a handful – because I've really liked them, and if I wasn't doing this professionally, and I'd just met them in a bar or at a club, I probably would have anyway. So what the hell.' She finished the champagne in her glass. 'That's what I tell myself anyway. Then it doesn't feel like I'm a…you know. But I wouldn't do it with someone I didn't really fancy, however much I was offered. And some of them are really scary.' She twirled her glass by its stem, perilously, and looked across at him. 'If you know what I mean?'

They stood beneath the arches waiting for her limousine to arrive. She had put on an expensive looking coat trimmed in fur.

'Don't worry,' she giggled. 'It's synthetic, but I'll kill you if you tell anyone.'

'Can I ask you something?' Rob said. 'If I had asked, and matched your price, would you have slept with me?'

She looked up at him, trying to decide if he was just curious, or if this was his way of saying that he wanted to.

'No,' she said, not unkindly.

'Why not?'

'Because Robert, when clients ask this many questions, they are either from the vice squad, the inland revenue, customs and excise, or immigration. It's not worth the risk. And in your case, although I think that under normal circumstances it could have been a distinct possibility, I believe you have an obsession you need to work out first. I don't plan to be part of the therapy.'

He watched as a Mercedes with smoked windows drew up. The commissionaire opened the door to let her in. Professional to the last, she turned to smile and wave at him, ducked her head, and disappeared.

The commissionaire tipped his hat respectfully to Rob, expertly palmed the note, and raised a hand to hail a taxi for a waiting couple. It had cost him seventy six pounds for the Lunch, thirty pounds for the Champagne, ten in tips, and six hundred for the two hours. Seven hundred and sixteen pounds, to learn what he had already suspected. That to the rest of the world Angel was a high earning, high class prostitute, with no friends, and no discernible past.

Lost in thought, Rob was about to enter Green Park Underground Station when he remembered the brown paper carrier bag in the luggage room of the Ritz Hotel. He cursed, and hurried back against the growing tide of Christmas shoppers and early revellers. Seldom had he felt this alone. As he doubled back he failed to notice the man bending suddenly to tie a shoe lace. Had he done so he might also have registered that the shoe in question had no laces.

16

He carried on past the entrance to the Underground, across the park, and down towards Hyde Park Corner. He needed the open space, the absence of crowds.

The occasional couple sauntered arm in arm. Nannies trundled their charges in gleaming push chair versions of four by fours. Leafless trees stood proud like sentinels. In the grass below, the tips of winter flowering crocus poked through the frost hardened soil. He walked head down, the collar of his jacket turned up against the chill North Easterly, oblivious to the two men in Burberry overcoats fifteen metres back, matching him stride for stride. At the furthest extremity of the park, he came out from the shadows of the trees lining Constitution Hill by the marble pillars of the memorial gates. He stopped for a moment to raise his hand, and shield his eyes from the glare of a harsh winter sun. A black Mercedes four wheel drive pulled into the curb alongside him. The nearside rear door flew open. He began, instinctively, to step back, and found his way blocked by a pair of burly chests.

'Get in Mr Thornton.' Said a cultured voice from within the car.

He looked to his left and right. There were no Guards here, ceremonial or otherwise. No police in cars, or on mountain bikes. Just an endless stream of traffic whose drivers had a single objective; to make their exit safely from this pitiless roundabout. Two pairs of hands propelled him towards the car. They met with little resistance.

'Very wise Mr Thornton,' said the occupant of the car as one of the followers climbed in beside Rob, and the other joined the chauffeur in the front. 'I only want a little chat, but if you had thought to refuse me the opportunity…well, lets just say that my staff can be very persuasive.'

As the vehicle moved smoothly away Rob turned to face his abductor. Here was a man of a similar age to him. A little taller perhaps, short blond hair with an inclination to curl, fresh faced, with a redness to his cheeks that suggested country living. He wore a dark pinstripe suit, and what Rob could have sworn was the unmistakeable tie of an Old Etonian with its pale and dark blue stripes.

'I do hope you'll excuse this unannounced appointment Mr Thornton,' the man said. 'But it's so much more convenient for us both than having to ask you come to the office. This way, hopefully, we can have it done and dusted within a few minutes, and have you back where you started.' He waited for a response. When none was forthcoming, he said: 'No questions? Very good. So much simpler if I do the asking. You can call me James, and I shall call you Robert; unless you would prefer that I continue to call you Thornton?'

Rob nodded his acquiescence.

'Good. All that you need to know is that I represent Elite Executive Escorts.' He saw Rob's eyes flick to his tie. 'What did you expect?' he said.

'Eastern Europeans, Russians, Turks, Chinese, Yardies perhaps?' He shook his head slowly. 'We haven't quite sold off the crown jewels yet, although I admit the time is fast approaching. I first saw a niche in the market while I was still at Eton. And during my time in the Guards it became increasingly evident that there was a great unfulfilled want for really high class companions. Ones you could be proud, and unashamed, to have on your arm. Girls that could pass as one's sister, or girl friend and might hold out the promise of further pleasures in store, but not broadcast it to the world. Do you see Robert?'

'I see.' Said Rob

The man called James smiled a knowing smile. 'Of course you do. You've met our Sam. So you will understand that it means being highly selective. We look for young women who could quite easily grace the pages of Vogue or Tatler, and equally the centrefold of Playboy or Maxim; but who have not. Because their beauty, grace, and companionship, is not for common exchange. It is the exclusive preserve of our valued members. Do you see?'

'I see,' Said Rob.

'That is why we become concerned when someone takes an unhealthy interest in one of our associates.' He read the expression on Rob's face, and held up a neatly manicured hand. 'Now don't be disappointed in Sam, she merely confirmed what we already suspected; that you had booked her with one intention in mind. To enquire into the whereabouts of another of our associates; Angel to be precise.'

'I don't deny it,' Rob said. 'But I don't see why that should be considered unhealthy.'

James leant back, his face falling into the shadows. 'Come, come Robert,' he said, 'Don't be so disingenuous. You must know that we are concerned that Angel appears to have gone missing.'

'And now you know that I'm as concerned as you.'

'Ah yes, but you see we don't quite understand why. Perhaps you could enlighten us?'

Rob wondered how much he could safely tell them. It was difficult to think under this kind of pressure, and he sensed that the man on his left, and the other one up front, would be carrying something even more persuasive than the knife with which he had been threatened in Clissold Park. He decided on a highly selective version of the truth. 'I met her at a party in Manchester last week,' he said. 'She was with one of your members. When I heard that she'd gone missing, I became concerned. I thought I'd see what I could find out.'

There was a moment's silence. When James spoke this time his voice had dropped a level, and taken on a softer yet menacing tone. 'You say you met her. What does that mean exactly?'

'We spent some time talking, dancing, while her companion was talking business with the host.'

'Did you pay her?'

'No, of course I didn't. Apart from anything else I didn't know she was an escort.'

James chuckled. 'Lucky for you she had come with someone else, or you would have owed us a considerable sum. How did you come to know she was missing?'

'She happened to mention that she was staying at the Midland.'

'She would never disclose where she was staying.'

'Well she did. I went to the hotel and found out that she'd booked out. I was coming down to London to stay with my mother for Christmas so I thought I'd look her up. I went to her flat and found that she'd not been back there, and the landlord and her neighbour were concerned.'

'How did you know where she lived? Even I don't know that?'

'She told me.'

'I don't believe you.'

'Well she did. How else would I know?'

'And how did you know she worked for us?'

'As we parted, she told me the truth about what she did, and said that if I wanted to spend some time with her again – I could reach her through the agency.'

Through the one way tinted windows Rob could tell from the brightly coloured window displays that they were travelling down Oxford Street. It was slow going this close to Trafalgar Square but he knew there was no way he could safely exit this car.

'Well this is quite a coincidence,' James was saying. 'Because we are looking for Angel too. She has not booked in for almost a week. Her monthly payment is overdue. She would normally have called us, and made a bank transfer. And there is something else that disturbs us greatly.' He turned and leaned forward so that they could see each other's faces. 'You see, when we were told that you had asked specifically for Angel, repeatedly, and expressed your willingness to wait until she was available, we became suspicious. Particularly since you were a new member. So we looked you up on the Internet. And guess what Robert?'

Rob's heart sunk, his diaphragm like an iron fist beneath his ribcage.

'Among the details of your illustrious career, your qualifications, and notable cases, we came across a much more recent story; involving no less than a charge of rape.'

'The accusation was withdrawn, no charges were brought.'

'So we believe. But let's face it Robert, you of all people will know that tells us absolutely nothing about innocence or guilt. Especially in cases of rape. Two questions remain; who made the accusation, and why did she withdraw it?'

'An Anjelita Rosa Covas.'

James sighed with exaggerated melodrama. 'You disappoint me Robert. I took you to be far too intelligent to waste our time on guessing games, and half truths. You see we were curious. We don't believe in coincidence. So we contacted the client who had booked Angel for a long weekend – coincidentally in Manchester – and you'll never guess what he told us. But of course, you will won't you, because not only were you there at the party, but you also paid our client a visit, just yesterday.'

Rob saw little point in answering. It hadn't been a question.

'So what are we to think? The person accusing you of rape turns out to be our very own, and highly valued associate, Angel. She mysteriously withdraws the charges, and equally mysteriously disappears. And here you are scouring London for her. Now why is that?'

He had no idea how to answer, other than with the truth, the whole truth, and nothing but the truth.

If what you tell me is true,' James said when Rob had finished. 'And I have no reason to suspect otherwise since you must know we will be able to check the bulk of it, then that suggests a limited number of explanations. Perhaps Angel made the mistake of taking on a second, and even more problematic non-paying, client on the same evening. Too late she tried to cover her mistake by shouting rape, came to her senses, and disappeared to avoid further embarrassment. Or possibly you did rape her, and in the cold light of day she remembered her previous experience in court, and how that ended tragically for her sister, and with the guilty parties going free. She simply could not face going through with it. Of course it's equally possible that someone frightened her into withdrawing her accusation. So persuasively in fact, that she felt she had to disappear?'

'Meaning me?' Rob responded. 'In which case, why the hell would I go to these lengths to try to find her?'

'Good question. Because you're frightened that she'll tell the police that you put pressure on her. Because you have decided that the only safe way to preserve your reputation and career is to see that she disappears permanently.'

'That's ridiculous!'

'And then again,' James continued unperturbed. 'Perhaps you've already disposed of Angel, and this supposed search is just an elaborate attempt to cover your tracks.'

It dawned on Rob that these were precisely the hypotheses that he would have advanced for the prosecution. And if he was honest with himself they were the reason why he'd kept his search, and findings, from the police. In truth, every one of them was a plausible scenario. And in each of them, one way or another, he was implicated.

'Well I know that I didn't rape her,' he said. 'And if you ask the police you'll find that they don't believe that I did either.'

'In which case, how do you account for her disappearance?'

'Well for a start, you said it yourself. Perhaps she came to her senses, was embarrassed that she'd made a fool of herself, and just wanted to get away. Maybe she came to her senses in another respect. She wants a fresh start, away from your agency, from her work as an escort.'

'Ignoring your unkind implication that Elite Executive Escorts is somehow inappropriate work for Angel, I think your explanation simplistic and unlikely.'

'In which case she's been abducted. For all I know, by you. This charade could just be you covering up your tracks.' The atmosphere in the back of the vehicle seemed to chill; as though the air conditioning had been turned to low. The man on his right placed his arm across the back of the seat, and pressed closer. A hard irregular shape beneath his arm pit pressed into Rob's shoulder.

James moved back into the shadows. 'Because I understand that you are under stress Robert,' he said. 'I am going to ignore that last remark, and focus instead on our mutual goal. We both wish to find the whereabouts of Angel. If we find her, I promise that you will be the first to know; if only to keep you out of our hair. If, on the other hand, you find her before we do, you will firstly inform us, and secondly, give her a message. Tell her to call us. If she wants out, she knows there are procedures. It's all in the contract. Nobody simply walks away.'

'What procedures? How do I know she'll be safe?'

'Come now Robert, Angel is our associate. She pays us to protect her. If she wants to leave the agency she has merely to give due notice, and pay two months rent. If she wishes to leave straight away, then three months rent. Believe me, she can afford it. And to be honest, from what you have told me she was not entirely honest with us about her past. If we had known about her unfortunate experience she would not have passed our risk assessment. Something like that can have unforeseen circumstances,' he paused dramatically. 'As indeed it seems to have done.'

You're telling me, Rob reflected. I could do with a copy of that risk assessment. I'll take it with me the next time I'm invited to a party.

The four by fours came to a halt. He could see the Wellington Memorial Arch through the window. They were back where they'd started.

'Make sure you keep in touch,' James said. 'As a member you'll find it really easy. Just ring the number, and ask for me. Or you can send an email.' He made it sound like a simple business deal. 'Of course we won't have any problem in contacting you Robert. It was rather careless of you to use your own credit card, and your real name. Few of our clients do you know. Most of them get a personal assistant to register on their behalf.' He leaned back into the light; smiling, almost chatty. 'But we always find out anyway; usually by the end of the first date. As you know from first hand experience, our girls are very, very good.' He held out his hand. 'Good bye for now then. So nice to have met you. If we need a barrister any time we won't hesitate to look you up. And I wouldn't recommend you do anything silly, like memorising the licence plate. We would consider that a breach of faith. And what's the point? All we've done is give you a lift, and have a little chat.'

The rear seat passenger withdrew his arm, shifted his weight, opened the door, and waited for Rob to get out. He thrust the brown paper carrier bag into his hand, and stood there waiting for him to move away. When Rob reached the crossing point he looked back and saw the four by four receding at a leisurely pace down Grosvenor Place.

He stood there for a moment trying to decide which had scared him most: The Turkish knife; the Russian threats; or the softly spoken Old Etonian with the fresh face, and firm handshake. It was, he decided, a close run thing. Altogether too close.

17

It was a typical Christmas Eve; cold, crisp and dry. Flickering icicles, and flashing snowflakes, hung from sofits. Snowmen vied with deer pulling sleighs for the remaining patches of urban lawn. Santas laden with parcels hung from ropes, and climbed up drainpipes. America had reached the outskirts of London.

MPVs and four by fours lined the roads around the Green, where a constant stream of people made their way to the doors of St Catherine's Church. He found a seat six rows back on the left hand side, from where he could see his mother in the choir, preparing to start the first of the Advent carols that would lead seamlessly into the traditional favourites celebrating the Saviour's birth. As he sat there, in the packed pew, memories came flooding back of past Christmas's in another church to which he walked, from the comfortable five-bedroom detached, arm in arm with his sister, and his parents. The church where his father played the organ, and his mother took her turn to read the lessons and the prayers of the faithful. Where he was baptised, inducted into the mysterious Sacraments of Confession, and Communion, and was confirmed as a Soldier of God. Where from the age of eleven he would be woken early twice a week, and on Sundays, to serve Mass for Father Malachy, the

Parish Priest, who smelt perpetually of an musty mix of smoke from cigarettes, altar candles, and incense, mingled with the aroma of whisky poured from the bottle of Powers he claimed was reserved for special occasions. Rob remembered with a smile that such occasions had seemed to come with increasing frequency as the priest approached retirement, at seventy five.

He found himself standing and kneeling in all the right places; singing the carols with enthusiasm. The responses to the priest's invocations tripped automatically from his lips. He recognised, like an old friend, the general sense of wonder, awe, and celebration, that seemed somehow to epitomise his understanding of what was meant by faith: the unthinking acceptance of what ought to be. At the communal Sign of Peace, he joined in, giving and receiving with a simple handshake, and felt himself wrapped in the arms of this congregation. He felt an incredible sense of peace, of warmth, of belonging. He knew that the sensation would be transitory, but in that moment he welcomed it, and found it strangely healing. He even took Communion; partly from habit, partly to reassure his mother. But also because right now he needed all the help he could get. He had convinced himself long ago that mortal sin was a concoction; a device of organised religion to control the ignorant. Nevertheless, as he approached the altar he found himself repeating the Act of Contrition. In the time that it took for the host to dissolve, he had prayed that Anjelita was safe, and for a speedy resolution to his search. He had prayed for his mother, his sister Angela, and had made promises he knew he would never keep. When he looked up, and across at the choir, he saw his mother smiling back, and felt a twinge of guilt. But then guilt was the price you paid for this particular brand of faith. He wondered if the roots of his need to find Anjelita had their origins in that lonely confessional box at the age of seven. His religious upbringing had instilled a moral code of which he was proud, and which, despite his non attendance, guided him still. But with it came responsibilities; obligations that he felt, but no longer fully understood.

His mother turned up the gas fire, poured two small glasses of brandy, and insisted that they opened their presents. He left till last the two that he had discovered on his office desk just as he was leaving for London. He could tell from the writing that the first was from Anna.

'Anna,' his Mother said. 'That's a nice name. Do I know her?'

'No Mum. You don't. She happens to be my pupil.' He said, removing the silver paper star that hid the sellotape seal.

'Well,' his mother observed. 'She seems to have gone to a lot of trouble. And you know what they say about pupils having crushes on their teachers.'

He unfolded the red and gold wrapping paper to reveal a second hand paperback entitled: The Real CRACKER: Investigating the Criminal Mind. Inside the cover she had written:

I saw this and immediately thought of you! Never know when it might come in handy. Thanks for all your help and advice. Merry Christmas. Anna.

He smiled, and passed it to his Mother to inspect.

'Not exactly a Keats first edition is it?' she said. 'I'd have thought she could have run to something new.'

'I told you Mum. She's just a pupil. It was a nice gesture, that's all. I didn't get her anything.' Which in retrospect felt like a big mistake. After all, she was the one that had tracked down Anjelita, and her website alter ego Angel. And she'd got nothing for her efforts. Not even a card. He resolved to put that right as soon as he got back to Manchester.

The second package was slimmer. The wrapping paper was green, overprinted with jolly Santa Claus in their traditional red and white costumes. His name and address was printed in large type on a standard address label. There was no stamp.

'Who's that from Robert?'

'I don't know.' He said, turning it over. 'There's no return address. Someone must have left it on my desk at work.'

'How exciting. You've got a Secret Santa.'

'Secret Santa? What's that?'

'You know. When you put all your names into a hat, and you draw a name out in turn, and then you have to buy a present up to a certain value for the person whose name you draw. Only nobody's supposed to know who drew which names. Then when you open your present you have to guess who it's from; the identity of your Secret Santa. Sometimes they give you little clues. It's great fun. We used to do it in our staff room. I bet that's what it is.'

Rob shook his head. 'There's nothing like that at Weir Chambers. Or if there is, nobody's asked me to join in.' He turned it over slowly, and felt gently along the sealed edges.

'I am just going to pop into the kitchen,' he said, getting up. 'I think I'll open this with one of your kitchen knives.'

'There's no need to do that Robert' she held up a pair of scissors she had been using to cut the label tags. 'Here, use these.'

'No really Mum, I don't want to risk cutting what's inside.'

In the kitchen he placed a piece of polyroll in the sink, and put the package on top. He took a pair of oven gloves from the drawer, and put them on. Using the smallest vegetable knife he carefully slid it under the sealed edges making sure that his face was as far from the sink as possible. The wrapping came away cleanly to reveal a plain white envelope. It was not sealed. Nevertheless, he opened it with care and slid out a colour photograph. It had been taken on Deansgate in the centre of Manchester; within the past fortnight. He could tell because Waterstone's window held their Christmas display. In the centre foreground, waiting to cross the street, was someone he had cause to recognise; whose face he knew he would never forget. Edward Robinson, pederast, and child killer whom he had prosecuted, and against whom he had failed to secure a conviction. Not his fault. But it was one of those cases that would haunt him until his dying day. Curious, he turned the photo over. A message was printed on a piece of copying paper that had been stuck to the back of the photograph.

This day is born, in Bethlehem
A child pursued by Herod's men

Such monsters still exist today
One has become my latest prey
This gift for you is out of sight
All will be clear by morning light.

Happy Christmas Robert.

He had no idea what it meant, or from whom it had
come. It seemed his mother had been right. He had
his own Secret Santa. He read it through again. The
word *prey* sent a chill through his heart.

18

He slept fitfully again that night, and sleepwalked through most of Christmas Day. His mother had been right on another score. A procession of neighbours, and fellow parishioners, called to wish her Merry Christmas, drink a glass of sherry, and have a nosey at her son made good. There was a brief respite during the Queen's Speech when his sister Angela rang from Melbourne. He always enjoyed talking with her, her husband Gerry, and the niece and nephew he had never seen. Gerry, had left the Metropolitan Police, seduced by promises of rapid promotion, a better standard of living, less paperwork, sunshine, and outdoor living. By the sound of it, apart from having to keep a wary eye out for funnel web and red backed spiders, it had more or less turned out that way.

Despite his best intentions, and urged on by his mother, he ate too much of everything during their Christmas dinner, and walked the streets in the bitter cold for an hour to prevent himself falling asleep. It was a temporary respite; the blood sugar high replaced with a vengeance by a flood of insulin that left him feeling drained, and more depressed than ever. After an hour of *It's a Wonderful Life* his eyes began to close, he excused himself, and retired early.

As though seen through a kaleidoscope, his dreams tumbled one into another. He awoke feeling refreshed, and strangely hopeful. In the absence of papers to read over breakfast on this Boxing Day morning, his mother switched on the news. It was the second headline story that caught his attention. To be specific, it was the face that flashed up on the screen. Incredulous, he watched as the news reader spoke over a series of photographs and video clips.

"The body of Edward Robinson, fifty seven years of age, was found late yesterday evening in undergrowth beside a disused stretch of canal in East Manchester. First reports suggest that he had been shot some days previously, and his body dumped there. Edward Robinson stood trial in 2001 accused of the systematic abuse and murder of two children in Salford. Following a lengthy and high profile trial he was, controversially, found not guilty, but was subsequently imprisoned for nine years on a lesser charge of conspiracy to incite child abuse, and downloading and distributing images containing child pornography. Four months ago he was released early, on parole."

At this point a piece of video film showed Robinson outside the Crown Court with his solicitor, and in the background Rob himself, and DI Tom Caton, the senior case detective, moving disconsolately away.

"Inevitably, there will be much speculation that one of the possible motives for this killing could be revenge, or some form of vigilante action, by those close to the child victims. The police are currently playing this down, and have emphasised that all lines of enquiry are open. They have appealed for anyone who may have any information regarding Mr Robinson's death to contact them directly, or via CrimeStoppers, as soon as possible."

'Are you all right Robert?' His mother asked from across the table. 'You've gone a nasty shade of white.'

He felt as though he was going to be sick. He pushed his chair back, got up, and poured himself a glass of water at the sink. It tasted harsh and brackish as it always did down here. *"Anyone who may have any information…"* He had information, but he had no idea what it meant. He just knew that he had to get back up to Manchester and find out.

'Wasn't that you on the television just now?' his mother said. 'Did you have something to do with that case, is that it?'

'I'm sorry Mom,' he said, I've got to get back to Manchester straight away.'

'Don't be silly Robert. There aren't any trains or buses until tomorrow. And in any case, you don't look fit to travel. I think you must be going down with something.'

'Then I'll take a taxi.'

Have you any idea how much that will cost? Assuming you can get one today, which I very much doubt.'

He slammed the glass down. 'Oh for heaven's sake Mother, just leave it alright? I'm going back, and that's an end to it.' He stormed out of the kitchen leaving her sitting there, shocked, and a little shaken. He had not called her Mother for years.

He found an Asian taxi firm in Slough that was only too happy to take his money. This was after all not one of their own religious festivals, and there was the bonus of being able to charge as much as the market would stand. For Rob, the money was an irrelevance.

He spent the entire journey going over and over the Robinson trial. There had to be a clue there somewhere. Someone, he reasoned, unhappy with the verdict, and who felt that he had a debt to repay to Rob, must have sent the photograph, and carried out the murder. But was it the same person who sent the text from Anjelita's phone? Where was the connection? How could there possibly be one? When the trial took place, he reminded himself, Anjelita was still in Portugal, approaching her own nemesis. No matter how many times he analysed it he was damned if he could see a link. Edward Robinson had been as guilty as hell. He had the means, and the motive. He had even admitted his involvement to other members of the international paedophile ring which he had helped to co-ordinate. But he had been careful to dispose of all of the physical evidence that could have linked him directly with the murders, and had claimed that his confession was simply a case of vicarious bragging. The case hinged on whether he had the opportunity to commit the crime. Unfortunately, the key witnesses placing him in the vicinity at the time that the children were abducted, cracked under cross examination, and - most telling of all - his mother had provided an eleventh hour alibi. The same mother who, four months after her son walked free, had plunged from the Bennett Street road bridge onto the tracks, and into the path of a Pendelino intercity express.

By two thirty in the afternoon he had dropped his case off at the apartment, made the phone call, and was waiting in reception at Longsight Police Station. A uniformed auxiliary came to collect him and took him up to the Major Incident Suite. He was shown into the office of the senior investigating officer. The name on the door was Detective Chief Inspector Tom Caton. With him was DS Hale. They rose to meet him.

'Mr Thornton,' Caton said, arm outstretched. 'I don't suppose either of us expected to meet again this soon in relation to Edward Robinson. Not like this anyway.'

Rob shook his hand, and exchanged a smile of embarrassment with Beth Hale. 'I can't say that I did,' he said, sitting down in the remaining easy chair. He was conscious that they were watching him with a mixture of curiosity and expectation.

'DS Hale is here because she worked on the original case.' Caton explained. 'She was our liaison officer for the bereaved families.'

'It was that job that convinced me to apply for the Sexual Crimes team,' she told him. 'I thought at least I could do something that would prevent it happening to other children,' she smiled grimly. 'How wrong could I be?'

'You were rather vague on the phone Mr Thornton,' Caton said. 'But we're all ears. We need all the help we can get on this one.'

Rob told them about the original text message, but not about what he and Anna had discovered on the internet about Anjelita and her sister Rosa, nor about what he had been doing, and had discovered in London. He had convinced himself that they didn't need to know, and that it would only serve to change the relationship between them adversely; particularly the relationship between himself and DS Hale. She had been quite clear in her warning to walk away from Anjelita. He also showed them the wrapping paper, envelope and photograph left for him at the office.

'Have you got your phone with you?' Caton asked him.

'Yes.' He took it from his pocket, switched it on, retrieved the message, and handed it over.

Caton brought up the number of the sender, and returned the call. 'Unobtainable,' he said. 'But at least it's going to be easy to trace the owner.' He reached over to the desk behind him, pressed a button, and spoke into the intercom. 'Ged, can you come in here please?' Addressing himself to Rob he said. 'I assume you tried to return the call at the time?'

Rob nodded. 'Yes. The phone was switched off.'

There was a knock at the door and a prim and efficient women in her mid fifties entered. 'Yes Sir?' she said. Caton handed her a piece of paper on which he had written the sender's number. 'Ged, give this to Mr Wallace and ask him to let me know the name on the contract, and to get a trace on the phone itself – or at least the chip. I'd like that ASAP. And ask Mr Benson to come in as soon as he gets back in. Tell him to bring a pair of gloves, and a couple of evidence bags.'

'Of course Sir.' She took the paper and left.

'Jack Benson is our senior Scene of Crime Forensic Officer.' Caton told Rob. 'He'll see what trace's have been left, and if any of them bring up a match on the database.'

'Won't you need my fingerprints, and DNA, for

purposes of elimination?' Rob said.

Beth Hale looked a trifle embarrassed. 'That won't be necessary,' she said. 'We do already have them.'

It was Rob's turn to colour up. As much with anger as embarrassment. 'I wasn't charged,' he said. 'Let alone convicted. They should have been destroyed.'

'Technically speaking, although we are no longer investigating a case of rape or sexual assault, it is reasonable to link her disappearance with that allegation,' she responded. 'Even though Ms Covas withdrew her complaint in writing, I'm sure you can see our dilemma? She is still missing, and we have no idea of her state of mind when she made that withdrawal.'

'So you're saying that I'm still a suspect?'

'No. I am saying that until we find Ms Covas, we are obliged to keep on file all of the evidence we've gathered related to her.'

DCI Caton could see that tempers were rising. 'Given that you have just offered to give us a new set of samples,' he said. 'Surely the fact that we already have them on file shouldn't be an issue. It saves us both the bother. In any case, you must know that the law now permits us to keep the DNA of anyone arrested for a recordable offence, regardless of whether or not they are charged. But if it really concerns you that much, I'm sure an exception could be made. Perhaps DS Hale can give you a guarantee that yours will be destroyed as soon as the investigation into Ms Covas's case is closed, and that you'll be notified personally when that's happened.' He looked pointedly at Beth Hale, who was clearly angry to have been placed in this position..

'Of course.' She reluctantly agreed.

Rob could see that he'd overstepped the mark. His own objections to proposals for a universal DNA database from birth, and his personal insecurity, had got the better of him. Caton was right. As the law stood there was nothing he could do about it. If anything, he'd shown himself up, and alienated Beth Hale. 'Of course I don't have any objection to you having my DNA, fingerprints, and blood samples, and I'm grateful to DS Hale for your offer.' He said. 'I'm sorry I lost it there for a moment. What with being accused of rape, the disappearance of Ms Covas, that text message, and now this…' he pointed to the photo lying on top of its envelope. 'It's all been a bit too much.'

'Fair enough,' Caton said, eager to move on. 'What's your take on these messages? You must have thought about it.'

'I've spent all day thinking about it. At the time, I assumed the text message was from Ms Covas. Now I'm beginning to wonder if it was something to do with Robinson. Perhaps he was already dead?'

'It's possible,' Caton said. 'Initial findings suggest that he was killed six days ago. The day you received that text.'

'How can you be sure?'

'The degree, and nature, of early stages of maggot infestation. And the fact that someone had tucked a copy of Thursday's Manchester Evening News inside his jacket, immediately after he was shot. We know it was after, because it covered the exit wound in his chest. Forensics tells us the blood and fluids on it had freshly congealed.'

'But I don't see any connection between Ms Covas and Robinson,' Rob said. 'Do You? After all, she was still in Portugal when Robinson was sent down.'

They stared at him intently. Surprise etched on their faces. 'How do you know that?' Caton asked.

'Well...I don't, not for a fact,' Rob said hastily covering his mistake. 'But when we were at Vince's apartment she gave me the impression she had only been in England for a few years.' He watched them trying to make up their minds; wondering whether to give him the benefit of the doubt.

'But what if she was lying to you?' Beth Hale said. 'What if it was all part of some larger deception?'

'Like what?' Rob asked.

'I don't know. Maybe she was in league with someone else. She can't have turned up at that party by accident. And she can't simply have disappeared either.'

'So you're suggesting that she may have been stalking me?'

'Well someone was. Still is, if that message is anything to go by.'

'We could always see what the FTAC have to say,' Caton suggested.

'FTAC?' Rob said.

'Fixated Threat Assessment Centre' Hale told him. 'It's a national organisation run by the Metropolitan Police specialist operations department,' she looked across at Caton. 'But isn't that really for prominent persons – royalty, politicians, diplomats?'

'It is,' Caton replied. 'But I suppose it could be argued that Mr Thornton is a prominent person. If nothing else, he's defended some people who are. It might be worth a try. I'll get on to them.' He turned to Rob. 'Unless there's anything else, I'm afraid that DS Hale and I have work to do?' He made his point by standing. 'I'm assuming that if you get any more of these messages, or suspect that anyone might be following you, you'll contact me straightaway.' With that they all shook hands, and Rob was shown out.

Several people commented on how peaky he was looking when he arrived at Chambers the next morning. Nobody recalled who had left the package addressed for him on the Thursday before. It had been chaotic with the Christmas post on top of the normal deliveries. Tasha did remember picking it up with the post and putting it on his desk, but had no idea when it had arrived.

Anna was bowled over by the flowers he had bought for her on his way in from the stall beside St Ann's Church.

'They're gorgeous. You really shouldn't have.' She said.

'Well I left in such a hurry,' he said. 'That I forgot to leave you a Christmas card, so it was the least I could do, especially after the way you stood by when…well you know what I mean.'

'So tell me,' she said. 'What did you find out in London?'

He told her everything. Not just because he needed to tell someone, but because he felt he had to. Just in case something happened to him. For the first time he believed that was a distinct possibility.

'Stalker!' she exclaimed when he'd reached the

end. That's so scary.'

'Thanks,' he said. 'That makes me feel much better.'

'No, you know what I mean. You don't think it's that Russian Dimitri, or that man from the agency?'

'Think about it Anna. They didn't even know I existed before I went down there and started asking questions.'

'So that leaves Anjelita Andrades. I mean, the fact that she has so many aliases is weird to say the least. Never mind that she accused you of rape.'

'If you'd met her landlords, and her boss, not to mention some of the clients she must have had, I think you'd want to protect your identity. Besides, we know she was in Portugal when Robinson was sent to jail. I can't see any possible connection between the two of them. We'll just have to see what the FTAC has to say. In the meantime, I need you to do some work on the Barry Moss case. I need you to check a precedent for me, and have a look at the statements by the main witness for the prosecution,' he handed her a manila folder. 'It's all in here. Let's meet up again at lunchtime. I've got to see Henry about some briefs he's picked up. It's always the same after the Christmas break. There are more relationship breakdowns and acts of senseless violence than any other time of the year. So much for peace and goodwill.'

As soon as his meetings were over Rob logged on to the internet and typed Fixated Threat Assessment Centre into the search bar. There were two articles from the Times, one from the Guardian, several from organisations representing patients with mental illness, and several from sites purporting to be the guardians of freedom and liberty. They told him all he needed to know. Following fears of a growing terrorist threat to politicians, and members of the royal family, the Home Office had commissioned research into VIPs world wide, who had been the victims of stalking. The FBI, the Capitol Hill Police protecting US politicians in Washington, and the secret services of a number of European countries, provided information and assistance. As a result of the findings the FTAC was very quietly – some said secretly - set up. According to an official statement its role was to 'assess, manage and reduce potential risks and threats from fixated individuals, against people in public life, particularly protected VIPs.' The Centre consisted of a small team of police officers, civilian researchers, a forensic psychiatrist, a forensic psychologist and a forensic community mental health nurse. Much had been made in the media of concerns about their powers to forcibly detain suspects under the Mental Health Act, without charges being brought.

Well, Rob decided, I am a person in public life, but a very long way from being a VIP. On the other hand, if this is a stalker, and that stalker murdered Robinson, and heaven forbid has abducted or killed Anjelita Andrades, then they have to be interested.

The phone call came at a quarter to twelve. It was a Detective Inspector Jamieson. Jamieson had been well briefed by Caton, but still asked Rob to go over his account again. Then he asked him a series of questions.

'Did you receive the text message before or after news of your arrest had appeared in the papers and on television?'

'After.' Rob replied.

'And had you had any such messages at any time in the past year or so prior to receiving that text message?'

'No.'

'Have you ever had the feeling that you are being watched? That someone is following you?'

Rob thought of London. He had been followed twice and had never noticed; too lost in his own thoughts. 'No, he said. Never.'

'Well then you're very lucky; most people do at some time or other. But at least it suggests you're not normally paranoid.'

Ron registered the use of the word normally; implying, that it didn't mean that he wasn't at this moment in time. 'No, I'm not,' he asserted. 'The text was for real, and so was the package.'

'Hold you hair on,' said Jamieson. 'I'm not suggesting you are. It's just important to establish these things. Anyway, I'm afraid this doesn't look like one for us I'm afraid. Right now this should be dealt with by Greater Manchester Police as part of their murder enquiry. There hasn't been any specific threat to you. Only an implication that, just possibly, someone has committed a murder which he or she thinks would gratify you. That doesn't mean it was done for you, and certainly not that you might be a future victim. Now if you should discover that you are being stalked, or receive a threat against your life, or liberty, then we would be happy to liaise with DCI Caton.'

'And that's it? There's nothing you can do?'

'Well, not unless you can come up with a suspect,

or even a motive why someone might want to do this.'

'And there's no advice you can give me?' He found it impossible to keep the frustration out of his voice. Jamieson softened accordingly.

'Look,' he said. 'I'll put you through to our senior forensic psychiatrist. I'm sure she'll be able to give you a few pointers. Other than that, all I can do is wish you good luck.'

Dr Eve Hammond was a little more sympathetic. 'If we became involved with every case of stalking in this country we would simply be snowed under,' she explained. 'The Government has had to prioritise, but I do appreciate how worrying this must be for you. The best I can do is tell you what to look out for. Put you on your guard, and maybe give you a way into discovering who it is that is pestering you.'

Pestering, was definitely not how Rob would describe it, but he assumed she was trying to reassure him.

'First of all,' she continued. 'Let's dispel the popular belief that there is a single typology of stalker. There isn't. They are not all lonely, insular, and obsessive, nor are they likely to be suffering from a diagnosed mental illness such as schizophrenia. The one thing that could be said of them is that they all suffer to one degree or another from some form of personality disorder. Often, they are described as intelligent and articulate. If you met them in a normal social setting such as a bar, or at a party, you could well find them amiable and polite, attractive even, and utterly believable. Interestingly, that tends to make it that much more difficult for victims to have their concerns about such a person taken seriously.' She paused, and Rob thought he could hear here drinking something.

'The most common pattern is a former partner, particularly someone with whom you have had sexual intimacy, even a one night stand; the most powerful trigger of all being rejection after such intimacy. The film Fatal Attraction was surprisingly close to the truth you see. But it could equally be acquaintances or colleagues at work believing themselves to be in love with you, and deluding themselves that you are in love with them. Then there is the growing breed of cyber stalkers who use the web to frighten, and control their targets, from the relative security of their own home. They are probably the exception when it comes to describing a typical profile. Males make up the majority of such stalkers. They will often turn out to be small, untidy, dirty and inadequate geeks, with a wispy moustache or beard, and an unhealthy interest in pornography.'

'That doesn't sound like my Secret Santa.' Rob said.

'Secret Santa?'

Rob explained.

'Ah, I understand,' she said. 'Well you'd be surprised how many incidences of stalking begin with anonymous cards or presents around Christmas, and St Valentine's Day. Anyway, you're quite right. Yours certainly doesn't fit that profile. No, I am afraid yours is much more likely to belong to one of two groups: vengeful, or delusional.'

'It seems to me this person may belong to both,' Rob said.

'That's very insightful of you, and perfectly possible I'm afraid.'

'Why afraid?'

'Because the vengeful stalker – who is most often male by the way – is the most dangerous, primarily because they are driven by a desire for vengeance. Usually for some real or imagined hurt. The imagined part of course refers to someone who is delusional. In your case, it rather sounds as though someone may be fixating on you; imagines that they owe you a debt; and is repaying that debt by harming others on your behalf. As a kind of proxy for you. Equally this person may be seeking to gain your affection.'

'Well if they are, it isn't working.' Rob reflected. 'Killing or harming others on my behalf is the last thing I would wish. It would only make me feel responsible for their deaths.'

'Ah, well. That's another possibility.' Hammond said thoughtfully. 'If this is a really intelligent person, have you considered that the messages might be ironic? That your Secret Santa is not seeking to please you at all, but wants you to feel responsible? Is actually punishing you? You know, the juxtaposition of that rather primitive, childlike poem, with the cold blooded execution of the victim, is particularly chilling.'

Rob didn't need telling that. He was already well aware of the fact. Far from reassuring him, the conversation left him feeling more concerned than ever.

19

Anna had done a great job on the tasks Rob had given her. By the time they'd discussed them, and finished the irresistible smoked salmon sandwiches she'd brought back from Philpott's on Brazenose Street, there was no time left to discuss what he'd learned from Doctor Hammond. His afternoon was full of meetings with solicitors, and their clients.

'I could come over to yours this evening,' she said. 'Or if you don't mind slumming it, you could come over to mine?'

'I don't think either of those would be a good idea.' he told her.

She looked crestfallen, and started to rise. 'If that's how you feel, I understand. It must be hard to...'

He reached out, and grasped her arm, stopping her in mid tracks. 'It's not that. Sit down for a moment, and let me explain.'

She sat down, needing to be convinced.

'Look Anna. It's something the psychiatrist from the FTAC told me. Sometimes a stalker – especially one who is sexually obsessed or vengeful – will seize on someone close to the object of their fixation as either an obstacle to their delusionary relationship, or as a proxy target. Either way, I can't take the risk of putting you in harm's way.'

Her worried expression softened into a smile. 'I'm touched,' she said. 'But I'm a big girl. I can take care of myself.'

'Like Anjelita Andrades did, or Edward Robinson?'

That rocked her a little, but she came bouncing back. 'If this person is watching you, or is close to you, then surely they'll already know about me. That I'm your pupil. That I spend more time with you than anyone else in these Chambers. If what you say is true, they probably know about the first time I went to your apartment. I'm already at risk by association with you.'

She was right of course. And it simply added to the mounting weight of responsibility he felt. 'So why make it worse?' he said. 'Make it even more likely that you would be targeted?'

She put her hand over his. It didn't feel like an intimacy; just a reassuring gesture from a colleague. 'Look,' she said. 'You can't do this on your own. You're too involved to stay objective; to ask all the right questions. Why don't we stay a bit longer than usual after work? It will look as though we're catching up. There's nothing unusual in that. Then if you leave first, and I wait for a decent interval, if you are followed, well whoever it is won't know we were here together.'

And so it was decided.

They sat at the table, blinds drawn against the wintry evening gloom, mugs of coffee to hand. Between them lay a legal pad, and a biro.

'I have a suggestion,' Anna said. 'About how we might tackle this.'

'Go on.'

She picked up the biro, and held it out. 'Why don't

you do two lists: one of all the people who could possibly – in your wildest dreams - think they owed you something; and another of everybody who might be out to get you?'

He took the biro, and smiled wryly. 'OK. Let's start with the first one first; I have a feeling it's going to be a hell of a lot shorter.' He wrote the heading: *People Who Owe Me.* And then added two columns beneath it: *People I Successfully Defended and Victims/Victims' families whose perpetrator I Successfully Prosecuted.* He wrote a name in the first of the columns, sat back, and began chewing the end of his biro.

'I hope you don't mind, but I've got a couple of other suggestions for you Rob,' she said fighting hard to control her impatience.

'Mmm,' he replied, continuing to stare at words on the page.

'First of all, if you do it this way we'll be here all night. I think you should just brainstorm them as fast as you can. Not try to make a decision on each one in turn. If there are any really unusual ones in there the odds are that they're more likely pop out at you from a list. Secondly, if you keep chewing that biro you're going to end up with ink all over your lips, and a serious case of blood poisoning.'

Rob wiped his mouth with the back of his hand, checked it, and threw the biro into the bin. He took a pen from the inside pocket of the jacket draped over the chair next to his, removed the top, and began to write. On more than one occasion he had to leave the table to consult the records on his computer. When he finally lay down his pen there were seventeen names in the first column, and over a hundred in the second. He showed her the list.

'You're right,' she said, pointing to the first column; those he had successfully defended. 'There are not as many as I expected.'

'That's not because I have a bad success rate,' he reminded her. 'Quite the reverse. It's just that I tend to appear more often for the prosecution than the defence.'

'I noticed. Why is that?'

'Because the burden of proof is so much greater now that everything has to scrutinised by the Crown Prosecution Service, a much smaller percentage of innocent people are brought before the courts.

'And you have a moral objection to defending people you suspect to be guilty?'

'You know I do. We've had this conversation before.'

'You're lucky to be able to pick and choose. As soon as I finish my training, and get called to The Bar, I'm going to have to take what's offered which, let's face it, is going to be whatever morally squeamish Barrister's like you turn your noses up at.' She said it lightly; mainly tongue in cheek although the gist of it was true. The ferocity of his response took her by surprise.

'Well we've all been there. All I can promise you is that the harder you work, and the more you prove yourself, the greater the degree of choice you're going to get. If you want to wear your heart on your sleeve you can stick to Legal Aid cases, do loads of Pro Bono, and live like a church mouse. On the other hand, you can swallow your conscience, and cherry pick the most lucrative briefs regardless of how undeserving and guilty your client may be. Or you can sell your soul to the Crown, and prosecute all and sundry, consigning innocent and guilty to jail with an equally clear conscience, because after all, justice is blind, and the judge and jury are the ones who make the decisions. Welcome to the legal profession. '

She stared at him speechless. Not because of what he had said, but the bitterness with which he said it. This was not the Robert Thornton she had come to know and admire; regard as a brilliant mentor, and role model. She realised that she had massively underestimated the stress he was under.

'Let's get on with this shall we?' he said, bending forward, and beginning to strike one at a time through names on the list. When he finally sat back she could see that every one of them had been deleted.

'I'm sorry for the way I snapped at you,' he said. 'That was uncalled for.'

'I'm the one that should apologise,' she replied. 'I ought to have realised this isn't the time to be having one of our little debates.'

It was enough that they were able to smile at each other.

'It didn't take you long to eliminate those,' she said, nodding towards the list.

'I'm not surprised. Most of them were patently innocent, so it was never that difficult to prove, and certainly not just down to me. There were some where I had to fight bloody hard, and in most of those cases their gratitude was commensurate; until they got my bill. And not one of them had the makings of a murderer; after all, they were innocent of the charges brought against them.'

'Unless you did a better job than you realised?'

He looked at her. 'You mean what if one of them wasn't actually innocent?'

'It happens. Just like victims of a miscarriage of justice in the other direction. The innocent sent to jail. Did you never have cause to wonder about someone on that list? If they might have duped you, as well as the system?'

He went back over the names, intently this time. Against three of them he paused, and put a question mark. 'These two, I did wonder at the time if they might have been pulling the wool over our eyes. Just a little too smug when the verdict was announced, when normally you'd expect them to dissolve in tears or be overjoyed. But this one,' he placed the nib of his pen against a woman's name. 'Was a case of shoplifting; the third time she'd been caught leaving the same store with goods unpaid for. Her defence was confusion due to a course of prescribed medication. Her doctor was very convincing; as was she. Hardly grounds to pay me back like this, guilty or otherwise.'

'What about the others?'

'Lennie Milham? A rather nasty murder. It was alleged that he'd fallen out with a fellow punter at the Belle Vue dog track. They had a massive bust up in front of scores of witnesses. Promises of dire revenge on both sides. Then two nights later the victim was found with stab wounds in his back, and his throat cut. Unfortunately the police made a mess of the procedures. He was questioned initially without a solicitor, and his house, car, and garden were searched without a warrant. They found the murder weapon in a bin in his back yard, and that was that. They never bothered to look for any corroborating evidence.' We were able to show that the victim had been a nasty piece of work himself. Among other things he was an enforcer for a firm of debt collectors preying on the poor and vulnerable, and he was rumoured to have been a grass. There were plenty of other people with a good reason to want him dead. Somebody else could easily have planted the weapon. And Milham did have an alibi, even if it was rather dubious.

'So he walked free?'

'Oh yes. But it didn't take a lot of work on my part, and I think he could tell I didn't like him. He wouldn't feel he owed me, nor that he had a reason to get back at me.'

'And the last one?'

'Matty Bartlett? He was accused of grievous bodily harm.'

'That's more like it, surely?'

'Not really. He'd been drinking in a pub in Stockport. A fight broke out around him. He'd got caught up between two rival gangs. They were using bottles, chairs, broken glasses. He was a big lad Matty. Very handy with his fists. He'd laid two of them out cold, before the police arrived. One of them was in a coma for four days. The police were extremely efficient in arresting everyone involved, and a lot less efficient in taking statements from witnesses, other than those actually involved. All I had to do was get a private detective to have a word with the bar man, track down some of the other people present in the bar that night, and hey presto, Matty walked free; self defence. Strictly speaking, although he was undoubtedly defending himself, he almost certainly went way beyond the reasonable force allowed by the law. But you'd have to have been caught up in a pub brawl to know how difficult that it is. I think justice was done. He was grateful, but definitely not homicidally so. He runs a fruit stall in Market Street. For the first few months he used to insist on not charging me for my fruit and greengrocery. It got embarrassing so I told him I'd have to shop else where. After that he started charging me. But I have a feeling I still get a bargain.'

'Sounds like you may be stalking him, rather than the other way round?'

Rob had to laugh at that. 'OK,' he said. 'List two.'

The title was admirably short; Out To Get Me. Again he created two columns: Ones I Defended Unsuccessfully, and Ones I Successfully Prosecuted. Rob worked at it while Anna freshened up their coffee. This time he was five minutes faster. Mainly because of the duplication in the second column – defended unsuccessfully - with those he had already recorded from the victim's perspective, as successfully prosecuted.

He pursed his lips. 'There are some pretty mean characters down here I have to admit,'

'Like who?'

'He started to run his finger down the second column: 'Murder; rape; GBH; importation of drugs; Murder; Murder; Multiple murder, gang reprisal; armed robbery; aggravated assault; rape; rape; armed robbery; drug trafficking, people trafficking, murder, keeping a brothel – actually a chain of brothels involving women trafficked from Eastern Europe, and the Far East; conspiracy to commit terror; rape; serial murder; rape; money laundering...'

'OK. OK,' she said, holding up her both hands. 'I've got the picture. Nice company you keep.'

He smiled. 'You'd better get used to it, or settle for cases of "Had an Accident? Not Your Fault?"'

'Well let's face it, it sounds like any one of these could bear a grudge, and have the nature and means to act on it. Always assuming they're not still locked up inside.'

'Even then, they've got plenty of contacts on the outside willing to prove themselves, or do it for the money. But I still don't see it. People like this tend to direct their anger at anyone who may have grassed them up. At rival gangs. Not even at the witnesses; the time to have a go at them is before it comes to trial, not when the verdict's been handed down.'

He paused while he thought about it. 'It's just occurred to me,' he said. 'That it's even more complicated than I thought. On top of all of these,' he tapped the lists. 'There are witnesses I've called – and especially those I've had to get subpoenaed, and ones called by the other side and cross examined - who have been publicly humiliated, exposed, and whose business, profession, marriage, relationship, may have been ruined as a result.' He brushed his hand through his hair. 'You know Anna, I always felt somehow that putting the wig and gown on somehow divorced you from those consequences. Isn't that we're taught? It's like a dramatic production. We strut the stage; play our part; and when the curtain comes down we move on, and leave it all behind. A momentary reflection on our performance, the reviews, the audience response; then pick up the cheque and start rehearsing for the next one.'

'I think you're being a bit hard on yourself,' she said. 'I've seen you outside of the court room. I know you care about what happens to your clients; the witnesses even; about justice.'

'Maybe not enough.'

'Don't be daft,' she said trying to raise his spirits. 'You keep telling me that there is always a reason why someone is in that dock, and in that witness box. Each of them is responsible in their own way. And even if they have been blown there by fate, that's hardly our fault. *"Don't let yourself become emotionally involved. Just like a nurse or a doctor you can feel compassion, recognise a need, but beyond doing your job you can't get involved in that way. The minute you do, you cease to be able to function properly. You're no use to anyone, and a risk to those around you."* You told me that.'

'You're right,' he said. 'And so was I. Thanks for reminding me. I suppose this just goes to prove how difficult it can be sometimes.'

'Unless you've got the skin of a rhinoceros and heart of stone; speaking of which, isn't that another list?'

'What do you mean?'

'What you said that psychiatrist told you. What if it's personal, romantic? Rejection following sexual intimacy?'

He felt himself blushing. 'I don't think so.'

'What do you mean you don't think so? Have you never been with a woman? Apart from Anjelita obviously.'

'No, but I think it highly unlikely. Anyway I'd rather not go there.'

Anna's frustration with him began to show; as much as her steely determination. She sat bolt upright, and waited for him to look at her before she spoke. 'But you have to.'

'Look,' he replied. 'This is embarrassing.'

'Why?' She was relentless. 'Because up until you jumped in the sack with Anjelita you were a lonely saddo?'

He grinned sheepishly. 'Hardly that.'

'Well what then? I suppose it's because I'm a girl that don't feel you can discuss your peccadilloes with me? Fine down the pub with the boys, or in the rugby club, but not here with me. Well I'll have you know I'm not exactly a wilting wallflower. You're looking at 21st century woman. If you hadn't had any other women in the past two years that would really concern me.' She screwed up her eyes, deliberately provoking him. 'Hang on, that's it isn't it? You're actually gay. Anjelita was just an experiment to find out if you're bisexual.'

'No I'm not,' he said firmly. 'And this conversation is stretching the limits of the pupil/master relationship too far.'

Her tone softened. 'Don't you think it's a little late for that?'

There had been just three women in his life in the past two years, averaging about four months each time. Two of them were ended by mutual consent. 'Frankly,' he told her. 'Once the first flush had worn off we realised we hadn't as much in common as we thought. We just got bored with each other.'

'And the other one?'

'A solicitor in Henry's Mayhew's practice. She finished with me.'

'Dumped you? Why?'

He hated the term dumped. Perhaps it was a sign he was approaching early middle age. 'Because she thought I was getting a little to serious.'

'Were you?'

'I suppose I was. I'd started wondering whether it was time I settled down, thought about a long term relationship, children; marriage even.'

'Did you tell her?'

'I didn't need to. She seemed to pick up the vibes.'

'We women are good at that.'

'Anyway, she told me she wasn't ready for a long term commitment. It was fun while it lasted. Thank you, and goodbye. PS. I hope we can stay good friends?'

'And have you?'

'No. As far as I know she has a practice in St John's Wood. She's in a new relationship according to Henry.'

'Don't you think you should check?'

'What's the point? We parted amicably enough. It was her idea after all. Anyway, I know for a fact that she couldn't be any part of this.'

'If I remember rightly, you assumed that Anjelita Rosa Covas was a safe bet. Look where that got you.'

'Well I just do. So let's leave it at that.'

Anna gave the impression that she was accepting defeat gracefully, while promising herself that she'd make her own enquiries in the morning. 'What about all the people you've never appeared for or against; simply given advice?' She said, changing tack. 'Some of those might have followed it, and felt let down?'

Rob put his head in his hands. 'God, I'd have no idea where to start. In most cases I wouldn't know if they took my advice, let alone whether it worked out for them or not.'

'You would if they'd complained.'

'That's a point. There were a few who went to the Bar Council, but nothing ever came of them. And there was the odd stroppy letter.' Rob looked at his watch. 'But it's getting late. I think we'd better leave it there, I'm going brain dead. I'll dig those out tomorrow.'

She picked up her bag. 'I'd better get going. I suggest you get an early night. And double lock your door.'

'Thank you Anna,' he said as he stood up. 'I really appreciate this. You were right. There was no way I could do it on my own.'

'You're welcome.' She smiled and headed for the door. Rob thought she looked a good deal older, far more mature than her years, and more attractive than he'd realised. As she reached the door she turned and grinned at him. 'Just make sure you remember you said that when I ask you for a reference.'

The door closed quietly behind her. He turned his attention back to the pad, and continued to stare at the lists in the vain hope that something would leap out at him. Eventually his eyes began to burn, and his head to throb. He placed the pad in his briefcase, put on his jacket, clipped the pen back in his pocket, and left.

The agency cleaner called from the bottom of the stairs. 'Goodnight Sir.' She was new. The third in as many weeks. East European, pretty, her English way above par; wasted in this role.

'Goodnight.' His reply was perfunctory. Had she been seven feet tall, dressed in a corset, and wielding a meat cleaver, it was unlikely he'd have noticed. His mind was on other things.

20

As he left court Rob spotted Harry Richmond heading in his direction. Desperate to avoid him he turned his back, and pretended to stare over the balustrade at something on the landing below. It was a ruse doomed to failure.

'Rob! There you are,' Harry said, slapping him on the back. 'Stanley said you had a prelim' in the Regina V Barry Moss case. Any joy?'

Rob fell into step alongside his colleague as they made their way out of the building. 'Not really,' he said. 'Not that I expected the judge to knock it back this early in the proceedings. The trial is set for the middle of January.'

'Bloody hell,' Harry said. 'That's rushing it a bit. Doesn't give you long to prepare.'

'Well there's a lot riding on this one,' Rob told him. 'And the police don't want their star witness getting cold feet, never mind the resources tied up in protecting him. The Home Secretary probably put a bit of pressure on the Lord Chancellor's Office. You know how it works.'

They walked a few paces in silence. Rob was not in the mood for idle conversation, and Harry was wondering if it was safe to broach the matter. He decided to get there as subtly as he could, which for

Harry Richmond was about as delicate as asking a date if she was on a diet. His opening gambit was a feint.

'How was Christmas?'

'Alright.'

Then Harry went for the jugular. 'Did you ask Peter Burnmoor? You know…see if he could trace her number? Maybe get an address?'

Rob knew that Harry could always find a way of checking. Not for the first time he decided to tell a partial truth. 'As matter of fact I did,' he replied. 'I did my best to follow it up, but I hit a dead end.'

'So that's it then? You're going to leave it?'

'I think so.'

Harry looked genuinely relieved. 'Thank God for that. I was getting worried about you. You've looked like death warmed up since this kicked off. Which reminds me. I got an invite from Vince to a New Year's bash he's hosting. He told me to tell you you're not invited.'

'As if I'd go.'

'Well as it happens I'm not going either.'

Rob looked across at his friend. 'Well you didn't have do that Harry, but thanks anyway. It's nice to know I've got your support.'

Harry laughed. 'That's not why I told him I wasn't coming. It's just that I've already promised Jane I'll take her to 235.' He saw the look on Rob's face, and hurriedly added. 'Don't get me wrong. I probably wouldn't have gone anyway. But if you had a choice between an evening with Vince's crowd, and Manchester's newest, smartest, hip live venue, which would you choose?'

'You've just told me I don't have a choice.' Rob reminded him. 'Anyway, who is Jane?'

'A legal exec' over at Woodside; very hot; mummy and daddy are loaded; and she thinks I'm simply amazing.'

'That doesn't say a lot for her judgement.'

Harry nudged him playfully. 'It's not her judgement I'm interested in.'

They waited in silence for a tram to pass, and the lights to change to green. Once again it was Harry who broke the silence. 'That was a funny do about Robinson,' he said. 'Weren't you with the Prosecution?'

'Yes.' Rob replied starkly. Having exhausted his least favourite topic, his friend had managed to home in on his second.

'Looks like someone decided to do the State a favour, and mete out their own punishment.' Harry probed.

'Maybe.'

'Bit of coincidence though. I wouldn't be surprised if the police get in touch.'

'They already have been.'

Harry stopped, and gripped Rob's arm. 'You're kidding? What did they say?'

He shook off the grip. 'Look Harry,' he said. 'I really do appreciate your concern. But I'd rather not talk about any of this. The last ten days have been a nightmare. Can we talk about something else? No Vince, no Anjelita, no Edward Robinson. Something completely different?'

Puzzled and concerned, Harry studied his friend closely. For a moment he considered pushing his luck.

Forcing the issue, in case it helped; like bursting a boil. The image made him feel queasy.

'Fair enough,' he said, and started walking again, along Deansgate. 'Look, why don't you come with us on New Year's Eve? You live just opposite; even if you are on the nineteenth floor. You won't need a taxi, just the lift.'

Rob shook his head. 'Thanks, but I've no one to come with. The last thing you need when you're trying to pull, is me playing gooseberry. And anyway, I don't feel up to it right now.'

'No but you will by the weekend. Look, I know that thing with the Covas girl was horrendous. I can't begin to imagine how you felt when the police came knocking. But it's just like riding a horse. When you fall off, you've just got to get right back on again.'

Rob stopped dead in the middle of the pavement, and stared in amazement at his colleague. 'I can't believe you just said that.'

Harry had to think about it for moment. When it finally dawned on him he put his hand to his mouth. 'Oh God, I'm sorry.' He said, sounding mortified. Unfortunately, what started out as an impressive act of contrition was spoilt by the twitch at the side of his mouth that spread slowly into a nervous laugh. Rob found himself joining in, until the two of them were howling with laughter; so much so that passers-by began to give them a wide berth.

Rob realised that it was the first time that he'd laughed since Vince's party. It had been at something Anjelita had said. The recollection was enough to sober him up, and bring back the nagging sense of guilt.

'Are you coming for a drink after work?' Harry asked as they stood on the steps of their Chambers. 'It is Friday you know.'

'No thanks Harry,' Rob said. 'I'm going to pass on that. I've got some stuff to get out of the way. Give me a clear weekend.'

Undaunted, Harry tried again. 'I tell you what. Why don't you ask that pupil of yours - Anna what's her name – to come with you on New Year's Eve? You can always ditch her if something better turns up.'

Harry, you're simply incorrigible,' Rob told him. 'Aside from the morality, if I were to do that, can you imagine what it would be like working together for the rest of the year?'

'Better than spending New Year's Eve sitting all alone in your castle in the sky, watching the fireworks go off all around you,' Harry told him. 'How sad is that?'

How sad indeed, Rob reflected as he packed his briefcase for the weekend. Of course he could ask Anna if she'd like to go, on the strict understanding that it was a date of convenience. But it was probable that she'd already made plans. Anyway, she'd gone back to London for a few days so it wasn't as though he could ask her face to face. He didn't want to start something that might lead to misunderstanding; unrealistic expectations on her part, and embarrassment on his. It was likely he'd have other offers, but they'd all involve friends or colleagues who knew him well. He could picture how, when the champagne began to flow, the conversation would turn inexorably, and painfully, to the accusation of rape, or the murder of Edward Robinson, or both. No, he decided, better lonely in the apartment with his books and music, than among a booze fuelled crowd of merrymakers.

Approaching midnight he had finished his work, given up on the list of names on his legal pad, and despaired of finding anything worth watching on the television. Unable to contemplate sleep, he poured himself a whisky, and went out onto the balcony. Perched on the end of the Great Northern Tower, his apartment faced South. Not the best of outlooks during the day across the flat roof of the Great Northern Warehouse, and the sliced loaf curve of the G-MEX exhibition centre, it did at least catch the bulk of the day's sunlight. At night, however, there was a different kind of magic. He leant on the hand rail and looked up at the night sky. This high up, despite the light pollution from the city, he was able to see a number of twinkling constellations. Lowering his gaze he could just make out the low dark mass of the Pennine hills at the south-eastern limit of his view, the red and white snakes of traffic on the Mancunian Way - appearing and disappearing between the university buildings - and straight ahead, bisecting the night sky, the blue glass blade of the Beetham Tower. He could see people the size of ants in the Sky Bar of the Hilton Hotel. A wail of sirens troubled the gentle city hum. Blue lights were flashing in the tiny triangle of space where Watson Street and Great Bridgewater Street met. He watched and wondered until the wind whipped up, and an icy chill in the breeze forced him inside.

He wandered aimlessly from room to room, unable to sleep, until an inexplicable uneasiness led him back out onto the balcony. The sirens had ceased, but the static flashing lights had multiplied. He closed the floor to ceiling patio doors, pulled the blinds, slipped on his coat, set the alarm, and left the apartment.

He stood at the line of police tape that had already been unravelled between the lights on the island at the bottom of Watson Street and those on the other side of the road. Rob had no idea what had drawn him here, but felt a growing sense of foreboding. Further down the street towards the Bridgewater Hall, in the centre of the tunnel created by the massive brick railway arch, shadowy shapes scurried in an out of the beams from police vehicles, and spotlights that had been set up on portable stands. The flashing blue lights, from the cars diverting the traffic away from the scene at either end of the tunnel, bounced off the roof and walls, imparting to the shadowy figures a spectral form.

'An accident is it?' Rob asked of the policeman on the other side of the tape.

'I couldn't say sir,' he replied, stamping his feet against the cold. 'Even if I knew...which I don't. If I were you, I'd get off home. I don't think there's a lot to see. And even if there was, I doubt that you or I will get to see it.'

Rob had no idea why he was standing here, colder by the minute. It was not in his nature to rubber neck accidents on motorways. He actually despised those who did. But whatever it was that had had drawn him, was keeping him here. Suddenly he was caught in headlights, and turned as a black van, with the words Tactical Aid Unit written large and bold on the side, pulled in to the side of the road behind him. That could only mean something other than an accident. A fight perhaps, a serious assault; something requiring protection, or a detailed search.

'What the hell are you doing here?'

He turned towards the voice, and saw Gordon Holmes striding towards him.

'Mr Thornton,' he said. 'I wonder if you'd come with me please sir?' He nodded to the constable who lifted the ribbon of tape for Rob to duck under. 'I rather think the Boss would like a word with you.'

'What's going on?' Rob asked as they walked a little way into the tunnel.

'Good question. We were wondering that ourselves,' Holmes said. He stopped beside a police van parked across the centre of the road. 'You'd better wait here while I tell Mr Caton. Can't have you contaminating the scene can we? That would really set the cat among the pigeons.'

As Holmes walked forward, his overshoes intensely white in the glare of the lights, Rob looked over the roof of the car, and beyond the second perimeter of tapes. A white tent had been erected. Inside, backlit figures moved slowly, jerkily, like the puppets of a Burmese shadow theatre. He watched as Holmes reached the entrance to the tent, and lifted the flap. One of the figures, bending forward from the waist, straightened up, turned, and left the tent. As he stepped into the light, DCI Caton followed the direction of Holmes's outstretched arm. Rob tried to read the expression on the Detective Chief Inspector's face as they stared at each other. He thought he detected, in equal measure, astonishment, puzzlement and suspicion; although the latter could easily have been a figment of his own imagination. The pair of them came towards him.

'Mr Thornton,' DCI Caton began. He sounded serious, focused, and formal. No Rob or Robert this time. 'Would you mind telling me exactly what you're doing here?'

'I was on the balcony of my apartment, and I heard the sirens, saw the flashing lights. I wasn't ready for bed, so I thought I'd come down, stretch my legs, and have a look.'

'And your apartment is where exactly?'

'On the south corner of the Great Northern Tower.' DI Holmes chipped in, reminding them both that he had been there before.

'The nineteenth floor.' Rob added. 'The balcony looks right down towards the junction here.' He pointed at the traffic lights behind him.

Caton studied him closely. 'I didn't take you for a voyeur Mr Thornton.'

'Well you were right Detective Chief Inspector,' Rob told him. 'I am not. As I said, I heard the noise, and saw the lights. I was wide awake, and curious. That's all.'

There was a long pause before Caton spoke again. 'You haven't had any more little messages then? On your phone, your computer…on a card perhaps?'

'No I haven't,' Rob replied. As the implications hit him his stomach fell through the floor. 'You've found another body haven't you?'

'Have you got your mobile phone on you?' the

detective asked, ignoring his question.

Rob removed it from his hip pocket and switched it on. They waited for the screen to light up. 'Three messages,' Rob said, holding it up for the others to see. He opened each in turn. The first two were texts. One was a sales pitch from his service provider telling him he'd earned thirty free minutes. The other was from Harry Richmond to say he'd wangled a couple of extra tickets for tomorrow night - New Year's Eve - just in case. The voice message was from his mother.

'Robert….Robert…is that you Robert? Are you there? God I hate these voice whatsits. Robert. You left a pair of socks under the bed. I've washed and dried them, and posted them this morning. Give me a ring to let me know you've received them. Robert….'

He gave Holmes the phone so that he could check them himself, and turned to DCI Caton. 'So who is it then?'

Caton waited until Holmes had finished with the phone and handed it back. The two of them watched him for a reaction as Caton said: 'Lennie Milham.'

Even in the scattered and reflected light it must have been obvious to them that Rob's face had paled. 'Lennie Milham,' he repeated lamely. 'Are you sure?'

'If you recall, I was involved in that investigation Mr Thornton,' Holmes said.

Not thoroughly enough, was Rob's recollection, but this wasn't the time or place to remind him that Lennie's quick walk to freedom was wholly down to sloppy police procedure.

'And DI Holmes tells me you were involved as well?' Caton said, inviting an explanation.

'I was the lead for the Defence,' he said. 'Not that

it's something I'm particularly proud of. It was an easy case to defend, and the CPS should never have let it go ahead. It was an embarrassment for the Crown and the police, and a hollow victory for me. There was more than a fifty fifty chance that Milham was guilty, if only the evidence had been secure.'

'So you defended him. Everyone knew he was guilty. And now he's dead?' Caton made it sound like cause and effect.

'It's just as likely,' Rob said, more in hope than certainty. 'That this has nothing to do with those messages. That someone close to the man he killed decided to even the score.'

Caton nodded. 'That's true, Mr Thornton. But why here? In the middle of the city. Why not nearer his home or his usual haunts? Instead we find him dumped just a few hundred yards from your apartment block. We know he was dumped, because there are none of the blood patterns we would have expected to find had he been killed beneath these arches. And what's more it already looks as though he was killed in the same way that Robinson was killed.'

'How was he killed Chief Inspector?'

'They were both shot Mr Thornton. Quite expertly as it happens, from about twelve feet away. So no likelihood of blood spatters on the perpetrator. And, since both bodies were moved after they were killed, we're not going to find any cartridges or bullets.'

'But there will be trace evidence?'

'Oh yes. Even despite the rain that had fallen on and around Robinson's body, we'll recover some trace evidence. But without a suspect to link it to that's unlikely to take us very far. So, Mr Thornton. Firstly, if you do receive any messages I want to know straight away; day or night. Secondly, I hope you're still bending your mind to who might want to reward or punish you by systematically taking out people you have defended or prosecuted. And since we don't see any connection between the two victims, other than the fact that they're dead, you might want to ask yourself if you know of anyone who knows about these cases, and their link to you. Someone who has the potential to act as a vigilante. Able to kill repeatedly in cold blood. Don't worry about giving us too many names. Our business is elimination. And right now, just one name would be a start. Now if you'll excuse me, we'd better get on. We'll be in touch in the morning. I suggest you get home, and watch your back. Would you like a constable to accompany you? '

Rob shook his head. Still stunned from what he'd just learned.

'No thank you,' he said. 'I'll make my own way back. I'll be alright.'

'Well see you are,' Caton said as he turned away. 'Right now you're all we've got.'

The lift doors opened. As Rob emerged into the hallway on the nineteenth floor, his phone began to ring. There was a new text message.

> *Lennie, Lennie, what's he done?*
> *Killed some people with his gun,*
> *Some with crack, and some with coke,*
> *He was a really nasty bloke.*

You know that he deserved to die,
No tears to shed…no reason why.

His hand began to shake, and the phone slipped from his grasp. As he stooped to pick it up he heard a ping, and the doors of the second lift opening. He turned, his heart thumping in his chest. Out into the hallway stepped his new neighbours, the Masons; a young architect, and her kitchen designer husband. They were laughing, arms around each other, until they saw Rob standing there. That stopped them in their tracks.

'Are you all right Mr Thornton?' asked Sheila Mason, clinging tighter to her husband.

Rob took a deep breath, and pulled himself together. 'Yes. I'm fine thanks.'

Richard Mason uncoupled himself, and stepped forward a pace to get a better look. 'Well you don't look too good,' he said. 'Is there something we can do?'

Rob could tell what was running through their minds. Was he drunk perhaps, or on drugs? Sleep walking? Having a kind of fit? 'No,' he said, 'I just had a bit of bad news that's all.' He held up his phone as evidence. 'I'll be all right, really I will.'

'Well if you're sure?' Said Mason.

'I'm sure. But thanks for asking.'

Conscious that their eyes were burning holes in his back he fumbled for his keys with his free hand, opened the door, and went inside. He put on the chain, locked and bolted the door, and leaned his back against it for a moment. When his hands had steadied, and the pulsing veins in his neck had subsided, he switched on his phone, and speed dialled the number Caton had given him.

It was gone nine in the morning when Rob finally crawled out of bed. For the past hour or so, he had been suffering with stomach cramps, and a tension headache, but had been too tired to do anything about it. Instead, he had lain there with his head between both pillows, trying in vain to block out the light; to block out everything.

He was in the middle of eating a slice of toast, and drinking a second mug of strong black coffee, when the entry phone buzzed. It was DI Holmes.

'Morning Mr Thornton,' the detective said, more cheerfully than warranted by the night's events. 'I'd like to ask you a few questions, and have a look at your balcony if I may.'

Rob led him past the kitchen, across the living and dining area, to the patio windows which he opened, allowing the detective out onto the balcony, and a gust of cold air into the room.

'Nice planters.' Holmes remarked, as pushed one of the aluminium chairs aside, and crossed to the furthest edge of the balcony. He leant on the handrail, just as Rob had done the night before, and stared down towards the bottom of Watson Street .

'Nice view, too.'

Joining him, Rob could see that the tapes were still in place, and a motorcycle officer was turning back motorists intent on reaching one of the car parks. 'Checking up on my story?' he asked.

Holmes turned to face him. 'Most important part of the job, sir; checking. Of course you already know that. When we fail to check it makes your job that much harder; or easier, depending on whose side you're on.'

Rob had no idea if he was being facetious, ironic, or simply stating the obvious. 'It wasn't my fault, or yours, that Milham was killed,' he said, hoping to bridge the uncomfortable gap between them. 'Even if he had been put away, someone could have got to him. Had him stabbed with an improvised knife.'

'Possibly, and I don't say that he wouldn't have deserved it. But he wasn't was he? Because he wasn't inside. So we'll never know. What we do know is that someone shot him in the head, and dumped his body down there as present for you. And we would like to know why.'

Rob could feel his hackles rising. 'And you think I don't.'

Holmes smiled thinly. 'Good. In which case perhaps we could go inside so that I can get those questions out of the way, and you can get back to your breakfast?'

Holmes left with a detailed list of Rob's movements for the past twenty four hours. Where he had been, what he had been doing, who he was with, and who might have seen him. He had copied down verbatim the message on his phone, and taken a note of the sender's number. He also had a copy of the lists of names on Rob's legal pad. The names Rob had pored over again and again. Rob had given them gladly. Not just to get rid of him, but because he was willing to do anything to stop this nightmare. Any questions that was, apart from what he had been doing in London over the Christmas Weekend. But he had a feeling that eventually he would have to come clean about that too. Then they would wonder why he'd kept quiet about it in the first place. Sooner rather than later, he was going to have to pluck up the courage to tell them.

21

He stayed in the apartment all day. For dinner he cooked a fillet steak with oven chips and wild mushrooms, and washed it down with three quarters of a bottle of La Bastide Saint Dominique Chateauneuf du Pape. He was waiting for a DVD to load, and trying to choose between finishing off the wine or moving on to brandy, when the phone rang. It was Harry Richmond. He was shouting over all the noise in the background. It sounded like a bar.

'Rob? Thank God you're in. Now listen. I've got Jane with me, and her friend Jules. Jules has been stood up, and since I've got two spare tickets for this evening, this is your lucky day.'

'Look Harry,' Rob began. It was obvious that his friend either couldn't hear or did not want to, because he simply soldiered on.

'Jules is abso…bloody…lutely gorgeous.' He shouted. His voice dropped for a moment, and Rob could just make out him saying to someone. 'Yes you bloody are. If I wasn't already taking Jane, I'd snatch your hand off.' Whatever the reply it caused a bout of laughter. Then Harry was shouting down the phone again. 'Seriously Rob, she's beautiful. Lovely personality, very sensible, and most importantly, she has definitely no psychopathic tendencies.'

'I'm sorry…' Rob began. He was immediately drowned out again.

'Don't be sorry mate, you haven't time. Get yourself dressed, you're coming out with us. No arguments, no excuses. Put your tuxedo on, it suits you. We'll pick you up in half an hour. You can give us a glass of champagne to start the evening off.'

At which point Harry ended the call, leaving Rob sitting there staring blankly at the phone.

MANCH235TER was emblazoned in two foot high pink neon lights above the wide doubled panelled glass doors. On each of the doors, in turn, the numbers had been etched in turquoise blue. Rob had been meaning to join the club. Not least because he was told it was as sophisticated as a casino could be, and it was literally yards from his apartment block. And now Harry had signed him up as a member, and here he was. Not as he had planned, and not in the right frame of mind to appreciate it. But what the hell? At least Harry had been telling the truth about the girls.

They were walking arm in arm ahead of him through the doorway and into the foyer. Jane and Jules. Both five foot ten in their high heels. Blonde, curvaceous, size tens squeezed into figure hugging black sequined dresses with shoe string shoulder straps. Joined at the hip. From behind, had he not known differently, he would have taken them for twins. The only distinguishing feature was their hair. Jane's in loose flowing curls held high with a band; Jules's silky, straight, and feather cut, the ends of which met to form a perfect oval where her cleavage began. Harry had been right about another thing.

They were both intelligent. No vacuous footballer's wives here. Smart, independent; going places. Under different circumstances he would thought himself fortunate this evening, and made a real effort.

By ten past eleven they'd had a flutter in the casino, and drunk champagne in a bar furnished in wood and burgundy leather, where the vertical glass surfaces were lit in muted gold like a fantastical aquarium. They had even made an initial foray onto the dance floor. Rob managed little more than desultory conversation. When he told Jules that he'd already eaten he got the distinct impression that she was relieved to be able to go to the buffet alone.

Rob leaned on the balcony, and looked down on the seething mass of people swaying to pulsating rhythms, captured, then released, by the roving spots. Half of the people here tonight had come in formal evening wear, the other half in fancy dress. It looked, sounded, and felt, like a metro-multicultural Mancunian Mardi Gras. He felt completely out of it. Disembodied. Just as he had known he would.

One of the spots captured Jules on the edge of dance floor, dancing with a handsome Asian man in a midnight blue tuxedo, and matching bow tie. It was the opportunity he had been waiting for. He made his way down to the bar where Harry was collecting drinks for Jane and himself.

'Harry,' he said. 'Thanks for tonight. I'll see you right for the tickets tomorrow. I'm going now. I can't take anymore of this.'

Harry turned fast, spilling Jane's champagne down

the front of Rob's jacket. 'Now look what you've made me do,' he said, trying to brush it off with the sleeve of his jacket. 'You can't leave yet. What about Jules? Who's going make sure she gets home safe?'

'If not you and Jane, then probably the guy she's dancing with,' Said Rob. 'I warned you I wasn't up to this. She'll be alright. Just make sure Jane keeps an eye on her, like she probably does every other time they go out together.'

Harry stood there, elbows clamped to his sides, trying to protect the drinks as people pushed past on their way to the bar. 'What the hell am I going to tell them?' He said.

'You'll think of something. Tell them I was taken ill.'

Rob turned and walked towards the exit.

'The way you've been tonight they won't find that hard to believe!' Harry shouted after him.

A flurry of snowflakes fluttered down as he stepped out into the street. The sweat on his face and neck cooled rapidly in the cold night air. He turned up the collar of his tuxedo, and set off, melting the dusting of snow on the pavement with every step he took.

Whether it was the amount he had drunk, the nervous energy he had expended, or the culmination of several days without a decent night's sleep, mattered not. Within ten minutes of arriving home Rob's jacket was on the hook behind the door, his trousers and underclothes clothes lay in a heap on the floor beside the bed, and he sprawled upon it, fast asleep.

22

Sunday 1st January

Twenty miles away to the West, is a three bedroom detached house in a leafy suburb of Horwich, considered by Greater Manchester Police, and the officer to whom it belongs, a safe house. It was now one fifteen in the morning. Michael John Thomas turned back the bedclothes, and listened. Nothing stirred. According to the clock on his bedside table it was over an hour since he and his minder had switched off the television, and turned in for the night. From next door he could hear the sound of light snoring; the inevitable effect of the turkey curry, and the brandy with which they had seen in The New Year, lying heavy on the stomach of police constable Burton. Thomas swung his feet silently to the floor, padded over to the chair where his clothes were piled, and put on his trackie bottoms, hoodie, and trainers. From under the mattress he retrieved the mobile phone on silent ring he had hidden there.

He slipped out of the house, and onto the pavement. He had already marked out a ten year old Fiat Punto on a driveway three doors down. No alarm, left as often as not unlocked. It was six weeks since he had seen his new girl friend Janice, although they had exchanged cards and a single present through his minders. He calculated that he could get to his mate's sister's house in Swinton within half an hour, spend a couple of hours with Janice as arranged, and still be back and in bed long before the eight o'clock changeover. He was certain that there was no way that Harry Moss knew anything about his mate's sister, or where she lived. Janice would have been on soft drinks all night, slip away from the party at the Duke of York, and drive over from Higher Broughton to Swinton. She knew to keep looking in her wing mirrors. The slightest sign that someone was following, and she'd bail out. He pulled up his hood, and stepped out onto Fearnhead Avenue. Nothing could possibly go wrong.

Rob woke at seven thirty. Much as he would have done on a work day. This morning there was no need to rush. He lay on his back and listened. Even up here, cocooned by the insulated panel walls, and toughened double glazed panes, he could hear the sounds of the city coming to life. The hum of engines, the squeal of tyres protesting at the traffic lights, the roar of souped-up cars accelerating, the thump of in car music systems. Most mornings he could hear the thud...thud...thud of the rotor blades as the traffic helicopter passed uncomfortably close; but not this morning. Today there was an eerie silence. Not even the corporation street cleaners astride their motorised vacuum cleaners were out this early on New Year's Day. He guessed that it was a combination of his body clock, and the unusual silence, that had woken him. Not that he felt tired. It was the best night's sleep he had had since Boxing Day. The beep of his mobile phone put paid to his plan to lie there a little longer. He assumed that it was Harry ranting about leaving him in the lurch the night before, and ignored it. Slowly, nagging doubts crept up on him. No longer relaxed, he sat up, switched on the bedside light, and picked up. It was not from Harry.

Twenty minutes later, Rob switched on the engine of his BMW. He took his road atlas for Greater Manchester from the side pocket, and laid it on the passenger seat. Not that he was likely to need it, but it would be good to have some idea of where he was going. He checked the text message again.

It's time my friend you came to me.
My latest present you should see
My gift should ease your daily grind
I'm only trying to be kind.
Anjelita sends her love,
And if you want to save this dove,
Then come alone, and tell no one
For I'll be watching, with my gun!

Happy New Year, Robert.

Directions follow.

Not for a second had Rob thought of contacting DCI Caton. The confirmation that Anjelita Andrades was still alive was all that concerned him. He reasoned that if this person had wanted to harm him he would have done so by now. Why would he go through the charade of killing Robinson, and Milham? And if he could do that in the city centre, and the police still had no inkling of his identity, then how much easier to kill Anjelita in a place of his choosing? His brain told him that he was behaving rashly in telling no one; without a weapon or a plan, flying by the seat of his pants; certain of his own invincibility. His heart and his innate arrogance told him otherwise. There was no other way. He slipped into gear, backed slowly out of the narrow parking bay, and sped off towards the exit.

Ten minutes later a second message ordered him to leave the city on the A6 at Chapel Street, and follow it onto the A580 in the direction of Liverpool. The roads were almost empty. He hit a succession of green lights that meant that even sticking to the speed limits he made good time. He was passing Pendleton Heights when the next set of instructions came through. They directed him onto the M61, and to follow the signs for Preston. No sooner had he joined the motorway than another message told him to exit at Junction 6, and follow the signs for Horwich. Throughout the journey he checked his mirrors. On the longest stretches, it was obvious that there was no one behind him. He glanced at the road map trying to guess where he was being taken. It was hopeless. The permutations were endless.

The route took him down a long dual carriageway past the imposing giant space ship that was the Reebok Stadium; home to Bolton Wanderers Football Club. As he reached a roundabout with what looked like a silver V2 bomber buried nose first in the centre, he heard the sound of wailing sirens. In his rear view mirror Rob could see a pair of police Range Rovers, lights flashing, tearing towards him. Heart racing, he pulled over to the side of the carriageway. He sat with the gears in neutral waiting for the brake lights to come on as they pulled over in front of him.

They sped past towards the next roundabout, where one turned left towards the Middlebrook Retail Park, and the other carried straight on in the direction in which he was to travel. He waited until they had disappeared, then slipped into first, and pulled away.

At the roundabout with the Beehive pub he turned left as directed. He realised that was heading towards Horwich town centre when the next text came through.

Stop. And Wait.

Conscious of the cycle route at the side of the road, he pulled into a recessed driveway beside a sign that read St Joseph's RC High School and Specialist Sports College. He switched off the engine, and stared at the phone in the hands free cradle; willing it to beep. Five minutes passed. Two police cars and a police van went by in the direction of the town centre. An officer in one of the cars gave him a long hard look as they went past. Rob felt sure that had they not had something pressing to respond to they would have stopped, and questioned him. He feared what that pressing appointment might be; and prayed that he was wrong.

The final message was more detailed than the rest. It led him through the town centre to the end, where the road forked left at a roundabout. He turned almost immediately right between two tall stone pillars marking the entrance to Lever Park, and onto

Lever Park Avenue, where a sign welcomed him to the West Pennine Country Park. He realised that had been here before; for the outdoor cycle events at the Commonwealth Games in 2002. Substantial houses on this tree lined avenue gave way to a narrow tarmac road that snaked its way between thick woods. He passed a succession of waymarked paths on his left, and Rivington and Blackrod High School on his right, until he reached the sign for a zigzag bend beyond a large stone cottage and retaining wall. He braked to walking speed, and turned sharp left as instructed down a wide track between two trees. Ahead of him a wooden barrier, fixed and locked between two hefty posts a metre high, barred further progress. He switched off the engine, and took stock.

Ahead of him, beyond the barrier, still discernible despite an inch of snow, the partly metalled track stretched out in a straight line as far as he could see. Foot high posts on either side, a metre apart, formed a continuous line of grey against the snow that led the eye towards the vanishing point. A line of naked sycamore trees, growing out of snow covered banks of earth, bordered parallel paths on either side.

He put the phone in his inside pocket, opened the car door, and got out. An involuntary shiver ran through him, and he pulled his coat close, wishing that he had thought to wear an anorak instead. His legal training kicked in as it dawned on him that there was every chance that he would destroy whatever evidence there might be here. In the track beside the car were a set of tyre tracks partially filled with snow. A car had driven in from the other side of the trees, and had left by reversing out onto the road. Rob opened his boot, removed the tyre lever, placed it in the right hand pocket of his jeans, and fed the part that protruded beneath his belt to hold it in place. Even through his clothing the metal was cold against his skin. He shut the bonnet, locked the car, and started walking slowly forward.

23

Even before he reached the barrier he could see that there were two sets of footprints heading away down the path ahead; one large, one smaller. He stopped, and began searching either side of the path. On the path to the right of the track, beneath the trees, he found what he was looking for; a single set of the footprints, the larger of the two, returning. An icy fear took hold of him, and he began to run.

Three times he fell on the frozen ruts, smearing his coat with muddy slush, grazing the palms of his hands, bruising his knees and elbows. Each time he scrambled to his feet, and hurried on. Within a half a mile he could see the outline of a ruined castle through the bare branches. Where the track rose towards the imposing stone walls he caught a glimpse beyond them of steel blue moonlit water beneath a lowering sky.

He reached the first of a series of rounded towers, and slowed to walking pace. His chest was heaving, his throat burning. Each exhalation of breath sent a cloud of steam into the frosty air. High above his head pairs of arrow slits in the curtain wall stared down like sightless eyes. He followed the wall around to the right until he reached three huge blocks of stone strewn in front of an opening in the wall, beyond which a roman arch marked the entrance to a roofless courtyard. He stood still, and listened for a moment.

The only sound was the mournful cry of a bird out on the reservoir. He took a deep breath, and walked towards the arch.

A breach in the wall at the furthest side of the ruins exposed a group of Canada geese bobbing on the troubled surface of the lake. To the right, three Gothic archways were set into buildings composed of thick blocks of the same grey millstone as the castle walls. The two pairs of footprints he had been following traced a path towards the central arch. The single set returned from the same direction. Rob put his hand inside his coat, and withdrew the tyre lever. It was so cold, and his hand so wet with sweat, that he worried that it might freeze to his palm, and burn the skin. Logic told him that whoever it was that he thought this weapon might protect him from was long since gone. And yet he clung to it, just as he clung to a forlorn hope that he would find her alive.

Still conscious of the need to preserve the evidence, instead of following the trail under the archway, he moved to his left, and climbed a small bank to reach a narrow window through which he was able to see inside. The building consisted of a roofless circular enclosure. Propped against the far wall, facing the doorway, was a body covered from head to foot in a veil of snow. The head slumped forward. Thick red blood had congealed on the top of the skull, and was crimson upon the chest. Rob felt his legs going from under him. He clung to the wall for support and retched into the virgin snow. A pair of swans, disturbed by the sound, lifted off from the reservoir behind him, and flew gracefully away.

The woods reverberated with the sound of sirens. PC Gerry Burton, the owner of the safe house, was the first to arrive. He found Rob Thornton, huddled and shivering, sheltering from the icy sleet beneath the arch of a tower entrance. Rob watched as the policeman entered the enclosure where the body lay, and returned a minute later, white as a sheet, and cursing like a trooper. Rob was led out of the ruins by another officer, and placed in the front passenger seat of a police Range Rover that had travelled down a different track with other search and emergency vehicles. He was offered a drink of tea in the metal top of a vacuum flask. As he warmed his hands, and sipped his drink, he was able to watch the scene unfold before him.

Lines of tape were slung between iron poles hammered into the frozen ground. Officers stood in huddles, stamping their feet, clapping their hands, talking into their radios, or muttering to each other; their breath hanging in the air like cattle in a yard. Every now and then one of them would point towards Rob's vehicle, and the others in the group would turn, and look directly at him. In some of their expressions he read pity; in others suspicion. Three men and a woman arrived in a van, donned white protective suits, latex gloves, and overshoes, and walked in file into the courtyard, each of them carrying a small black case. A police photographer and a video cameraman arrived, and sought instructions. It was surreal. A living nightmare. It came as a relief when the door was pulled open, and Detective Inspector Holmes stared up at him.

'Well, well, well. If it isn't Mr Robert Thornton,'

the detective said with ill disguised sarcasm. 'Fancy you being here.'

'I'm glad to see you Detective Inspector.' Rob said.

'Well I'm sorry to say it's not mutual.' Holmes told him. 'Now if you don't mind I'd like you to come with me. My Boss wants a little word with you.'

It was warmer in the Mondeo. Rob tucked his hands under his armpits in a vain attempt to lessen the stabbing pains as the blood flooded back into his frozen fingertips. He was sandwiched between them in the back. It was Caton who spoke first.

'It was good of you to call me Mr Thornton,' he said, with scarcely less irony than Holmes had been able to muster. 'What we don't understand is how you knew where to find him?'

'Him?' Rob looked from one face to the other trying to make sense of what he was hearing. 'It's a man?'

Holmes stared back at him. 'Of course it's a man. What the hell did you expect?'

'Who?'

Caton watched him closely. 'You really don't know?'

Rob shook his head. He was already beginning to feel ashamed of the relief he was feeling. 'No I really don't know.'

'It's Michael John Thomas.' Caton told him.

'Thomas? The key witness for the Crown against Moss? I thought he was…'

Holmes finished it for him. 'In protective custody? Well join the club. So did we.'

'But that means the case will collapse,' Rob said,

thinking out loud. 'The CPS is bound to pull the plug.'

'Very convenient for your client Mr Thornton,' Caton said. 'What you might call a good result.'

'Now that's hardly fair,' Rob began to protest. 'It's not my fault.'

'Isn't it? Moss is your client. You mysteriously find the body of the key witness - not during a stroll around the city centre, or popping down to the shops - but in the middle of nowhere. And you want us to believe that it has nothing to do with you?'

Rob could see his point. A child could see it. 'Well, not directly.' He said.

'Indirectly will do for a start,' Holmes told him. 'Perhaps we can agree on that?'

Rob's shoulders were beginning to cramp. He removed his hands from under his arms, and sat on them instead. The tyre lever dug into the hollow beneath his ribs. 'You're right I suppose,' he agreed. 'Indirectly.'

'You suppose?!' Holmes was nearly incandescent. 'We've got three dead bodies in the space of five days, every one of them linked directly to you, and you suppose it might indirectly have something to do with you? Get your head out of your arse man, and wake up before it's too late!'

'All right Gordon,' Caton said a little less firmly than Rob might have hoped. 'I think we can assume that Mr Thornton's got the point. All we need him to do now is to tell us exactly how he ended up finding Michael Thomas before we did.'

They listened intently, Holmes taking notes, as Rob took them step by step through the morning's events.

He gave them his mobile phone, and watched as they forwarded the texts one by one to their office, and asked for a trace to be set up on the sender's number. When they had finished Caton handed him back his phone. 'So why didn't you ring us Mr Thornton? Did you really think you could save Ms Covas all on your own? Come to that, how did you even know the sender of these texts was actually holding her, or that she was still alive?'

'I honestly don't know,' Rob replied. 'I just didn't believe I could take the risk that contacting you would result in him killing her.'

Holmes leant forward. 'So you came charging in here all on your own, armed with what exactly? Your razor sharp wit?'

Rob knew better than to admit that he had the tyre lever hidden beneath his belt. He had a feeling these two were sufficiently angry with him to charge him with possessing an offensive weapon with intent to commit GBH; or worse. 'I wasn't thinking straight.' He said.

'You can say that again.' muttered Holmes.

'You still haven't been entirely honest with us have you Mr Thornton?' Caton said in a tone all the more menacing because it was delivered softly.

'Rob's mind was racing. 'I'm sorry,' he said. 'I don't know what you mean?'

Caton's eyes bored a hole into Rob's head. 'This obsession with Anjelita Covas,' he said. 'Or should I say Angela Andrews?' He smiled thinly, and nodded as he picked up the tell tale signs on Rob's face. 'You see, we managed to trace the phone from which the first text you received was sent. It was registered to an Angela Andrews, with an address in North London. We asked our colleagues in the Met to pop in, and have a word with her. I wonder if you can guess what they discovered? Not only did Ms Andrews turn out to be our very own Anjelita Rosa Covas, but there had also been a number of people calling at her flat wondering why she hadn't been home since her trip up North. One of whom, bore a remarkable resemblance to you Mr Thornton.'

The two detectives stared at him in silence, waiting for him to respond. Rob had no choice. He told them everything.

The windows were steamed up. The sleet had turned to snow, covering the outside of the car in a white cocoon. Holmes sat back and whistled through his teeth. 'Bloody Hell! Covas, Andrews, Angel, Andrades, she's got more aliases than Mata Hari.' He said.

'And she's still missing,' Rob reminded him.

'Alright Mr Thornton, keep your hair on.' Holmes retorted. 'You're lucky we haven't charged you with obstruction. Come to that, we still might.'

Rob turned on him. 'Don't you think you'd be better occupied trying to find her, and the lunatic that's holding her?'

Holmes twisted in his seat, squaring up to him. As they glowered at each other, shoulder to shoulder, brow to brow, Caton leant across the two of them, pushing them apart. 'Stop this!' He demanded. 'Gordon, get out and clean the snow off the windows. Then park yourself in the driving seat. As soon as I've spoken to the senior investigating officer, and explained the connection with our two murders, we're taking Mr Thornton back to his car, and then all three of us are going back to the office to put this on the record.'

Rob was still sitting there when a text came through. He opened the in-box with foreboding, and started to read the message. He found it difficult because his hands were shaking uncontrollably. No rhymes this time. No riddles. No Robert. Straight to the point.

Did you like this present Thornton? How does it make you feel? Grateful? I doubt it. Powerful? I don't think so. Cheated? Impotent? Are you beginning to get the idea? I do hope so.

PS. Anjelita sends her love!'

Four hours later his shoe prints had been taken and photographed by the scene of crime forensic officers. He had been escorted back to Longsight police station, and had provided a written statement covering everything that had happened since Anna showed him the web site on which the tragic history of Anjelita Andrades had been exposed. Caton's team had linked the texts following Edward Robinson's murder to Robinson's own phone. Michael Thomas's girl friend had confirmed that the most recent set of text messages had been sent from the number of the phone he had been using secretly for the past three months. Neither phone was now active, or traceable. It was assumed that each in turn had been used, and then destroyed. Probably at the bottom of the reservoir.

Rob's head ached. He had been required to go over and over again the lists he had provided of possible but unlikely suspects. He knew he could walk away at any time. He felt certain their threat to charge him with obstruction was a bluff, and in any case he doubted that it would stick. He stayed and co-operated because he felt he owed it to them, and above all to Anjelita. Going it alone had got him nowhere and the bodies were piling up. It didn't take a genius to see that he needed help; in more ways than one.

Caton had even managed to get the Fixated Threat Assessment Centre to disturb Dr Eve Hammond on holiday so that she could talk with them by video link. This time it was evident that she was taking it far more very seriously.

'This no longer sounds like someone who really believes that they owe you,' she said after listening patiently to Rob's account. 'This is far more threatening. Not just for those who may have some connection with you like the three men who have been murdered already. Interesting that they are all men,' she added as an afterthought. 'But threatening for you in particular. This is far more in line with the pattern of a vengeful stalker. The definition is self-explanatory, but the triggers may be many and various. And in this case, rather more unusually, we appear to have a serial killer to boot.'

'These vengeful stalkers,' Rob said. 'Can you give me some examples. I can't for the life of me relate that term to anyone I have on these lists.'

'*For the life of you* is exactly what this is about,' she told him ominously. 'The first thing you have to realise is that this is someone who nurtures an extreme level of anger with you. That anger is being played out through his – let's assume for a moment that it is a him, even though it could just as easily be a woman – murder of these three men. By choosing victims with whom you have had a professional relationship he is trying to make you feel guilty; to shame you.'

'Well he's succeeding.' Rob told her.

She nodded. 'Of course he is. You would have to be particularly hard hearted – probably sociopathic – not to have those feelings right now. Your sense of guilt gives him power over you. It feeds his sense of control; of omniscience. It also places you in very dangerous territory. A place where you feel obliged to make contact with him. To negotiate your way out of this. To understand why he's doing it. To understand what it was that you did to provoke him in the first place.'

Rob knew exactly what she meant. He felt all of that and more. It was what had driven him to go to Rivington alone.

'But you see,' she continued. 'The likelihood is that you haven't done anything wrong. The fact that his whole motivation may be to take vengeance on you – to get even if you like – will almost certainly be based on some insignificant or imagined hurt. There is every possibility that you have never met. That you have had no relationship whatever, personal or professional, other than the one he may have fashioned in his own imaginings. And the most troubling aspect of all of this is that the less contact you have actually had with him, the more delusional, and therefore the more mentally unstable, he will be.'

'And the more dangerous.'

'Precisely.'

'So it's unlikely that he'll be on any of these lists I've compiled?'

'It's not impossible that he or she might be there, but I would say that it is highly unlikely.'

'So how the hell am I supposed to find him?'

She shook her head, and leaned in towards the web cam. 'I don't think that you are going to. Not until he or she is ready. And then it will be him that finds you. Given that you followed all of the instructions you were sent your stalker will believe that he has you exactly where he wants you. He can choose his time and place. And be assured, he will, and probably quite soon. '

'So what do I do?'

Eve Hammond sat back and folded her arms. 'What you should have done in the first place. Nothing. Don't attempt to reply to any of his texts. Don't respond to any of the instructions you've been given. Give DCI Caton your phone, and let the police take it from here. Get a new mobile phone, and give the number only to your family, closest associates, and the police. Take a holiday. And don't tell anyone where you're going.'

Rob could see from her expression that she was giving him the customary advice, but there was no real conviction behind it. 'But that won't stop him will it?' He said.

She sighed. 'No Mr Thornton. It won't stop him. It will probably make him angrier, and more determined. But it may make him more reckless… bring him out into the open where the police can deal with him.'

How much more reckless can he become Rob wondered as he opened the door to his apartment. Three men dead already. How many more to bring him out into the open, and what of Anjelita Andrades? Was he expected to leave her to become victim number four? He dropped his briefcase on the floor, threw his jacket over a chair, and slumped down on the sofa. He took out his mobile phone and checked for messages. There were none. He'd already decided to follow Dr Hammond's advice, and hand over his phone as soon as he had a replacement. He had also decided to take a holiday. With Thomas dead the Barry Moss brief would be going no further than the filing cabinet. The rest of his work was less urgent. And some of it his colleagues at Weir Chambers would pick up. Donald Weir had found it difficult to hide his relief when Rob had told him. Anna on the other hand was visibly upset. When he explained that according to Dr Hammond she was now in real danger herself because his stalker could well perceive her as an obstacle to his goal to get at Rob, she had pleaded with him to let her stay. He had urged her to go back to London at least until things had been resolved. Reluctantly she had agreed. She had some things to sort out she said, then she would leave later today. So now he was alone; with a holiday to plan, a phone to change, and a bag to pack.

He got up, went through to the open plan kitchen, put some coffee beans in the grinder, and filled the coffee maker. As he waited for it to pump through he went to the pictures folder on his mobile phone, and opened the one he had taken in the flat on Back Green Lanes in Islington. Anjelita and Rosa Andrades stared back at him. There was so much innocence in those smiles, so much love in their embrace. Both had lost their innocence within a year of that photo being taken. Rosa had taken her own life. Now Anjelita's hung in the balance. The coffee began to gurgle through the machine. Tears trickled down his cheeks. He knew one thing for certain. He was not going to walk away.

24

After a restless night, waiting for the phone to beep, Rob had a shower, shaved, and dressed. In the kitchen he discovered that he had run out of fruit juice, cereals and bread. Within ten minutes of leaving the Great Northern Tower he was washing down two paracetemol with a cup of coffee in Essy's Café on John Dalton Street, before starting on their full English breakfast. Today was going to be the day. His father would have said he felt it in his water. Rob now knew exactly what he meant. There was a pit in his stomach he was doing his best to fill. But the feeling never went away. He had a sense of foreboding, and at the same time an inexplicable urge to get it over with.

Breakfast demolished, he checked his phone for messages. Still nothing. The photo of Anjelita and her sister Rosa was now his screen saver. A constant reminder and driving force. He pocketed his phone and set off across the city towards the Northern Quarter where Peter Burnmoor had his office.

Burnmoor's agency was used, as a matter of course, by Henry Mayhew. He had done the rooting out of witnesses to the fight in the Stockport pub that had secured a not guilty verdict for Rob's client Matty Bartlett. Rob had never been to the agency before but had been many times to this creative quarter of the city.

Former warehouses and terraced houses now hosted a vibrant mix of fashion houses, art galleries, cafes and music shops by day, clubs, bars, and restaurants by night. He found the agency in a terraced property on Tibbs Street, tucked discretely between a clothes shop and a health food café. The sign on the small bronze plaque beside the door said simply Burnmoor. He turned the handle, and went straight in.

The agency was a tardis. Extended outwards into the former yard, and no longer used for residential purposes, the downstairs rooms had been stripped to the walls, and filled with modern office furniture, desk top computers, and flat screen technology. Along one wall stood a bank of files. Two men and a woman were busy at their keyboards, and a third man, fishing in a cabinet, had his back to Rob. Upstairs – apart from the unisex toilet – there were two offices. The largest and most comfortable belonged to Peter Burnmoor. He rose as Rob entered, and advanced from behind his desk, hand outstretched, a beaming smile on his face.

'Robert Thornton,' he said. 'Delighted to meet you at last. It's an honour.' He pumped Rob's hand up and down for added emphasis. 'I've seen you in court, of course, and I understand I have to thank you for quite a few jobs Henry Mayhew's put my way. Plus that little phone tracing number we did for you.' He led Rob over to a plush brown hide sofa beneath the rear window, and sat down beside him. 'Can I get you a drink?'

Rob shook his head. 'No thanks, I've just had a coffee.'

'Well if you don't mind,' Burnmoor said getting back on his feet, 'I'll just pour myself some water before you tell me why you're here. Refresh my brain so to speak.'

While the private detective filled a beaker from the dispenser in the corner of the room, Rob sized him up. If the stories were true, this former military policeman, and detective sergeant in the Metropolitan Police, had had a chequered career. Whilst not exactly leaving the force under a cloud, it was rumoured that he had chosen the right moment to move jobs, and cities. At six feet one, and fifteen stone, he was an imposing character. A decade desk bound had put too many pounds around his waist, but Rob would still have wanted to be on side in a fight.

'Right,' said Burnmoor, sitting down carefully so as not to spill his water. 'What can I do for you?'

'Well it's a little delicate.' Rob began.

Burnmoor took a sip of water. 'Delicate is my middle name.' He said, his face a mask of discretion.

'I want you to find a woman. A woman I have reason to believe is in danger. Being held against her will. It's imperative that she's found fast, and without alerting the person holding her.'

Burnmoor put the beaker down on the coffee table in front of them. 'Don't you think that's a job for the police?' He said.

Rob shook his head. 'They're already looking for her, and for the person who is holding her. But I've been warned to keep them out of this if I want to see her again.'

'Warned how exactly?'

'By text message.'

'Well that's something. I can trace the phone,' he paused and looked quizzical. 'But then the police will have done that already?'

Rob shook his head. 'He uses different phones each time and then gets rid of them.'

Burnmoor folded his arms. 'So tell me, what's this got to do with you?'

When Rob had finished telling as much as he was prepared to divulge - none of which included the connection with the murders, or the string of messages - Burnmoor got up, and walked over to a cream and chrome filing cabinet behind his desk. He leafed through it, withdrew a folder, closed the drawer, and returned to the sofa. He opened the folder and handed it to Rob. 'Is this the woman you want me to find?' he asked.

Robert stared in amazement at the photographs. There were six of them. They showed Anjelita Covas – whom he know knew to be Andrades - leaving the Midland hotel; crossing St Peters Square; sitting in a cafe drinking from a mug; staring into the shop window of the art deco House of Fraser on Deansgate; entering the hotel lobby. Two pages of typed notes gave an anodyne account of her movements across two days. She had done nothing it seemed except leave the hotel, go once to Bootle Street Police Station, window shop, have a drink of coffee on two occasions in separate cafes, and return to the hotel. More or less repeating the cycle on both days. The dates and time were printed across the top of the photographs. Notes had been scribbled on the back of each. Rob checked the dates. The seventeenth and eighteenth of December. Anjelita had disappeared on the nineteenth. He looked up at Burnmoor. 'I don't understand?' He said.

'Mr Richmond asked us to do a background check, and put a discrete tail on her. I think he wanted to see if there was anything that might discredit her accusations against you...if it ever came to court.'

Rob was stunned. 'Harry Richmond? He mentioned something about me getting a private detective on to it, but I made it clear it was the last thing I wanted at that stage. I thought it might prejudice my case. That it might look like harassment.'

'Well it looks as though he ignored your wishes,' Burnmoor said. 'No doubt he thought he was doing you a favour. Anyway, it only lasted two days; then he called it off. Didn't give a reason. But from what I read in the press I assumed it was because she'd withdrawn her accusation. We never really got anywhere with the background check. Given a little more time we might have done.'

Rob's feelings about Harry Richmond at that moment were mixed. He had ignored their conversation, and could easily have discredited Rob's position had it come to trial. On the other hand, if he'd only kept that tail on for one more day. Then it hit him. He had been told on the nineteenth that she had gone missing, but that was at half past ten on the previous evening. 'When exactly did you call the tail off?' he asked, barely able to contain his excitement. 'At what time on the eighteenth?'

Burnmoor picked up the folder and flicked to the back page. 'Mr Richmond instructed us at nine am on the morning of the nineteenth,' he said. 'I pulled Jack in straight away.'

Rob was on the end of his seat. 'So you're saying he was watching the hotel all night?'

Burnmoor shook his head. 'Not all night. According to this, he went home at midnight, and came back at six in the morning. He could hardly sit in the lobby all night without arousing suspicion. The same goes for outside. The only place he could park up for any length of time would have been the taxi rank at the side of the Central Library.'

Rob wasn't listening. He grabbed the folder from Burnmoor's hands and tapped it with his finger. 'Then he would have seen her leave the hotel,' he said. 'Half past ten on the evening of the eighteenth the police said. Why isn't there a photograph in here?'

'Burnmoor shook his head. I don't know? Maybe he got moved on, and drove round the block. Maybe he was distracted for a moment. It happens.'

Rob threw the folder down on the table. 'Is he here?'

'He was downstairs in the office when you came in. You must have passed him.'

'Why don't we ask him then?'

Burnmoor crossed to his desk, and picked up his phone. He waited, glanced across at Rob, and then looked out of the window. After what seemed an age, he cancelled the call, and tried another line. 'Aisha,' he said. 'Is Jack still there? I need a word.' The expression on his face told Rob all he needed to know. 'No, it doesn't matter,' Burnmoor continued. 'Thanks anyway, I'll try him on his mobile.' He put down the phone and walked back towards the sofa. 'He left just after you arrived. He's on a job - a footballer's wife in Alderley Edge would you believe. Lucky sod. I can't ring him yet, he'll be on the move. Company policy. No phone calls to or from a moving car. One of my staff had a bad smash up on the M60 last year, so I made the decision. It causes us problems, but it was my policy so I can't go breaking it now.'

'That's all right,' Rob said hiding his disappointment. 'I'd rather do it face to face anyway. Who is this Jack exactly?'

'Jack Walsh? Been with me all of nine months. A real find. Very quiet, bit of a loner really, but a natural.'

'What was he doing before he came to you?' Rob asked.

'Bit of this and that for the past few years. Mainly security work. But he had an impressive Service history. Saw action in The Gulf, and In Bosnia. Awards for Bravery. A glowing reference from his old CO. That's what persuaded me to give him a try.' He crossed back to the filing cabinet, and took out another folder. He removed a sheet of A4 from it, and handed it over. 'Here, see for yourself.'

According to his commanding officer, Jack Walsh had been a tank commander in the 7th Brigade of the 1st Armoured Division in January 1991, during Operation Granby – part of the Desert Shield response to Saddam's Hussein's invasion of Kuwait. Striking out of Saudi Arabia, together with the United States Seventh Corps who held overall command, his brigade, together with the 4th Armoured Brigade, had been part of the left hook that had caught out, and destroyed, the bulk of Saddam's elite Republican Guard. In 1995, now promoted to Sergeant, he served in Bosnia as part of Operation Grapple. In both theatres he had carried out acts of extreme bravery for which he had been awarded the Queen's Cross for Gallantry, and bar. In the desert, when another tank in his squadron had been hit by friendly fire, he had risked his life to rescue members of the crew. And again, in Bosnia, under sustained fire he had pulled two men from the vehicle in front that had been blown up by a land mine in a designated Safe Area. At that point he was the most highly decorated member of the regiment in modern history. His decision to leave at the end of his nine year term in 1996 had been a matter of deep disappointment. Rob wasn't surprised that he had wanted to leave it all behind. He could equally understand that his departure would have been seen by the regiment as the loss of a great asset in leadership, training, and recruitment potential.

'His photo's in the file if you'd like to see it.' Burnmoor said. He held the file out in front of him.

A sheet of A4 was stapled to the inside of the front cover. In the top right hand corner, above the date of birth, and contact details, was a head and shoulders shot of a short haired grim looking man approaching forty. As Rob stared at the photograph the colour drained from his face, and the room began to spin. He felt a hand on his shoulder, and heard a voice that seemed to come from far away.

'You know him don't you?' It said. He tore his eyes away from the photograph, and looked up into Burnmoor's anxious face. He nodded

'Yes, I know him.' he said. 'I once saved his life.'

'Look,' Burnmoor said, topping up Rob's coffee. 'He's doing some pretty sensitive stuff for me. If there is something I should know I think you'd better tell me.'

From Rob's point of view, telling Burnmoor everything would leave the private detective with no option but to contact the police himself. Anjelita Andrades meant nothing to him. His business and his reputation meant everything. In his position Rob knew that he'd feel the same. He was still trying to decide how to answer the question when Burnmoor pushed him harder.

'You're thinking that he's behind that woman's disappearance, aren't you?' he said.

'I don't know,' Rob told him. 'It's probably just a coincidence him turning up here. And you were right, there are any number of explanations as to why he might have missed her leaving the Midland that night. Either way, it's best not to let him know we suspect him of anything at all. Please don't tell him I've recognised him, or that I wanted you to track down Ms Andrades. Just give me time to think it through before I talk to the police.'

Burnmoor scratched his head. 'So how am I supposed to explain your coming here?'

'If he asks, just tell him I was lining up a job related to one of my briefs. Something I wanted you to handle personally.'

Burnmoor shook his head. 'That won't work. Everybody knows that Henry Mayhew acts as the go-between. None of you barristers would be seen dead coming here yourselves.'

Rob threw up his hands in exasperation. 'Well just tell him whatever you want, so long as you think he'll believe it. Please just carry on as normal. It'll only be until I've spoken with the police, and either they or I come back to you.'

He could tell that Burnmoor was not convinced. He just hoped that he would go along with it for now. Long enough to buy the time he needed. The trouble was he had no idea how long he actually had.

Half way back to his apartment he found out. His phone told him that he had text. He stopped under the glass covered walkway between the Town Hall and the extension building, took a deep breath, and opened his in box.

It's time we met. I have the girl. You can save her. BUT ONLY IF YOU TELL NO ONE, & Come ALONE. Instructions follow.

No rhymes. No mention of Anjelita. Something told him he'd been too late in sending Anna packing. His heart began to pound. Frantically he rang Reception at the Chambers. Tasha answered.

'Mr Thornton,' she said. 'I thought you were on leave?'

'I am, but I need to speak with Anna as a matter of urgency. Is she still there?'

Tasha sounded wary, and confused. 'Well...no. She left about an hour ago.'

Rob's heart sunk. 'Did she say where she was going?'

'Back to London. I thought you knew? She didn't sound very happy about it.' There was an unspoken question in her voice. Rob could imagine the rumours circulating Chambers about the reasons for his pupil's sudden departure. 'Did she say how she was getting there? When she was leaving?'

'Mid afternoon I think. From Piccadilly Station. But she did say she was going to pop into The Rylands Library first. To finish some research she's been doing. Why? Did you want to...?' She found herself speaking to a continuous tone

Rob was already sprinting across Albert Square. He darted perilously between the streams of taxis on the West side, and ran down the pedestrianised length of Brazenose Street. His onward rush scattered the queue outside Philpotts and sent flying a carton of soup belonging to an unsuspecting customer exiting at that precise moment. At the junction with Deansgate he could see the Gothic red brick library in front of him. The lunchtime traffic was at its usual standstill. He crossed the road and hurried through the automatic doors of the brand new glass and steel entrance. The concierge on the desk was pleased to see him, but concerned at his appearance.

'Mr Thornton,' he said. 'Are you alright? Can I help you?'

'Anna Gardener,' he said breathlessly. 'Is she still here?'

'Yes sir. She went up to Reading Room Reception on Level 4.'

Rob ignored the lift, and raced up the wide stone staircase almost stumbling as he swerved to avoid a couple on the second level landing. The woman at Reader Reception smiled as he approached the desk.

'Hello again Mr Thornton,' she said in a practised librarian's whisper. 'We haven't seen you here for a while.'

Rob could tell that she was reappraising him in the light of everything she had read, seen, and heard about his arrest and exoneration. Ordinarily it might have made him feel uncomfortable, but not right now.

'Anna Gardener,' he said. 'I understand she came up here?'

'Why yes Mr Thornton, she did. I asked her to use the Special Materials Room.' She pointed through the clear glass panels beyond which Rob could see three people busy reading books propped up on foam rests, and making notes. In the centre, over the back of one of the chairs, was Anna's jacket. In front of it lay a legal pad, and a large leather bound book .

'I don't understand,' he said. 'Where is she?'

'Oh, I can't say, Mr Thornton. She popped out about twenty minutes ago. But she's bound to be back. Her things are there as you can see, and her bag is still here in our holding area.'

Rob gripped her hand, pinning it to the counter top. 'If she comes back please ask her to stay where she is till I get back. Tell her it's really, really important. Tell her it's a matter of life or death.'

Flushed and confused, she pulled her hand away, and stepped back a few paces. The other member of staff on duty had witnessed this from the doorway to the collection store. He put down the book in his hand, and came to stand protectively beside her.

'Of course Mr Thornton,' she said, her voice wavering. 'I'll tell her.'

His sense of panic rose as he moved from floor to floor, racing down the huge stone spiral staircase, searching the dark and gloomy rooms on either side. Close to despair he entered the Historic Reading Room.

She was standing with her back towards him, beneath the delicate arching tracery of the Cumbrian granite roof. She was staring up at the white marble statue of Enriquetta Rowlands, the benefactor of this library, surrounded by the largest collection of rare books and manuscripts in Britain. He touched her gently on the shoulder, half expecting it to be someone else. It startled her from her reverie.

'Oh, Rob, it's you,' she said with evident relief, and not a little surprise. You nearly made me jump out of my skin.'

He took her by the arm. 'Never mind that,' he whispered. 'Let's get out of here. We need to talk.'

25

They sat in The Café at the Rylands. She with a skinny latte, and a toasted tea cake, Rob with a glass of mineral water. It was all he could face.

'You saved his life?' she said. 'So why wasn't he on the list of people who might have thought they owed you? He'd be number one on mine, no messing.'

Rob shook his head wearily. 'It was a long time ago. Instinctive. I never really gave it a thought afterwards. I didn't even find out his name.'

'So how come you're so certain that Jack Walsh is the man you saved?'

'His face. As soon as I saw it everything came back to me. As vividly as if it was yesterday.' The hand holding his glass began to shake.

She put her hand on his to steady it. 'It might help if you tell me about it.'

He put the glass down, and looked at her.

'Seriously,' she said. 'It's better out than in, my mother always says.'

It made him smile. Gave him the courage to remember. 'It was about ten years ago,' he began. 'I was up in town visiting an aunt who lived on her own in a flat in Praed Street, in Paddington. She was in her eighties, with tunnel vision. Registered blind, but it didn't stop her crossing the Edgware Road and Baker Street every day to get to the shops and the street markets. She would just hold up her white stick, and march across.'

Anna listened patiently. She sensed that none of this was relevant; just his way of getting there.

'I suppose,' he continued, 'When you've lived through what she did – brought up in an orphanage, rising to become housekeeper to the Duke of Westminster, dismissed because she'd fallen for a footman twenty years her junior, the Blitz, losing him to a freak accident - braving the London traffic is a picnic. When I left the flat I needed to stretch my legs for a bit, so I walked up to the Regents Canal, and followed it all the way to Ladbroke Grove, where I decided to take the tube. I have no idea why I chose to go that way. I'd never done before.' He looked into his glass as though expecting to find an answer there. 'If I hadn't, none of this would have happened…be happening now.' He swirled the water around in his glass, drank some, and set it down. 'I was waiting on the platform, southbound. It was a quarter to one in the afternoon; moderately busy. There were about twenty other people waiting. A man was standing stock still in front of me, staring down at the tracks. It immediately struck me as odd. He was motionless. Focused. Like those street artists you see these days that dress up, or paint themselves, and pretend to be statues. I heard the rumble of the train, and saw him tense. Then he stepped beyond the yellow safety line. It was the way he bent his knees. I knew he was going to jump. I wasn't the only one. I heard someone gasp behind me, and a woman off to the left had her hand to her mouth, and was pointing. The front of the train appeared in the mouth of the tunnel, the brakes were only just being applied. Without thinking, I rushed forward, grabbed his shoulders, and pulled him back and sideways. We fell to the floor. I felt a rush of wind on my face from the slipstream of the train. Above the squeal of the brakes, and the clatter of the wheels on the rails, I could hear someone screaming.' He looked up at her. 'Do you know, the strangest thing was that he didn't struggle? Just let me pin him there until the police arrived. As they led him away he looked back at me, over his shoulder. The look on his face was full of pain and anguish. The nearest I can get to describing it is that painting by Edvard Munch…'

'The Scream,' she said.

'That's it. The tortured figure, clutching his head in torment against a blood red sunset over Oslo Fiord. But there was something else as well; disappointment, reproach. I don't know. I didn't hang around. Just gave a statement to the Railway Police, and that was the last I heard until now. What I don't understand is how he tracked me down, and why?'

'How, is easy,' she said. 'He only had to check your name with the police. He could have said that he wanted to thank you. Or maybe he saw your face in the papers, or on TV. Let's face it, it's not as though you've been keeping a low profile these past few years. As for why? You'll only know that when we find him.

He shook his head. 'When I find him, if he doesn't find me first.'

'We've had this conversation before,' she said. 'You've got to leave it to the police. Especially now that you know it's personal.'

'I can't.'

'Why not?'

'You know why not.'

'Anjelita?'

'Yes.'

'You don't owe her anything. She tried to pull you down. OK, we don't know why, but she did. Has it never occurred to you that she might be working with this man…Jack Walsh?'

She could tell from his expression that it had never crossed his mind; not for a moment had he even considered it.'

'Well think about it,' she pressed. 'Isn't it a bit of a coincidence, her turning up out of blue at the same time that he's here? And as for the stuff I found on the web, how do you know a word of it is true? What's to say she didn't fabricate the story to suck you in?'

Rob pushed the glass away and put his head in his hands. It was too much for him to take in.

'You are going to have to tell the police,' she said. 'Now you think you know who it is, they can follow him. If he has got Anjelita – if that really is her name – they're equipped to deal with that. You're not. Come on Rob, you know it make sense.'

'Alright,' he said at last. 'I'll tell the police. But not till I've seen you on that train.' He pushed back his chair, and stood up. 'Come on. Let's get your things.'

He waited until her train pulled out, and then made his way back to the multi storey car park. He had never had any intention of going to the police. Anna had been right. It was personal. This was about him, and Walsh. Anjelita was the bait to bring them face to face. The minute he stopped taking the bait, he felt certain that Walsh would dispose of her. It was a risk he was not prepared to take. His connection with Anjelita had put her at risk, just as his connection with the three dead men had made them targets. If he had had any doubts about seeing it through to the end, the phone call to Burnmoor had quashed them. Walsh had not been in contact all day. His mobile phone number was unobtainable. He had not turned up at his appointment with the client, who had rung the agency to express her anger. It was all he could do to stop Burnmoor from ringing the police himself. He fingered the piece of paper in his pocket on which he had noted the address beneath the photograph in Walsh's personnel file. It was where he headed next.

He had been here for over an hour. The light was beginning to fail as evening drew in. Patches of shadow marked out the distance between the street lamps. Rob felt far too conspicuous parked up in his car on Newcastle Street. Not only was his the most expensive car in this part of Hulme, but he was in someone's designated parking space. It could only be a matter of time before they asked what the hell he was doing there. But it was the only place from which he could see the entrance to the address Walsh had given.

There was a tap on his window. He turned expecting to find an angry resident telling him to bugger off. Instead, a callow mixed race youth, astride a mountain bike, and wearing a hooded jacket, signalled him to wind down the window. In his right hand he held a package. Relieved that he had locked the doors, Rob released the window to create a gap of less than an inch.

'What do you want?' He asked.

'You'll afta do betta dan dat man.' The youth replied, holding up what looked like a medium sized Jiffy bag. 'I nevfa get dis fru dere.'

'What is it?' Rob asked.

'I doe know do I?, the boy replied, exasperated. 'Djoo wan it, or not?'

'Who gave it to you?'

'Look, I've ad enuff o' dis.' He placed the package against the windscreen, and cycled off at speed, pulling back the handlebars to execute a couple of contemptuous wheelies as he went.

Rob checked the mirrors, opened the window, and reached out to retrieve the package. He closed the window again, and stared at the jiffy bag on his lap. It was much heavier than he had expected. He turned it over to see if there was anything written on it. There was not. He opened his glove box and took out the combined bottle opener and corkscrew he kept there for emergencies. He levered opened the small knife blade, and slid it carefully beneath the sealed flap. Holding the bag as far away as possible from his face he gently shook the contents out onto the passenger seat beside him.

There was a video tape, a small brass key, and a handheld device with a small screen set in a black case. There were press buttons on either side. Across the top the name, Route-It. It didn't take a genius to tell this was a GPS satellite navigation device. Rob picked up the GPS. He turned it over and examined it. He had no idea how to switch it on, let alone use it.

He put it back in the Jiffy bag together with the key and tape, and placed the bag in the glove compartment, which he closed and locked. He had been in court enough times to know that just stopping at traffic lights with such a device on the passenger seat was enough to invite the smashing of a window, and an arm snaking in to snatch it. He checked his mirrors again, but could only see the outlines of other cars parked up. It was clear that his cover was blown. That's how both police and criminals liked to describe it. Here he'd sat thinking he was watching Walsh, when it was actually the other way round. He started up the engine, switched on the lights, and set off.

The tape was short, and graphic. Just like the text messages. With one terrifying difference.

She was sitting on a straight backed chair, wearing a white shirt tucked into a pair of belted blue jeans. Her hair was up. She wore no make. The bruises she had self inflicted had healed, but her face was pale and drawn. Her eyes stared straight at the camera, boring through the lense. It was almost as if she could see him. He could tell that she was petrified. She bent down and picked up something. As she straightened, he could see that it was a copy of the Manchester Evening News. She held it up to the camera which zoomed in until the date stared back at him. January 2nd. This morning's edition. The camera zoomed out again. She lowered the paper, and let it drop to the floor. After a short pause, during which her gaze shifted up she reached forward with her right hand and took a slip of paper the cameraman must have handed her. She read it to herself, and then looked up at the camera. He could see that she was fighting back tears. She swallowed, and then began to read out loud. Her words were charged with emotion; so faint that he could barely make them out.

'Robert. Tonight we meet again.' She paused, and looked up, listening. Someone was prompting her from behind the camera. She began again, louder this time. 'Robert. Tonight we meet again. I believe I have cancelled my debt to you. Now it is your turn. It would be a pity...a pity for Anjelita to have to suffer anymore. Come alone, and I...assure you I will let her go. Do not, and...' Her voice caught in her throat. She struggled over the words. '...and I will kill her.'

She looked up at the camera. Appealing. This was no act. He could see she was close to collapse. The camera lingered on her for a moment. She began to speak again. This time unscripted.

'Robert...I am sorry. Forgive...'

White lines began to flicker across a blank screen. He leapt to his feet, swearing. He punched the wall over and over again, venting feelings of anger, guilt, and impotence. Behind him, another picture appeared on the television screen. Only when the pain in his fist began to register did he turn, and see it. A piece of flip chart paper had been pinned to the back of a door. On it, printed with a felt tip pen, were a set of instructions. He realised that the nearest biro was in the kitchen beside the fridge. By the time he'd got it, together with one of the pieces of card he used to write messages on, the screen was blank. He cursed, and pressed rewind. At the appropriate place he paused the picture, and began to copy the instructions down. As soon as he'd finished he pressed play to see if he had missed anything else. There was nothing. He sat down on the sofa to read them through.

They told him to how to switch the GPS on, and at what time; ten pm. They gave him step by step instructions to select the route. He was to follow it to the destination. When he arrived he would find a padlock securing a metal cover. He was to use the key to unlock the padlock, raise the cover, and climb down the ladder he would find beneath it. He was to close the cover behind him. He would find further instructions at the bottom of the ladder. He was to bring a torch, warm clothes, and non slip shoes. He was to tell no one, and come alone. That was it. He read them through twice more, hoping to find some clues as to the destination; some inkling to the purpose of this rendezvous. It was hopeless. His mind began to create increasingly horrific scenarios. None of them with a happy ending.

His hand was really hurting now. The pain dragged him back to reality. He went into the kitchen and ran his fist under the cold water tap for several minutes. He splashed his face, and dried it on a tea towel. He looked at his watch. It was a quarter to seven. A little over three hours in which to sort himself out. Too long to wait; too short to find another way. He went through to the wet room, and began to strip.

At ten o'clock precisely, Rob stepped into Peter Street. A gentle misty drizzle settled on his hair and face. He was wearing trainers, blue jeans, and a dark blue fleece with matching anorak. His inside zipped pocket held the microlite torch he kept in the apartment for power cuts. In his left hand he held the GPS. He switched it on, and from the menu selected Route. He expected a map of the city to appear, just like the one on the satnav device in his car. He was disappointed. A single large dot pulsed in the bottom centre of the screen. An arrow extended from it showing the required direction of travel. He pulled up the hood of his anorak, and set off head down. The arrow led him east south east, down Windmill Street, behind the Radisson hotel – the former Free Trade Hall – and the Midland Hotel, across the square in front of the G-Mex centre, and south south west onto Lower Mosley Street. Opposite the Bridgewater Concert Hall, at the junction with Great Bridgewater Street, it led him west for a hundred metres, and then north into Weston Street. Close to the entrance to the NCP car park, the arrow stopped moving. The pulsing slowed, and on the screen five words appeared:

You have reached your destination.

Rob looked around in disbelief. According to the information on the screen he had travelled precisely seven hundred and seventy eight metres, in almost a complete circle from the point where he had started. He looked up and could see the balcony to his own apartment high up on the nineteenth floor of the Great Northern Tower. He looked back down at the ground but could see no sign of a padlock. He tried walking further down the pavement, and found the arrow leading him back. He began to cross the road, and was told that that he was moving away from his destination. It was only when he stepped behind the railings to one side of the car park entrance that he saw it.

The padlock secured a large rectangular metal manhole cover set into a raised concrete frame set in stone. Rob looked around to see if anyone was watching. Apart from the odd car that sailed past, a mist of spray in its wake, the street was empty. Even if a car were to drive off the road, and into the car park entrance he doubted that anyone would notice him. He was in shadow, and they would be concentrating on avoiding the walls and barriers. The padlock, like the key he held in his hand, looked brand new. It would have been an easy matter, Rob reasoned, for Walsh to use bolt cutters to remove the original lock, and replace it with his own. There were cameras in this car park he was sure, and it was manned, although the staff were rarely in evidence. He had no idea how Walsh had managed to spend time here unseen, let alone bring an unwilling victim. It was immaterial. He was here now, had not been challenged, and the key fitted perfectly. He slipped the padlock into his pocket and turned his attention to the lid. To Rob's relief, it was hinged; supported by sliding brackets on either side. On the side nearest to the lock an iron ladder, enclosed in a cage of steel rings, disappeared into a deep black hole. He shone his torch, hoping to catch sight of the bottom. He fancied he saw a flash of reflected light from a pool of water. He climbed gingerly over the edge, pulled the lid down behind him, and began to descend. He had the sensation of entering a tomb. Of descending into Hell.

26

On the way down he counted the rungs. There were thirty three. Above him was the car park. Above that, the G-MEX Conference Centre. Below his feet, were a solid stone and concrete floor, and a succession of small pools of standing water, no more than an inch or two in depth.

Despite the narrowness of the beam of his torch he was easily able to locate the package. It was fixed by gaffer tape to the iron bolts securing the ladder to the wall. Another Jiffy bag. He cradled the bag in the crook of his left arm so that he could shine the torch on it with his left hand, leaving his right hand free to reach inside.

As soon as his hand touched the heavy object he knew what this was. It invited his hands to curl around and cradle it. Not that the shape was that familiar to him. No more than it would have been to any man of his generation who as a child had played with toys assumed appropriate for boys. He drew it out into the microlite's harsh beam. It was a gun. Black, charcoal grey perhaps. Difficult to tell with out reference points. Not metal. Some kind of heavy plastic; a polymer perhaps. He had never held a real gun before. The handle was ribbed for the fingers to curl around. With the exception of the rearmost section, the barrel was flat and smooth – like a rectangular box. There was a guard around the trigger – he presumed to prevent it from being fired by accident. Immediately beneath the barrel, in the same gun metal grey, was a box like device, the size of a small video camera, at the front of which was a lens. Like a torch. He had no idea what it was. Gingerly, ensuring that the barrel was pointing away from his body, he turned the pistol on its side. Along its length were etched a number of letters and symbols. He changed the angle of the torch so that he could make them out.

Lock 19   AUSTRIA   9x19

And then it struck him. What he had taken for a squiggle around the L of Lock, was in fact a G. This was a Glock pistol. 9 millimetre. There had been a case where he had been asked to appeal a British Army court martial. It concerned the accidental firing of a Glock pistol that had resulted in a near fatal injury. He had not taken the brief, but he recalled the details. He felt he should put it in the pocket of his anorak, but was frightened that it might go off. There were protrusions on the grip, and beside the trigger. He wondered if one might be the safety catch. He realised that even if he could decide he would have no idea which was off; which on. He unzipped the left hand pocket of his anorak on the basis that if it did discharge it would do the least damage, and slipped it gingerly inside.

There was something else in the bag; something white. Rob pulled out a crude map drawn by hand on a piece of A4 printer paper. He turned it over to check the other side. It was a letter head. For the Burnmoor Agency. He shivered again. Assuming that Walsh was behind it, he was no longer at pains to hide his identity. Which could only mean that he had no expectation that Rob would live long enough to reveal it. Then why give him a gun? Was it a cruel trick? Perhaps the magazine was empty. Bar pressing the trigger, there was no way of finding out.

The map showed what looked like a continuous tunnel that ran through four separate larger areas of varying size. Rob knew that the Great North Eastern railway had loaded and unloaded goods and materials for the warehouses immediately above him. Perhaps this had been a store, or wagon way. The map gave him no clues as to the purpose of this underground network. It did, however, tell him where he was, and where he needed to be. A cross in one corner of the third of the larger areas bore the legend:

YOU ARE HERE.

Beside another cross, just inside the fourth, were the words:

WE ARE HERE. THE WW2 WARDEN'S POST. WAITING.

He folded the map in two to make it easier to handle, and began to explore the chamber in which he stood, quartering it with the torch's beam.

As far as he could gauge the space was some twenty metres long by eight metres wide. The walls were of old red brick, dusted white with what he presumed was either mildew, or crystallized salt that had leached from the mortar, or the bricks themselves.

Brick arches had been built to further strengthen the roof. Two lines of yellow cable, high up the walls, snaked along the side of the chamber and disappeared around a corner. It suggested there was, or had been, power down here. Emergency lighting perhaps. But he could see no lights. It sounded from the map as though this place had been used as an air raid shelter during the Second World War. It made perfect sense. It would take a very special bomb to drill its way through the six levels, the basement, and reinforced roof of this complex. Towards the end furthest from him two huge brick pillars, several metres apart, four metres wide and several metres deep, rose to the ceiling. In the one closest to him, at head height, an opening the size of a door revealed a hollow centre. Some kind of lift or winching shaft, was his best guess, for whatever was moved between these levels at the height of the Industrial Revolution. He checked the map again to see if these shafts were marked. They were not. He took a bearing on the ladder down which he had climbed, and started walking.

The exit from the chamber was into a tunnel the width of a small street, strewn with broken bricks and a century's accumulation of dust. He kept close to the left hand side, trailing his hand along the dank wall to aid his balance. In less than a minute he found himself in another chamber; much larger than the first. The ceiling was high and vaulted. He heard a scurrying sound, and his heart skipped a beat. He lowered the torch, and followed the sound. A rat the size of a domestic cat stopped, and froze for a moment, caught in the centre of the beam. Its beady eyes seemed to glow. He could see the whiskers on its face twitching; slivers of silver. Then, as suddenly, it was gone. As he moved the beam across the floor he discovered that it was lower than the stone flags on which he was standing. Seven courses of brick, and one huge stone block, lower. Four stone steps led down into the basin. As he raked the beam back towards him it picked out a massive stone bollard, a metre high, close to the steps. He knew exactly where he had seen one of these before. At Salford Docks. It was a mooring bollard. He could see it now. He was standing on the former tow path of an underground canal. A canal that must have linked the basin at Castlefield with the railway terminus of the Great Northern Eastern Railway. The winching shafts in the other chamber would have raised and lowered the goods between the canal bed below him, and the railway yards above. He checked the map again. From the shape and size of this chamber, he could tell that he was in the second of the chambers. According to the map, Walsh and Anjelita were waiting in chamber four. He had set off in the wrong direction. Cursing, he turned around and hurried back.

Hurrying was his first mistake. He tripped on a piece of broken stone and fell full length. In an attempt to cushion his fall he instinctively rolled to his left, hitting the stone floor with his shoulder. His head struck the side of the tunnel. The torch went flying. And there was darkness.

When he came round his head was aching, his hands and knees stung, a floating rib in his left side hurt like hell where the gun had been rammed against it. The pain in his shoulder was excruciating. He levered himself into a sitting position, his back against the tunnel wall. He felt his shoulder. The pain ran the length of his collar bone; where it met his shoulder, the bone protruded. He wondered if he had broken his shoulder, or dislocated it. He unzipped the front of his anorak part of the way, and using his right hand gently manoeuvred his left arm until it was inside the anorak; the hand tucked beneath his right armpit. Then he zipped up again as far as he could get it to go. It was the nearest he could manage to a sling. The effort, and the pain, left him feeling sick. He sat there for a moment cursing his stupidity; feeling sorry for himself. He knew that he had to find the torch. On hands and knees he inched forward. Each contact worsened the pain in them, but none of that compared with the pain in his shoulder. He found the torch, and felt the glass lens cover. It appeared to be intact. Making a silent prayer he clamped the torch between his knees, and turned the end with the fingers of his right hand. The beam appeared. He placed the end of the torch in his mouth and shone it on his right hand.

The whole of his palm had been cut and grazed. The wounds were bloody but superficial. He thought about washing away the dirt and dust in the water in the chamber ahead of him. Then he remembered the rat, and thought better of it. A friend of Harry Richmond had caught Wiels disease while water skiing and had died a painful death. Instead he wiped it lightly on the side of his jeans, the knees of which were scuffed but intact although blood was seeping through the one on the left. He touched the side of his head where it had struck the wall, and felt a bump the size of a walnut. When he brought his fingers away they were red, and sticky. He swore to himself, wiped his hand on his jeans again, took the torch from his mouth, clambered painfully to his feet, and moved slowly, and carefully, down the tunnel.

Beyond chamber three the level appeared to change. A set of steps headed down into a smaller chamber. To his right, a huge stone arch rose up to support the wall on his left. Below him, at the foot of the steps, the beam showed a small, box like, brick building – no more than three metres high – jutting out into the chamber. A curved and metal pipe protruded from an aluminium funnel set into the flat roof. As the beam panned down it caught an opening, perhaps a foot high and eighteen inches wide, two thirds of the way up the wall facing him. It also captured Anjelita's ashen tear strewn face. Her mouth was taped. Her eyes blinked in the torch's glare A gun – not unlike the one in Rob's pocket - was hard against her right temple.

Rob was no longer aware of the pain in his body. Adrenalin coursed through his veins. His heart raced. Before he could think what to do or say a voice filled the chamber, bouncing off the arches and the walls, echoing down the tunnels. It was a voice he had never heard before, except in his imagination. Low and measured. Exuding confidence and control. Strong, yet somehow fragile; pained. A mass of contradictions.

'At last Robert. We'd almost given up on you. No. Don't say anything. And don't move. Just stay where you are. Sit down on that step. And switch off that torch. You no longer need it.'

Rob did as he was told. As the light went out another came on. It illuminated the whole of Anjelita's head and face, and as much of the chamber as a trio of church candles might have done. She turned her head to the side and Rob could see her only in profile. Her shadow, greatly magnified, flickered on the opposite wall. The hand holding the gun moved until the tip of the barrel rested against the base of her neck.

'So you came Robert,' said a disembodied voice out of the shadows of the warden's post. 'And now do you remember? Do you know who I am?'

'Jack Walsh.'

'Very good. And you remember when last we met?'

'On the Underground. I thought you were going to kill yourself.'

There was a pause. He thought he heard something like a deep sigh.

'You were right. I was. Until you came along.'

Rob had no idea where this was leading, but reasoned that it was best to keep him talking. Wasn't that what they said; keep them talking? Something will turn up, he told himself. It had to. 'But I don't understand Jack,' he said, as calmly as he could manage. 'Why would you want to take your own life. You were a hero...are a hero. You saved the lives of those men. Why would you take your own? I don't understand.'

This time the voice was louder, more strained. Rob sensed there was a bitterness there, and anger barely held in check.'

'No you don't. Why should you? That's why you had no right to interfere. Why you had no bloody right to interfere in my life. Or in my death!'

The gun wavered. Anjelita appeared to cringe, seeking refuge against the wall. Rob sat up, alert. His hand felt for the bulge in his anorak pocket. The gun in Walsh's hand steadied, and then moved back a fraction allowing Anjelita to straighten up. Strands of hair fell across her face. Walsh began to speak again.

'You say I'm a hero? I'll tell you about that. The twenty Fifth of February 1991. The second day of Desert Storm. We were in amongst the elite of the Americans. Out of Saudi and into Iraq at last. We wanted to show the Americans what we could do. I was in too much of a hurry...I wanted us to be right up there with the action. I pushed our tank ahead of the line. Our troop commander accelerated to get ahead of us...to slow us down. We were too near the enemy positions when the air strike was called up. They were hit because we were too close to the Iraqis...because I forced the pace.'

'As I understand it,' Rob said. 'It was a lot more complicated than that. You hadn't been issued with proper markings capable of being identified from the air. The Americans had the technology to enable them to recognise their own vehicles – you didn't. Their pilots were National Guard – trained at weekends. No combat experience. Gung ho. You can't blame yourself for any of that.'

'There you go again. Thinking you know better!' He was shouting now. His voice ringing off the curved brick ceiling. 'I was there...I was fucking well there! Where were you? At home in bed? Watching it on the television like it was some kind of computer game? Well I'm telling you, and you're bloody well going to listen!' His words echoed through the tunnels, and faded. Then there was silence.

When he spoke again his voice had gone quiet. Almost a whisper. Muffled by the wall between them. Rob had to strain to hear.

'I forced the pace. I *forced* the fucking pace. We should not have been there. They should *not* have died.' He paused for a moment, adjusting the torch as though his arm had begun to cramp. The beam jerked away from Anjelita's face for a second. It settled again. She opened her eyes, startled. Fearful that something was about to happen. As Walsh began to speak again, she bowed he head and closed her eyes. He could see her willing it all to end.

'You think I saved the life of those men?' Walsh demanded. 'You think there was a fairytale ending? Or maybe like *The English Patient* he falls in love with his nurse, and she with him? Gerry had ninety per cent burns. He was due to get married that summer. His fiancé couldn't take it. He didn't even want her to. They were never going to have proper sex...let alone children. He wasn't going to walk again, let alone work. He couldn't sit or lie still for more than five minutes at a time. He couldn't sleep at night. I went to see him just the once...I could barely bring myself to look at him. Not because of his injuries... what he looked like. But because of what I'd done to him. Not just the once...twice. I'd put him in harm's way, and then made sure he'd live to suffer for the rest of his life. He tried to put me at my ease. Put on a brave face,' he choked at that. 'A brave face; can you believe I said that? He didn't have a face – just a mask with a hole for his eyes, and what was left of his mouth. Not his ears mind. He didn't have any. The more he tried to thank me, to pretend he was grateful, the worse I felt. I couldn't wait to get out of there. And he knew. He understood. I turned just the once…as I got to the door. His eyes had followed me. I could tell he was thinking. *Why did you pull me out of there? Why didn't you let me die with the others?* The day they took the bandages off what was left of his hands, he began collecting the pain killers. That's what they reckoned anyway. He'd pretend to take them. God knows he had enough places to hide them. A whole week they reckon he waited…to be sure he had enough. Seven days he let them think his pain was under control. God, he must have been in agony. Do you know how many seconds there are in a week? I do. Six hundred and four thousand, eight hundred. That's bravery. Not what I did.'

He was quiet for a moment. Rob didn't know what to say. Walsh was right. There was nothing he could say.

'Do you know where we were headed when they got Gerry's tank? Kuwait. It meant crossing the road to Basra. Does that mean anything to you? Does it?

Rob's brain wasn't functioning down here. He had a feeling he should know; that it was on the tip of his tongue.

'The Highway to Hell,' Walsh told him. 'That's what they called it. Now do you remember?'

Rob did. He recalled being fascinated and appalled in equal measure as the television footage panned across the columns of black and burning vehicles strewn either side of the road.

'The Yanks told us it was like shooting fish in a barrel. Mile after mile of lorries, trucks, cars, and requisitioned buses. One thousand four hundred of them. Anything that could move was on that road. There was the odd tank or two, but bugger all that had the capacity to fire back.'

He went silent again.

'We arrived as night was falling. What I remember is the smoke, and the smell. The air was rank…a mixture of burning diesel fuel, charred flesh, and human hair. There were people - American soldiers and civilians returned from the desert where they'd taken shelter - moving among the wreckage, prising open the boots of vehicles. Taking whatever they could find. It was impossible to know who was looting, and who was simply trying to retrieve their own belongings. Out troop commander said not to intervene. We just trundled on by. There was a boy… about seven…sat in the ditch beside the road. He had his head in his hands. Rocking to and fro. His mouth was wide open, but no sound came out.'

Just like your face on the Underground platform as they led you away, thought Rob.

'And we just trundled on by.' Walsh repeated in a monotone. 'We just trundled on by.'

This time the silence dragged on. The beam of the torch clung stubbornly to Anjelita's face. Water dripped like a metronome, slowly and methodically, from the high roof. Each staccato contact with the tunnel floor echoing for a fraction of a second. It felt as though all the clocks in the world had stopped. And time stood still.

27

Just when Rob thought he could stand it no longer, Walsh began to speak again. 'I don't know how I managed to get it together after that,' he said. 'But I did. They said I'd get flash backs. They were wrong. I didn't. Not then. I got on with the job. Threw myself into it. Got promoted. I had to go to the Palace to get my medal. It made me sick to the stomach. I felt like screaming...*I don't deserve this! Don't you get it? It was my fault!* I just wanted to get out of there. Then there was Bosnia. We baby sat the humanitarian convoys, and had to watched while the killings went on. The massacres, the genocide. You tell me what was humanitarian about that? Standing by while they got on with it. Laughing in our faces. Mining the tracks the convoys used.'

Once again, he stopped talking.

Rob had no sense of whether he was remembering, or trying to forget. He decided to fill the silence; tentatively. Hoping to demonstrate empathy. To build the foundations of a relationship. He had the feeling this was a story Jack Walsh had waited a long time to tell. What was it Anna had said? Better out than in. Perhaps that would be enough. Perhaps it was all he wanted. To be heard. To be understood.

'That must have been hard,' Rob said. 'After all, you were trained to fight back. To protect the innocent. That was what you joined up for in the first place.' He waited for a response. When none came he decided to take the risk of continuing. 'At least you saved those lives. When the land mine went off?'

Walsh started talking softly. His voice barely audible. It was almost as though he was talking to himself.

'That was when it really started. The driver and the front seat passenger were dead. The truck was on its side, on fire. They told me the ones I pulled clear were fine. Just minor burns and shrapnel. They wanted to meet me afterwards, but I didn't want to see them. It would only have reminded me of Gerry. But that was the least of my worries.'

His voice cracked. Then he laughed. It was a strange sound. Haunting. Like a caged animal.

'That night the flashbacks started. And the panic attacks. They came in waves. Every day. Not just at night, but whenever it was dark or in a confined space. I couldn't get in a tank or an armoured car. I got pains in my chest, stomach cramps, I could hardly breathe. My heart would suddenly start to race. I'd break out in pools of sweat. They gave me sedatives…and Beta Blockers. Anti-depressants …Valium and Prozac. The gaps between the attacks increased but they didn't go away. Or the flash backs. The funny thing was, it was never Gerry I saw…or the blazing truck. It was that kid in the ditch on the road to Basra. The bottom line was, I could get through the day but I couldn't function. Not as a soldier. They wanted to invalid me out. I didn't want that. I asked if I could resign. They said I would lose a load of benefits. I didn't care. I just wanted out of there. With some dignity. And to sever all my links with the Army. I thought that would do it. I was wrong.'

This time the silence went on and on. Anjelita wasn't moving. It was as though she was in a trance. Rob felt compelled to try again.

'What happened Jack?' he asked as gently as possible. This time the response was almost instantaneous.

'I lasted three months on the outside. Then they had me sectioned. Admitted to a secure psychiatric hospital.'

Rob could barely believe it. 'They sectioned you? The Army sectioned you?'

The light from the torch moved slightly. Rob imagined Walsh shaking his head.

'Not the army. My parents.'

'Your parents?'

'I would have done the same. I was living with them…if you could call that living. They thought I was going to kill myself. They were right. They didn't know what else to do.' He paused, as though gathering himself. When he spoke again his voice had hardened. 'Do you know how they found out I was going to kill myself Robert? Do you?'

Rob had no idea. 'No,' he said.

'The police contacted them. They were holding me in a cell in Paddington Green Police Station, on the Harrow Road. They were told I had just been prevented from throwing myself in front of a train on the Hammersmith and City Line.'

A chill ran through Rob. He had forgotten how cold it was down here.

'The police surgeon's advice was short, and to the point. If I was sectioned, there was a chance that I'd get the help…the treatment I needed. If not, it was certain that I'd finish the job that had been so rudely interrupted. What choice did they have Robert. You tell me that? What choice did you give them?'

Rob thought it unfair. The logic twisted. He knew there was no point in saying so. But he could see it all coming together.

'They tried more drugs. When that didn't work, they tried electroconvulsive therapy. And then electro therapy. I suffered memory loss. The panic attacks went away, and the flashbacks became less frequent. Then there was psycho-therapy. It was pointless. I went along with it because I just wanted to get out of there. My memory began to return. And with it the flashbacks. I didn't tell them...but they guessed. Then one day a woman from the British Legion came to tell me that my father had died of cancer. I think the doctors expected me to crack up again. But I was just numb. Six months later she was back again. My mother had died in her sleep she said. A heart attack they thought. A broken heart more like. That got to me. I pleaded with them to give me something. To let me just slip away in my sleep like she'd done. There was no way they were going to do that. Instead they gave me Stelazine. Waited until the psychiatrist said I was stabilised...then they kicked me out... discharged me.'

He began to sob. It was the most distressing sound that Rob had ever heard. Somewhere between a child and a wounded animal. Anjelita heard it too. She lifted her head and turned it ever so slowly until she was facing Rob where he sat on the edge of the pool of reflected light. She looked puzzled and confused. No wonder Rob thought. She has been held captive for over a fortnight. Now the man with the gun to her head was cracking up. He wanted to tell her it would be alright. To reassure her somehow. The best he could do was nod, and mime the words instead.

Rob knew this was approaching its climax, whatever that might be. He might never get a better chance. He slowly unzipped the left hand pocket of his anorak, praying that the sound of the sobbing would mask what little noise he made. He had no idea if Walsh was able to see him. As a precaution, he inched his backside up onto a higher step; further into the shadow. It was awkward trying to get his hand around the pistol grip from this angle, and so instead he eased it out barrel first, praying that it would not go off. The torch like device beneath the barrel caught against the zipper and became stuck. As he tried to work it free Walsh coughed twice. Rob froze.

Walsh began to speak. He sounded totally different. Like another person. This voice was older; deeper; menacing. About every word there was an air of finality. It brooked no interruption. Anjelita recognised it too. Where there had been supplication and confusion in her eyes, there was now terror.

'I had nowhere to go,' Walsh intoned. 'Except that empty house. I had no job. But I had a purpose. I sold the house for instant cash to a speculator, and moved into digs. With my service record it didn't take long to get work with a security firm. I lied about what I'd been doing for the past three years. Said it was undercover work. I don't think they even bothered to check. It took me two years to find out who you were, and where you lived. I moved North. Got a job with Burnmoor. You know the rest.'

'But I don't understand what it is you want.' Rob said. 'What Anjelita has to do with all of this. Why can't you just let her go?'

'She was just a means to an end. To get you here.'

'How did you know I would try to find her? That I would care what happened to her?'

'Because everything I learnt about you confirmed what I suspected. You have a God complex Robert. That's why you do what you do. If you hadn't been a barrister you would have been a surgeon. You pick and choose the people you want to defend or prosecute. The deserving, and the undeserving. You feel you have the right to intervene in other people's lives. Just as you intervened in mine.'

Rob sensed that he was smiling now.

'Do you think you would have come if I'd simply asked you to?' Walsh continued. He waited in vain for Rob's reply.

'I thought not.' He continued. 'I was wondering how to manage it, and then I was asked to follow her. When I learned what she'd done - her connection to you - I almost pissed myself. '

So Anna was wrong. Anjelita had nothing to do with this. 'Why was it so important to get me down here?' Rob asked.

'Because I wanted you to feel something of what I felt. Experience something of what I went through. The terror. The confusion. The loss of control. It's funny, but the one thing that all the drugs and therapy did achieve was that I lost my fear of the dark; of confined spaces. In fact...I lost my fear of everything.'

In the darkness, Rob shifted his grip on the pistol until it fitted neatly in his hand. His index finger curled around the outside of the trigger guard. He had no idea how to get close enough. How to get Walsh to move the gun away from Anjelita's head for the time it would take to let off a shot. God, he couldn't even see Jack Walsh, and he had never fired a gun before. He began to sweat. He could feel his heart beating in his chest. If this was what Walsh had wanted him to experience he was succeeding. He knew that somehow he had to get him to show himself.

'What about the others?' he said. 'Robinson, Milham, and Michael Thomas? They had nothing to do with any of this.'

'Like me, their misfortune was to have crossed your path. You thought you'd do me a favour. I thought I'd repay it; threefold.'

'You thought that killing them was doing me a favour?'

'Are you saying that it wasn't?'

'Yes I am. It was the last thing I would have wanted.'

'Well there you are then. Now you're beginning to understand how it feels to have a prefect stranger making choices for you. Choices about life...about death. About my life...my death.' Walsh paused for a moment, collecting his thoughts, steading himself. 'You see, it was never really about me owing you. It was about you owing me. So now, you are going to put it right. Stand up.'

His voice was firm, inflexible, intimidating.

Rob stood. The pain throbbed in his shoulder.

'You have the gun?' Walsh asked.

'Yes. I have the gun,' Rob told him. 'But I don't

intend to use it. I don't even know how to fire it.'

'What you do or don't intend is irrelevant here,' Walsh replied. 'As for not knowing how, you needn't worry. It's child's play. Are you right handed or left handed?'

'Right handed.'

'Under the barrel - at the front – there's a tactical light. You'll find a small switch close to the lens housing; on the top inner surface – towards your body. When you've located it, press it down.'

Rob did as he was told. A thin red beam appeared, projected on the cavern ceiling where the gun was pointing.

'You see. You'll have no problem aiming. Now, place your index finger around the trigger. Gently now. There's no external safety catch. When you squeeze the trigger the safety disengages. Continue to squeeze, and the gun will fire. Release it, and the safety engages again. Like I told you; child's play.'

His voice was emotionally detached. Matter of fact. He was a sergeant again. Explaining the workings of the weapon to a raw recruit.

As he tried to steady the Glock, Rob stared at the laser beam darting across the ceiling. He heard the sound of something tearing, and a cry of pain. He looked back at the gaping hole that served as a window in the wall of the warden's post. It was Anjelita who had gasped. Walsh had torn the tape from her mouth. Now she was pressed up against the far side of the window. The gun was pressed firmly to her right temple. And Walsh had come forward into the square of light. It was the same face as that in the photo Burnmoor had showed him. A little older. It could have been the effect of the light at such close range, but his face looked pale, and drawn; his eyes black rimmed, his jaw set firm. There was a chilling resignation in his eyes.

'So now you pay me back,' he said. 'For what you did all those years ago. And for the years in between. It's very simple. All you have to do is point that pistol at my head, and pull the trigger. Then it will all be over. For you, for her, and for me.'

Rob's hand began to shake. 'Please don't make me do this,' he said. 'I can't do it.'

Walsh's reply cut through the air like a knife.

'Yes you can. And you will. Or she dies. I am going to count to ten. By the time I get to ten either you'll have pulled that trigger, or I'll have pulled mine. That's it. There's nothing more to say.' He started counting. 'One...two...three...four...'

Reluctantly, Rob raised the pistol until the laser found a spot on Walsh's temple between his ear and eye. The gun was relatively light, but he had difficulty holding it steady. Anjelita's eyes were tightly closed, her lips moving in silent prayer.

'Five...Six...'

Rob pressed his arm into his side, and leant against the brick arch for support. Walsh turned towards him; the laser hovered above the bridge of his nose.

'Seven...eight...'

Now he was smiling.

In a moment of panic it occurred to Rob that Walsh's gun could still go off if he was struck.

'Nine...'

Rob squeezed the trigger. There was a flash, the deafening sound of an explosion, and the torch went out.

In the darkness, around the walls, and down the tunnels, echoed the sound of the gunshot...and a woman's scream,

28

Rob's knees buckled. He clung to the wall for support.
His ears hurt. He wondered if the drums had burst.
He was vaguely aware that Anjelita was still screaming,
but there were other noises. People shouting.

'Armed Police! Stay where you are! Stand still!
Stand Still! Throw the gun out in front of you. Do it
now!' There was a rising panic in the voices.

Rob realised that beam of the laser was tracing
patterns on the floor of the chamber beneath him. He
let go of the gun, and heard it clatter down the steps.
A powerful beam of light appeared, swept across the
floor, up the steps, and found him.

'Put your hands on your head! Turn and face the
wall! Do it now!'

He tried to speak. To tell them he was unable to
move his left arm. But the words would not come. He
raised his right hand, and placed it behind his head,
turned awkwardly, and leant against the wall. Arms
seized him, pressing his face against the rough brick
surface. Stabs of pain shot through his shoulder and
side. He was beyond crying out. His legs were kicked
apart, and he felt them pat him down. He was swept
off his feet, and carried down the steps, his legs
trailing behind him, onto the chamber floor where he
was unceremoniously dumped. Someone stood
astride him, the barrel of their gun just to the left of

his head. He sensed another behind him. The beam of light was angled on the ceiling illuminating the whole of the chamber. Six more men, in black from head to toe, guns slung across the front of their bodies, were between him and the furthest corner. One held the torch. Two stood beside the entrance to the warden's post from which a trousered leg protruded. From its stillness and the awkward angle, he assumed that it belonged to Walsh. Two more were carrying Anjelita, sobbing inconsolably, towards the tunnel entrance. Once they had disappeared the man astride him seized the hood of his anorak and hauled him to his feet. None of them spoke. As they marched him past the warden's post Rob had to look away. When they reached the mouth of the tunnel, he could contain himself no longer.

'He's dead isn't he?' he said. .

'Of course he's bloody dead,' DI Holmes told him as they waited for the ambulance containing Anjelita to pull away. 'No thanks to you.'

It took a moment to sink in.

'What do you mean, no thanks to me?' Rob said.

Gordon Holmes stared back at him; incredulous. 'I don't believe it! You thought you'd shot him didn't you? According to Firearms you didn't even fire the bloody gun. If they'd waited for you to make your mind up she wouldn't be in that,' he pointed to the departing ambulance. 'She'd be in a body bag.' He rubbed his chin vigorously. 'You were lucky the Boss decided to put a tail on you.'

It was Rob's turn to stare. 'You had a tail on me?'

'What did you expect? It was obvious you had no

intention of keeping us in the loop. The Gowned Crusader. That's what we'd christened you. Into the valley of death, and all that crap.'

'So when I went to see Burnmoor...'

'When you left we paid him a little visit.'

'And when I staked out Walsh's house...'

'We were staking you out. Sadly, they didn't spot him giving that kid the package, but then neither did you spot our men, thank God.'

'But you let me put my pupil on the train.'

Holmes grinned. 'And had it stopped at Stockport. There wasn't much she could tell us. But it confirmed our suspicions. We sent her on her way, and pulled in the Firearms Team. They were already on standby. When you went down that manhole, we nearly had kittens. Fortunately, that complex is fully mapped as part of the City's Critical Incidents plan. There's the entrance you've just come out of inside The Great Northern, and another under Granada Studios. Four men went down over there; two waited a decent interval, and then followed you down from the car park. The team who went in under Granada had to wade through three feet of water to get to the section where you were. Any deeper and they wouldn't have made it in time. Lucky for you again. Not so lucky for the poor sod that fired the shot though.'

He pointed to a group of officers, deep in conversation, twenty metres away; DI Caton, several senior officers Rob didn't recognise, and the members of the Tactical Firearms Team who had brought him out. 'He'll be feeling like shit. There'll be an investigation. Police Complaints Commission swarming all over them. They'll want to know why nobody shouted a challenge.'

'Why didn't they?' Rob wondered out loud.

Holmes stared at him as though he had two heads. Which was exactly how he was feeling.

'Why the bloody hell do you think? Because he had a gun pressed against her head. Because he'd already killed three people. Because he wanted to die. Because there was an amateur there with a gun in his hand, and no bloody idea what he was doing with it! They were more afraid of you than they were of him. And because, whether he intended to kill her or not, by the time they got there - thanks to you - it was too late to negotiate.'

An ambulance pulled up beside them. Holmes opened the door, pushed Rob inside, and jumped in after him. As they pulled away, Rob looked back through the rear window. The Tactical Firearms Team stood in a silent accusative huddle watching him leave.

29

Monday 15th January

'Thanks for seeing me,' Rob said. 'I'm not exactly flavour of the month with your colleagues.'

Detective Sergeant Beth Hale rose to meet him. 'You shouldn't be too hard on yourself,' she said sitting opposite him. 'I'm not sure they would have got him without you. Even if they had, there's a good chance that she wouldn't have survived a shoot out.'

'How is she?' Rob asked.

'Getting there.'

Rob sensed her reluctance to discuss it, and decided to change the subject. 'Walsh was psychotic wasn't he?' he said.

'I've spoken with Doctor Hammond.' She said.

Rob nodded.

'According to her, he was a candidate for suicide the moment that tank was hit in front of him. Psychotic? That's more difficult to tell. There was one stage in the hospital when they thought that he might be suffering paranoid schizophrenia. Then they realised he was talking to himself. Making up rhymes. He never wrote anything down, but he'd say them to himself, over and over again. That drug they gave him before he left the hospital - Stelazine – it can cause psychosis. Even trigger schizophrenia if there's a

321

tendency there. There was a packet of it in his house. Opened. He was still taking it. His hospital records are all over the place. Manic depression, possible bi-polar disorder. Frankly, it's all irrelevant now.'

Rob knew that she was right. The moment that he had acted to stop Jack Walsh from committing suicide, he had set in train a course of events that no one could have foreseen. Let alone prevent.

'How's your shoulder coming along?' she asked.

'Another week of physiotherapy,' he replied. 'And I'll be fine. It was just an AC joint separation. The collar bone slipping up over the shoulder blade. It's normally rugby players and cyclists that get it. Hitting the ground shoulder first.' He rubbed it self-consciously. 'It's going to stick out for the rest of my life though. A permanent souvenir.'

There was an awkward silence. She knew what he was dying to ask. He knew that she would be reluctant to respond.

He finally plucked up the courage. 'Anjelita Andrades,' he said. 'Why did she do it? I need to know.'

Beth Hale sighed. 'It was your need to know, that Walsh played on. It was the hook he used to reel you in. Can't you let it go?'

Rob shook his head. 'I have to understand. Especially now. After all of this.'

She fingered the glass of water in front of her. 'The truth is we'll probably never know. I doubt she could explain it herself. What happened in Vince's bedroom was probably a form of self-harm, as was the fact that she did the job she did. Punishing herself for her sister's death. Some women deal with rape head on.

They rage, and fight, and want to face the bastard in court. Or they join one of the support groups. Make something positive come out of it. Either way, they end up by putting it behind them – not that it ever goes away completely – but at least enough to enable them to move on with their lives. The ones we worry about are those that try to deny that it ever happened; The ones that block it out. Because with them it always surfaces somewhere down the line, when the pressure builds up. Like a dormant volcano. It's the same principle: the greater the resistance, the bigger, and more unpredictable, the eruption.'

'But Anjelita did try to face it up,' Rob reminded her. 'She went on that website. She sought help.'

Beth nodded. 'True. But she wasn't able to follow it through. It's like starting a course of antibiotics. If you don't finish the course, the infection develops resistance and comes back worse than before. For Anjelita, what happened with her sister was an unbearable complication. Not least because she blamed herself for all of it.'

'But why did she choose, of all things, to become an escort.'

'It probably wasn't a conscious choice. She came to England to put it all behind her. Once she was here her looks, her intelligence, the fact that she was alone, would have made her perfect for Elite Executive Escorts. She needed work. A Spanish woman she met – a part time salsa teacher at La Tasca in Islington – told her about the agency. It was good money. Respectable. No need to go beyond polite conversation unless she chose to.'

Rob grimaced. 'But she chose to with me. Was she

paid to do it? By Vince…or Jack Walsh?'

Beth Hale shook her head. 'No. She told me that she really liked you…was drawn to you. She thought you kind…*muy comprensivo,* she said. I looked it up. It means sympathetic, or empathetic.'

'And she paid me back by crying rape?'

'She never intended to. You have to remember that she was harbouring a deep seated hatred not just for the boys who raped her and her sister Rosa, but for the prosecution lawyer who destroyed Rosa in court, and the defence lawyer who did nothing to prevent it. Not to mention self-loathing and a sense of guilt that in some way it had all been her fault, or at the very least she should have been able to make it better for Rosa. In the aftermath of your love making she must have felt that she had betrayed her sister, and herself. She took it out on herself. Self-harm takes many forms.' She shook her head and sighed. 'And when that couple barged in and jumped to the wrong conclusion…'

'She went along with it.'

'I'm not sure she did it that deliberately. The impression I have is that she was simply too traumatised to make sense of any of it. The ambulance arrived, and then the police. She was frightened, angry with herself, and with you. Confused. When she finally realised what she'd done she did the right thing, and walked away.'

'Straight into the clutches of the one man on this planet who really wanted me to suffer.'

Beth ran a hand through her hair. 'And now this. It's going to take a lot of support and counselling if she's ever going to be able to live a normal life.' Her mouth was dry. She drank some of the water, and put the glass carefully back on the table mat.

'If she goes back to London, there are people looking for her.' Rob said. 'The Agency she worked for. Her landlords. Bad people.'

Beth nodded. 'Thanks to you, we know about them,' she said. 'It will be sorted. But best that she doesn't go back. She has money in the bank; enough to be able to move away. Buy a place. Not have to work for a while. Concentrate on getting well. Because, make no mistake, she is ill.'

'I'd like to help,' Rob said.

She shook her head. 'Please don't take this the wrong way, but you're last person we'd want to involve. For a start, she's feeling unbearable guilt about the charges she made against you. And simply having met you led to her being kidnapped, held prisoner, and ending up in that tunnel with a gun to her head. No, there may come a time when she'll be ready for the two of you to trade apologies, but it certainly isn't now.'

Rob started to object but she brushed it away; her voice suddenly hard, her body language assertive.

'Look, you showed you cared about what happened to her. And we'll let her know what you did; all in good time, when she's ready to hear it. But for now, just stay clear of her. And that's not a request. It's a warning. You do anything to jeopardise her recovery and I'll slap a charge on you of obstructing the police. You're a barrister, you count the number of times you withheld information. As a result, you put her life, and yours, at risk. If it hadn't been for our marksman, you'd have been facing a charge of manslaughter.' She had another sip of water. 'You have no idea how difficult it was for me to persuade DCI Caton not to report you to the Bar Council.'

Rob was genuinely surprised. You did that for me?'

Now it was her turn to look embarrassed. 'Yes,' she replied. 'But I'm beginning to regret it.'

You know,' he said. 'You're really attractive when you get mad.'

That made her smile. 'As opposed to really plain when I'm not?'

'You know what I mean,' he said. 'Look, I'm in need of some support and counselling myself. I don't suppose you'd care to help me one evening...say over a drink, or dinner?'

She looked at him appraisingly. 'I've got just three problems with that. Firstly, it seems to me you're a little quick to transfer your...I was going to say affections, but obsessions would seem a little more appropriate. Secondly, I'm not a therapist. And thirdly, I don't believe in mixing business with pleasure.'

It concerned him that this was the second time a woman had told him she suspected he was looking for a therapist. It wasn't enough to stop him from ploughing ahead.

'OK.' he said. 'You drop the charges, and we can call it strictly pleasure.'

She smiled at that. Rob thought it an endearing smile.

'For the time being,' she said. 'I'll reserve judgement on that. Let's start off with a drink, and see how it goes.' The smile broadened. 'And in case you were wondering, I'm not the kind of woman who puts it about on a first date.'

'Fair enough,' he said. 'I'm not the kind of man who would expect you to.

Not anymore I'm not.'

The Author

Formerly Principal Inspector of Schools for the City Of Manchester, Head of the Manchester School Improvement Service, and Lead Network Facilitator for the National College of School Leadership, Bill has numerous publications to his name in the field of education. For four years he was also a programme consultant and panellist on the popular live Granada Television programme *Which Way*, presented by the iconic, and much missed, Tony Wilson. He has written six crime thriller novels to date – all of them based in and around the City of Manchester. His first novel *The Cleansing* was short listed for the Long Barn Books Debut Novel Award. His Fourth novel *A Trace of Blood* reached the semi-final of the Amazon Breakthrough Novel Award in 2009.

Also By Bill Rogers
The Cleansing
The Head Case
The Tiger's Cave
A Trace of Blood
Bluebell Hollow
www.billrogers.co.uk www.catonbooks.com

If you've enjoyed
A FATAL INTERVENTION

You will certainly enjoy the other novels in the series:

THE CLEANSING
The novel that first introduced DCI Tom Caton.

Christmas approaches. A killer dressed as a clown haunts the streets of Manchester. For him the City's miraculous regeneration had unacceptable consequences. This is the reckoning. DCI Tom Caton enlists the help of forensic profiler Kate Webb, placing her in mortal danger. The trail leads from the site of the old mass cholera graves, through Moss Side, the Gay Village, the penthouse opulence of canalside apartment blocks, and the bustling Christmas Market, to the Victorian Gothic grandeur of the Town Hall. Time is running out: For Tom, for Kate...and for the City.

Short listed for the
Long Barn Books Debut Novel Award

Available in Caton Books paperback
ISBN: 978 1 906645 61 8

www.Amazon.com
www.catonbooks.com
www.billrogers.co.uk

Also Available in EBook & AudioBook formats

THE HEAD CASE

Roger Standing CBE, Head of Harmony High
Academy, and the Prime Minister's Special Adviser
for Education, is dead.

DCI Tom Caton is not short of suspects. But if this is
a simple mugging, then why is MI5 ransacking
Standing's apartment, and disrupting the
investigation? And why are the widow and her son
taking the news so calmly?

*SOMETHING IS ROTTEN IN THE CORRIDORS
OF POWER.*

Available in Caton Books paperback
ISBN: 978 1 9564220 0 2

www.Amazon.com
www.catonbooks.com
www.billrogers.co.uk

Also Available in EBook & Audio Book formats

THE TIGER'S CAVE

A lorry full of Chinese illegal immigrants arrives in Hull. Twenty four hours later their bodies are discovered close to the M62 motorway; but a young man and a girl are missing, and still at risk. Supported by the Serious and Organised Crime Agency, Caton must travel to China to pick up the trail. But he knows the solution is closer to home – in Manchester's Chinatown - and time is running out.

TWELVE BODIES
NO MOTIVE
THE HUNT IS ON

A COLD CASE IS ABOUT TO GET HOT.

Available in Caton Books paperback
ISBN: 978 0 9564220 1 9

www.Amazon.com
www.catonbooks.com
www.billrogers.co.uk

Also Available in EBook & Audio Book formats

Lightning Source UK Ltd.
Milton Keynes UK
178629UK00001B/10/P